A RAGING FIRE

SHEPHERD & ASSOCIATES SERIES - BOOK 4

JUDITH ERWIN

Emerald Cat Press

EMERALD CAT PRESS

Cover Design by: Judith Erwin
Cover Image: Licensed via Adobe Stock
Editor: John C. Boles

A Raging Fire/JUDITH ERWIN – First Edition

ISBN: 979-8-9938677-0-0 (Print-Trade Paperback)
ISBN: 979-8-9938677-1-7 (ebook)
Library of Congress Control Number: 2025925475

EMERALD CAT PRESS
Jacksonville, Florida

DEDICATION

For

MARY CAROLINE ERWIN

CONTENTS

CHAPTER 1

For more than a century, it was a house clothed in mystery, secrets, deception, and unexplained death. But on that moonless night, from high on a hill where it presided over a thousand acres, it was ablaze. Flames shot high enough above the roofline to be seen for a mile. The shrill sound of sirens, accompanied by flashing lights, pierced the late-night darkness as a convoy of fire, rescue, and police vehicles arrived on the scene of the antebellum mansion. Could the roaring flames consume all sins of the past?

Despite the property being a mile from the nearest town and hidden from street view by trees and shrubs, curiosity seekers began to assemble, adding an additional challenge for first responders.

In the burgeoning crowd of onlookers, a woman's voice called out, "Is anyone in the house?"

A police officer, attempting to control the crowd responded, "No idea, ma'am. Please stay back. This area must be kept clear."

The two-story, frame building was no match for the hungry fire. Built sometime in the early nineteenth century by a wealthy rice farmer, the plantation had evolved into a prosperous cotton farm by

1900. But crops no longer covered the land as scandal and neglect presided. For nearly twenty years, the mansion stood unoccupied and decaying. When it sold four years ago, massive renovation took place, but the new owner remained anonymous, disguised by a series of shell corporations leaving some in the nearby town to speculate for a while. With the passage of time, interest waned. However, the fire ignited renewed attention.

As an attractive TV reporter from nearby Charleston exited her van, followed by a cameraman, she said, "Joe, do you know anything about this place?"

He shrugged. "Got me. I just moved here a year ago. I didn't even know it was out here."

From a male bystander standing close to the van came a comment. "I think a drug lord bought it. Who else could afford it?

Before the reporter and her crew could complete setting up, another voice from the crowd shouted, "They've found a body."

CHAPTER 2

As Scarlett crossed the threshold of the Shepherd and Associates office after lunch, her raincoat and umbrella dripped a stream of water on the wood floor. "It's brutal out—" Catching sight of an attractive brunette in hospital scrubs standing in front of Liz Glover's desk caught her off guard. Likewise, Jake's German shepherd, leading the way, emitted a low growl before doing the doggy dance to shake rain from his coat. Scarlett tried to dodge the shower.

"Kai, it's okay," Liz said, which settled the shepherd. Focusing on Scarlett, she asked, "Where's Jake?"

"One of the attorneys in that insurance fraud case called while we were having lunch. They need him to testify today. I dropped him at the Courthouse before I picked Kai up at the groomer. He'll catch an Uber when he's done."

Upon hearing Scarlett's answer, the stranger's brown eyes registered alarm.

"And he didn't mention his appointment with Dr. Carden"—Liz nodded toward the stranger—"at one-thirty?"

Scarlett turned her attention to the young woman whose brown eyes projected a suggestion of urgency.

"Obviously he didn't. I'm sorry. He couldn't avoid it. Maybe I help you?"

"I can reschedule," Carden said.

Liz stood. "You don't want to go back out in this weather or waste your trip. Scarlett is Jake's associate. She can help you."

The look coming from Carden's eyes made it clear she was not in favor of the substitution. "That's okay. I'll just come back."

"Trust me," Liz said, "Scarlett is quite capable. and Jake could make it back before you are done. Let her at least take your information." A clap of thunder brought a reaction from all, including the dog.

Carden glanced at Scarlett and back toward Liz, apparently mulling over the proposal.

"It's vicious out there. Let me take your wet raincoat," Liz said, walking around her desk. "And I'll bring both of you a hot drink. Tea or coffee, Doctor?"

"I don't know. I really wanted to see Mr. Shepherd. I've read he is the best investigator in the area. I'll just come back when he's available."

"Liz is right," Scarlett said. "It's miserable out there. I can take your information. Hopefully, Jake will be here by the time I finish. The lawyer promised him he would be the first to go on the stand after the lunch break."

With a note of reluctance in her tone, Carden agreed. Before handing Liz her coat, she glanced toward Kai as he settled down beside the desk, half blocking access to the hallway.

"Come on back to my office. Don't mind Kai. He won't bother you, unless you have a weapon, which I doubt." Scarlett smiled. "Liz,

I would love a cup of tea if you don't mind. What about you, Dr. Carden?"

"Thank you, I'm fine."

Once the two were in her office, Scarlett introduced herself and said, "Do have a seat, Doctor, and tell me why you need a private investigator."

"Please call me Anna-Claire—Anna. Doctor sounds so pretentious." A framed photo on Scarlett's desk of her two Persian cats caught the doctor's attention. "You're a cat lover?"

Glancing down at the photo, Scarlett smiled. "I am. I own it."

"Me too. I've got a Maine coon."

"That's a magnificent breed. Well, we have something in common. But tell me how we can help you."

"This may sound crazy, but I need an investigator because I need to know who I am."

As Scarlett took a moment to process the woman's statement, she noticed sparks in the young woman's eyes build. "Who you are? Am I to take it you might have been adopted and want to learn who your birth parents are?"

"That's the starting point. And please forgive me for being insistent on seeing Mr. Shepherd. I don't mean to offend you."

"No offense taken. Jake does have a reputation, which he deserves, but he usually works on cases where a crime is involved. There are organizations out there that are very good at helping adoptees find birth families. Are you sure you need a private investigator?"

"I need a private investigator, and a good one, because there's something dicey about my adoption—maybe an illegality. I read about Mr. Shepherd in the local magazine and was impressed. According to the writer, he is the best in his field."

"She's right. If I were in trouble, there is no one I would rather have on my side. I think I know the piece you're talking about. But like I said, he usually investigates matters that involve a crime. There's rarely anything illegal about adoption, especially since you're an adult."

"I don't believe I was adopted under normal circumstances."

"Really? What makes you think that?"

"First of all, my parents never told me I was adopted. Yeah, I know it's not unusual. In the past it was common to keep adoptions a secret. During my youth, being adopted never crossed my mind, even though I really don't physically resemble either of the two people who raised me. But when I studied genetics in college, I began to give it thought. But even then, I figured I was a product of recessive genes. When it became popular to submit DNA to databases like Ancestry.com and 23andMe, I thought it might be fun to trace my roots. My father had passed away, and I told my mother I wanted to submit my DNA to one of the databanks. She became hostile, almost angry, saying it was ridiculous and a waste of money. She called it a scam and believed they made up the results."

Scarlett chuckled. "It does seem like science fiction, but DNA is a powerful element as you know, since you're a physician. But nothing you've said so far sounds irregular. Is there more?"

"There is. Mom was so upset, which I couldn't understand. Even if she thought it wasn't reliable, why was she so adamant that I not do it? I mean, it's not that expensive, and what could it hurt? I decided to blame it on her condition. My mother was in chemo for breast cancer at the time. Since she seemed so stressed, I decided to drop the subject. I didn't want to upset her. I dropped the idea. But after she passed away, I cleaned out the family home in Woodlawn to sell it since I live in D.C. I thought I might find a copy of my birth certificate in her files. When I didn't, I thought about that conversation and got a funny feeling. It had never occurred to me that I might be adopted, but when the thought popped in my head, I thought about the fact that I didn't really look like either one of my parents. Mom always said I looked like my grandmother's sister."

"I assume you have a Social Security number."

"I do. And I must have had a birth certificate. But when I applied to the Alabama Department of Public Health to get one in case I needed it, there was no record of my being born in Alabama. That nagging feeling came back. I even contacted my only aunt on Mom's side and my sole surviving uncle on my dad's side. They all said they were sure I was the biological child of my parents, but I know I'm not. I finally sent my DNA into a major database. Nothing in my profile they provided matches what I know about the family, nor does any potential match show the surname of any relative of either of my parents. If I was adopted, and I'll repeat I am *positive* now that I was, why would my parents go to such lengths to keep it secret? Why wouldn't someone in my family know?"

"Are you sure you were born in Alabama?"

"No. But that's where my parents always told me I was born. They moved to Virginia when I was very young. My dad was an army doctor. Do you have any idea of what it feels like to not know who you are? How many lies have I been told? I'm engaged and plan to have a family one day. How can I have children when I don't know my own background? Do I have parents out there? Siblings or cousins? Was I an illegal adoption? Even an abducted baby?"

CHAPTER 3

The word *abducted* barely escaped Anna's lips when the sound of Kai's enthusiastic bark countered the thunder outside.

"Jake's back," Scarlett said as she stood and walked to the door to get his attention.

As he came down the hall, he pulled off his jacket and loosened his tie. "I'm soaked," he said, as he reached her office. Before noticing Anna Carden, he began untucking his wet shirt.

"Jake, this is Dr. Anna-Claire Carden. She scheduled an appointment with you, but since you weren't back, I was about to begin an intake interview."

He gave a quick nod in Anna's direction. "Give me a couple of minutes, and I'll get back with you."

As Scarlett resumed her place behind the desk, Anna said, "So, that's Jake Shepherd."

"That's him."

"He looks like his magazine photo." She nodded as though agreeing with her own statement. "That article was written by the friend of a nurse at the hospital. I believe her name is Wendy."

"Wendy Carmichael. Yeah, I know the piece you mean," Scarlett said with a smile. "He tried to avoid her, but she was persistent and finally caught him in a weak moment."

"The article said he was highly decorated while an FBI agent and has a Yale law degree."

"All true."

"Impressive." Anna leaned forward, lowering her voice, "According to Callie, she's the nurse, Wendy Carmichael has a crush on him."

Scarlett grinned, raising her eyebrows. "I suspected she might."

"Callie thought he might ask Wendy out, but he didn't. I guess he's married."

"Nope." Scarlett rested her pen on the legal pad where she had planned to take notes. "He's definitely single. But since he's back, I think we should wait until he joins us before going into more detail about—here he is."

Jake sauntered in, rolling up the sleeves of his plaid flannel shirt and wearing jeans. "Dr. Carden is it? What brings you here?"

The doctor's demeanor changed, as if slightly intimidated by Jake. "I've recently learned I was likely adopted, and I want, actually need, to know who my biological parents are."

Jake frowned and gave a slight shake of his head. "Is this something you need for medical reasons?"

"No. Of course, it is important to know genetic health propensities. But it's hard to explain. I am kind of driven to know my story—the whole story. Since I realized I am likely not the biological child of the couple who raised me, I've been haunted by the uncertainty. I can't shake it. I wake in the middle of the night with questions burning in my head. Who am I? Do I have siblings? Did my mother not want me? Did she voluntarily give me up, or was I taken from her? Is she alive? Even not knowing what my cultural traditions might be bothers me."

"Tracking down someone who chose to delete you from her life may not be all hugs and kisses. You might be exposing a long-kept secret and create domestic chaos. Are you prepared for rejection?"

For an instant, she appeared wounded but quickly recovered. "It's a risk I have to take. Not knowing who my biological family is just isn't acceptable, whether we ever have a relationship. I need to know. Will you help me?"

"No need for an expensive investigation. As I recall, there are agencies around having success with locating birth parents."

"No." Her body stiffened. "I am aware of the agencies, but *my* case is complicated. I want it to be a little confidential."

With an expression crossed between annoyance and confusion, Jake said, "How is something *a little* confidential? In any case, I'm sure Scarlett can take care of you. If you'll excuse—"

Anna bristled, the soft brown of her eyes growing darker. "I need the best investigator possible, Mr. Shepherd. And I've been told that's *you*." She turned toward Scarlett. "No offense, Ms. Kavanagh, but I made the appointment with Mr. Shepherd for a reason."

"My, my," Jake said, his eyebrows rising. "You are certainly fervent in your mission, but tracking birth parents isn't on the list of services I offer."

"Your website says you take missing persons cases."

"You don't have a missing person case. I suspect your birth parents know exactly where they are and where they want to be. Scarlett has all the skills necessary to help you. It was nice to meet you." He turned and left, leaving Anna Carden speechless for a second.

As she turned toward Scarlett, she said, "My gosh! Is he always that abrupt? I've known doctors full of their self-importance but didn't expect it from an investigator."

Scarlett curled her lips, attempting to stifle a smile. "That's Jake, I'm afraid. You've just witnessed the worst of him. I spend a lot of time apologizing for his lack of social graces. But if your case takes a complicated turn, I expect he'll work with me. You'll see the best of him then. Jake may be a genius in his own mind with zero diplomacy, but trust me, he is that good."

Anna grimaced. "I'm sorry. I don't mean to question your expertise, but have you ever done a birth parent search?"

"In my law practice, I helped a couple of clients. However, this is *your* decision. If you don't feel comfortable with me, I understand."

She glanced around the office and noticed Scarlett's Harvard diploma. "You have a law degree from Harvard?"

"I do."

"Why are you working as a private inves—I'm sorry. That's none of my business."

"No problem. You're fine. I met Jake at a time when I was burned out with all the petty bickering and contentious nature of my family law practice. It may sound unusual, but working with him to dig out truth and help victims is gratifying. The law degree and my experience come in handy sometimes." Scarlett studied Anna's face for a sign of her intentions. "So, do you want to think about it and get back to me with your decision?"

As a minute or two passed, Anna sat quietly, fidgeting with the charms on a bracelet she wore. When she finally spoke, her tone was resolute. "No. I want you to start. But you are sure he will come in if the matter takes a sketchy turn?" She tipped her chin affirmatively as if emphasizing her statement.

Scarlett smiled. "Guaranteed. He likes to growl, but he can't resist a challenge. But I do have to warn you, the investigation may be expensive, and you have to be sure you'll be okay with whatever we find. You know the old saying, 'Be careful what . . .'"

With furrowed brows, Anna said, "I'm okay with the expense. I have a nice salary and an inheritance. Not knowing who I am is disrupting my life. I have to do it."

"I understand. We'll probably find it was a standard adoption, and one or both of your parents just didn't want it to be known."

"I think it was more than that, but where do we start?" As a clap of thunder caused both women to flinch, Anna opened the handbag on her lap. "Should I write you a check?"

"Not me. On your way out, you can stop by the desk, and Liz will take care of the retainer and explain our rates. For now, I need you to complete the intake form, answer a few questions, and sign releases authorizing us to obtain your various records. In addition, I need lists of any locations where your parents may have lived before you were born and the names of any people I can question about your parents." She handed the doctor a clipboard with a legal pad and a printed form for basic information attached. "While you do that, may I make copies of the paperwork you have in that manila folder you brought, which I assume contains your DNA report?"

"Of course."

When both finished, Scarlett said, "Did you send your DNA to any other company or upload your profile anywhere?"

"No. Just the one."

Before Scarlett could respond, Kai ambled into the office, taking her attention.

"Don't worry. He's just making his rounds, checking on everyone." The shepherd passed the client as he went behind the desk and nuzzled Scarlett. "Want a snack, do you?" She reached into a small jar on the desk and took out a couple of treats for him and then returned her focus to the client.

"Although you used a good company for your DNA test, let's submit a sample to some of the other companies for the purpose of confirming the accuracy of the report and giving you a larger pool of potential relatives. By the way, what are the major discrepancies in your report causing you to believe you were not raised by your birth parents, and have you received notice of any possible matches?"

"So far, only two distant matches on my father's side. The countries the report gave for my ancestry do not fit with what I know about my parents. Carden is a British surname, and from talking to family members of my parents, their ancestors were from the UK, the Netherlands, Sweden, and Germany. Unless the company mixed up my sample with someone else's, something is really wrong. According to the report, none of my ancestors were from those countries. My DNA report says my ancestors were from Italy, Greece, Spain, and France with a small percentage from Belgium.

"On second thought, before you send me the profile you received, let's get fresh samples to submit to at least one other company and a DNA lab. I doubt they made an error, but we should prove the profile is accurate before submitting to all the databases. We don't have kits in the office, but I'll have Liz send you several."

CHAPTER 4

Later that afternoon, as Jake cranked the SUV for their return home, he said, "So, Harvard, did the doctor hire you?"

"She did. But I'm definitely second choice. She read that article Wendy Carmichael wrote and thinks you're the pick of the litter."

He chuckled. "Of course, she did. You assured her I am, didn't you?"

"I apologized for your abrupt attitude and told her you are a genius in your own mind." As she settled into her seat, she glanced up through the windshield. "I'm glad the rain finally stopped." Her focus snapped back to him. "But you could be a little more diplomatic with clients, Sherlock. Your PR skills suck."

"Where did you get the idea that diplomacy is in my toolbox? That's your department. I like my cantankerous personality. Keeps people on their toes. Want to grab takeout or dig something out of the freezer?" He brought the vehicle to a quick stop for a red light, causing Scarlett to lurch forward.

"Takeout. But you also might try brushing up on your driving skills." She adjusted her seatbelt. "I'm not sure I should have taken the case. She asked me if I had experience with birth parent searches. I told her I had done a couple, but I didn't tell her I used a P.I."

His brow pinched together as he turned toward her. "Shame, shame, Harvard. Misleading a client? Not like you, whose integrity is above reproach." A smile crossed his face. "But I kinda like knowing you're not perfect."

"Yeah. Guess I've been around you too long. But I have the P.I. reports in my computer. I can follow what they did. Anna thinks her Social may be a fake."

"For the record, I don't mislead clients."

"Oh, right, Sherlock. I've seen your brutal honesty in action. I quote"—her voice deepened—"'Lie to me, and I'm out. Innocent, I'm your best friend. Guilty, I'm your worst enemy.' Yeah, maybe you never mislead clients, but you're darn good at misleading suspects and witnesses."

"That's fair play in the business. Back to your case. Liz can verify the Social through the administration's verification system." He made a sharp right turn.

"Anna tried to get a copy of her birth certificate, but Alabama, which is where her mother told her she was born, found no record of her birth."

"Don't they usually change a child's surname, if not the entire name, and issue a new birth certificate with an adoption? You're the family law attorney."

"Usually. I'm not sure whether I should try other states for her birth record or wait for more DNA results from the different companies, which will be at least six weeks or more." She reached over and scratched Kai under his chin as his head moved forward between the seats and over the console.

"Check the first three numbers on her Social to see if it was issued in Alabama."

"You can tell that?"

"For cards issued before 2011. Wouldn't hurt to start there."

She looked at him with a quizzical expression. "You know that how?"

"I know things. Liz can get you the list. Barbecue okay?"

"Whatever. Anna's father was also a physician and came from a wealthy family. Her parents left Anna a nice inheritance. That's why she doesn't have a problem with the expense of the investigation. I promised her you would help if it becomes complicated."

Jake turned toward her with a frown. "Oh, you did. What made you think you could rope me into a mommy-daddy search?"

"Keep your eyes on the road, Sherlock. I can rope you in because if it is a sketchy case, you'll be all over it."

"Think you know me, huh?" He turned into a barbecue restaurant.

"Yeah. I know you."

As he drove up to the takeout window, she said, "I want the chicken dinner, white meat, sweet sauce, and remember, you're using your barbecue card for the week."

***

When they reached the parking garage of their building after picking up dinner, Jake said, "Your place or mine?"

Scarlett mulled over the proposition for several seconds. "Yours. If we do mine, I'll never get you to leave. You take the food, and I'll feed the cats and then come up. But let's be clear, I'm not sleeping over."

"That's what you always say," he said, reaching across the console to pat her leg.

"I mean it, Jake."

"You always do."

"Damn it. Stop patronizing me." She socked his shoulder, causing Kai to emit a low growl.

"Easy, boy. I can handle it."

***

After dinner, Scarlett insisted on returning to her apartment to do research on Anna's case. Jake accompanied her to her unit on the floor below. When they reached the door, she turned to him. "You know, I think she's right."

"Really. That's good. Want to give me a clue as to who you're talking about?"

"Anna. The doctor. I think there is something not right about her background."

"Is this intuition, or do you have concrete evidence?"

"Don't mock my intuition. You follow yours all the time."

"Yeah. But mine's accurate. So, you are basing this conclusion on your gut."

Looking down at the cat figures on her door mat, she shook her head. "I can't explain it, but I have a really weird feeling. While I can't put my finger on what triggered my suspicion, I know Anna's smart and a scientist. They aren't prone to dramatize. It may turn into a case you'll be interested in."

"I'm pretty sure you'll let me know." He put both hands on her shoulders. "If you need me, Harvard, I've got your back."

Scarlett smiled. "I know that. What time do you want to leave in the morning?"

"Around eight—after—"

"I know. After you work out."

***

Liz was already at her desk when Jake and Scarlett reached the office the following morning. "I'll be out most of the day, doing interviews for Phil's case," Jake said as he passed by the reception desk.

"Anything you want me to do on this end?" the retired FBI analyst said.

"All good. Harvard can probably use some help on her new case."

Scarlett nodded. "Definitely, if you're not busy."

Liz stood, gathered up a pen, notebook, and her iPad. "Lead the way. I'm caught up on Jake's cases."

Jake proceeded to his office while the two women went into Scarlett's, followed by Kai. Before taking a seat, Scarlett dropped her portfolio on her desk and took a couple of dog treats out of the jar on the corner. Sensing a reward, the shepherd sat at attention, cocking his head from one side to the other as though listening for a command.

Liz scooted a chair up to the front of the executive-size Macassar ebony and white leather desk. It was a holdover from Scarlett's Atlanta law office. In contrast to Jake's organized clutter, Scarlett's office was meticulous. "Where are you starting?"

"Anna gave me all the information she has, which is very little. No birth certificate, no idea of where she was born other than it probably was not Alabama. I think the best place to start is the adoption reunification sites. Her mother could be looking for her and has registered.

That would be easy. But given how secretive her adopted parents were, it's likely a long shot. I do have a Social Security number we can start with, but Anna is afraid it's a fake. Jake said you can tell where it was issued by the first three digits."

"Given her age, it was issued before 2011. I'll get that right away and verify the number with the administration. Do you want me to register her with the various reunification sites?"

"That would be great. If you find the area where her card was issued, I'll work on collecting information from sources there. We need to submit her DNA sample to two or three of the major databases. If they all come up with the same profile, we can submit that to the rest."

"Give me the first three digits of her Social, and I'll check it right now." Liz opened the case of her iPad and booted it up.

"Two-five-two."

Within three minutes, Liz said, "Georgia. Most likely location is Augusta, but that number did cover other small towns in the general area of the state."

"What do you know? My home state. I know the adoption laws there. Records are sealed. Certain information can be obtained once the adoptee is an adult but requires a court order to open and consent of both sides. Why would her mother lie to her about where she was born?"

"Good question."

"Well, it's a starting point. I'll work on that while you authenticate the Social."

***

By the following day, Liz had verified the Social Security number and found it to be valid. Scarlett had placed a call to the attorney who bought her family law practice in Atlanta and handled a lot of adoptions. Although the lawyer was in court and unavailable, Scarlett left a detailed message with her paralegal, explaining what she needed and supplementing the request by email with a copy of relevant documents. Her friend responded with a text about forty-five minutes later, saying she had it covered.

On her way back to her desk from the restroom at approximately four o'clock, Liz stopped by Scarlett's office. "Have you heard from Atlanta?"

"Not yet. But I'm sure Vicky has contacts that can speed up the search. If she finds a record exists, to get information about Anna's birth, if adopted, will require a court order."

"That could take time." As Liz turned to leave, the ring tone of Scarlett's cell pierced the silence. She held up her hand to Liz, signaling her to wait. "It's Vicky."

Answering the call, she put the phone on speaker. "Hey, Vicky. Thanks for calling me back. Did you find any information on my client?"

"I found a birth certificate that matches your information on all four corners—name, date of birth, name of parents. It appears to be an original birth certificate as there is no record of an adoption."

"Are you sure? Parents? Date of birth? All match?"

"All match, but there is no sign of an adoption taking place in the state of Georgia. I'm emailing you the certificate. It came out of Augusta as you suspected. The father was listed as Captain Lawrence Carden, MD, so he must have been in the army and stationed at Fort Gordon."

After thanking her friend, Scarlett hung up, put the phone down, paused, and looked at Liz.

"Oh, my God. What do we have?"

CHAPTER 5

Before either Scarlett or Liz could say more, a low growl came from Kai, followed by a faint yelp as he trotted out of the office and sped down the hall, his claws clicking on the tile.

"Jake must be here," Liz said.

"I'll run this by him. Get his thoughts."

As Jake could be heard talking to Kai, the women waited in silence for him to pass by on his way to his office.

"What's up?" he said as he paused at Scarlett's open door. "Anything happen while I was gone?"

"Sort of. I just got off the phone with a friend in Georgia who did me a favor and researched Anna's birth records."

"And?"

"Jake, there's a Georgia birth certificate with the correct name, date of birth, and the names of Anna's parents who raised her, but no adoption record. What do you think?"

"Sounds to me like your client is either wrong about being adopted or somebody screwed up somewhere. Maybe your buddy just missed

the adoption. They are sealed, as you know, Madam Family Law Attorney."

"True. But since Anna's an adult, she is entitled to nonidentifying
information, including an original birth certificate. My friend, Vicky,
is sure the birth certificate is an original. But my intuition tells me
there's something more."

"Your intuition?"

With an indignant facial expression, Scarlett said, "Yes. My intuition. That shouldn't be a problem for you to accept given how often
you follow yours."

"When did I say you don't have valid instincts?" He pulled his
leather bomber jacket off, tossed it over his shoulder, lowered his voice,
and said, with a devilish twinkle in his eye, "Just not as good as mine."

With a flourish, Scarlett whipped an 8x10 photo out of Anna Carden's file and put it down on the desk with force. "Look at this family
photo of the Cardens. Anna's eyes are as brown as a bar of chocolate.
Neither of her parents have brown eyes. It is not genetically possible
for two blue-eyed people, or one blue-eyed and the other green, to have
a brown-eyed baby."

"Is that something you know, or are you guessing?"

"For your information, Shepherd, I took a genetics class in under-
grad."

Squinting one eye with a slight smile, Jake said, "Well, well, we're
learning more and more about you, Harvard." He turned to Liz. "Not
only is she a sharp lawyer, apparently she has forensic skills as well."

"Cut it out. I had a class and happen to remember a little. She isn't
the biological child of that couple. I am sure of it. So, if there was no
adoption, how are they her parents?"

"Tell you what. I'm sure you'll figure it out. Meantime, I'm going to check my emails, return a couple of text messages, and then call it a day. You onboard?"

Scarlett slid the photo back in the file. "Whatever."

As he left, followed by Kai, Scarlett turned to Liz. "What do you think?"

"It's certainly sketchy but might be as simple, although tragic, as a careless mix-up of babies by the hospital."

Scarlett nodded. "Yeah. I thought about a Florida case where that happened back in the 1990s. Certainly a possibility. To explore that theory, it would help to have hospital records for the time Anna's mother was a patient in order to identify other babies in the nursery." She shook her head. "But after over thirty years, those records may have been destroyed. Hopefully, genetic genealogy will turn up something." She began jotting notes on the legal pad from Anna's file.

"Are you planning to tell the client about this information?" Liz asked.

Scarlett looked up from what she was doing. "Not yet. I was just thinking of other possibilities. Her mom could have had an affair."

"Certainly possible. Especially if the military caused a separation."

"That's probably more navy than army in peacetime. But—" She dropped the pen on the pad with an expression indicating a sudden thought. "What about in vitro fertilization? I vaguely remember a case where the lab got the embryos mixed up. It wasn't discovered until the babies were about three months old. It was traumatic for everyone. Parents obviously wanted their biological child but had bonded with the baby they had."

"Those mothers must have been emotionally ripped apart, and how strange to think you had carried a baby for nine months that wasn't related to you," Liz said.

"Although I'm not a mother, I can't imagine what that would have been like." Scarlett picked the pen up again and jotted more on the pad. "There's another possibility. Artificial insemination with the lab mixing up the sperm."

"That makes quite a few leads to pursue, none of them illegal, unless. . . "

"Unless what?" Scarlett's brows pinched together.

"Unless, and this is off the rails. Unless Mom Carden wanted a different gene pool for her baby and bribed the lab into switching the sperm."

"No. That's almost science fiction—kinda creepy."

"When you've been around criminal activity as long as I have, nothing surprises you," Liz said. "I could see a woman not liking something about her husband, secretly using non-medical birth control, and then managing to obtain sperm for the insemination that matches what she wants."

"Wouldn't the sperm clinic want to involve the husband to match him to the baby?"

"She tells them she's single, widowed, maybe divorced."

"I could see Anna's mother protecting her secret if she used any of those methods of becoming pregnant or if she had an affair. She would not want anyone probing into the baby's birth details—wouldn't tell anyone. DNA was just gaining attention and probably not widely understood. I bet when she realized how easy DNA information could be obtained, once the genealogy databases became popular, she panicked. She may never have told anyone."

"Somebody knows," Jake said, stopping in the hallway by Scarlett's door.

Both women looked at him.

"Somebody always knows, and it's your job to find out who."

"Thank you very much, Sherlock, but I am aware of what I need to do."

Jake grinned. "Good to know. Ready? I'm starved."

"Before you leave, Jake, are you in or out of the office tomorrow?" Liz said.

"Out. I'm doing additional interviews with the client and a couple of alternative suspects in the Grainger case—may take a while."

Scarlett opened a desk drawer and claimed her purse. "Refresh my memory. What is the Grainger case?"

"Phil's arson."

"Oh, yeah. The upscale menswear shop that burned down."

"Uniforms arrested Grainger a few days ago. Phil says the evidence is all circumstantial, but the fact he was near bankruptcy in the business placed him at the top of the suspect list, plus he failed a poly. However, Phil doesn't believe he lit the match."

"Do you?"

"Will let you know after my interview."

"Question," Scarlett said.

"Yeah."

"How does a man whose business is near bankruptcy afford an attorney like Phil Madison plus you?"

"Easy. Rich wife."

"Hmmm. How rich?"

"Like wear-the-diamonds-once-and-discard rich."

"Wow! That's an image. Well, if you're out tomorrow, may I have Liz to work with me on Anna's case?"

Jake glanced toward Liz. "I have AI transcripts of today's interviews with the arson investigators. If you can do a quick review of those, then no problem with you working with Harvard." Looking back toward Scarlett, he said, "Ready?"

***

As they fastened their seatbelts in the SUV, Jake's phone rang. When he pulled it out of his shirt pocket, the Bluetooth connected it to the vehicle's audio speaker system.

"Hi, babe, what's up?"

"Daddy, I need you to tell Mom it's okay for me to go to the Raw Skipper concert with my friends. I know Hal is telling her bad stuff about concerts. He's such a D-bag sometimes. She says it's up to you."

"She does, does she? Good for Hal. So, Jackie wants me to be the bad guy."

"Please say yes. It's going to be so fantastic."

"I'm sure it is, Sabrina, but before I can go along with that idea, I'll need to talk to the adult or adults who are accompanying you." He gave Scarlett a dubious look, one eyebrow cocked.

"Dad, there are going to be five of us. We don't need an adult."

"No adult. No way."

"Daddy."

"Not going to happen, Scout. We've talked about this before. You go to a rock and roll concert only if there is a responsible adult along—someone I know and trust."

"That would probably have to be an armed cop."

"Funny, but not a bad idea. I could check with Pete and see if we have anyone willing to take the gig."

"Daddy, you like music. You should understand why I want to go, and you should trust me."

"All true. I do trust you. It's the druggies, pedophiles, and rapists that I don't trust."

"What if I Facetime you from the concert. You could see I was okay."

"And if you weren't, what could I do from the other end of a telephone? No, Sabrina. Unless a responsible adult accompanies you, you are not going. I'm sure you don't want me tagging along, but if Sonny, Brenda, or Randy is willing to take the job, I'll consent. Only way."

"That's not fair."

"Fair or not, that's my condition. Think about it and let me know. I'm thinking you don't have a ticket yet."

"Margaret's mom is getting them as soon as they go on sale."

"Well, we'll need two or you don't go. I'll pay for the tickets and the security."

The phone went silent for nearly a minute until Sabrina spoke. "I'll think about it."

"Good. I'm hanging up. Love you."

"Love you," she said with a grudge in her tone.

"Well, you just blew her vote for father-of-the-year," Scarlett said as the call ended.

"What? I'm doing my job."

"You need a teenage-girl guidebook. I'm sure it says on page one that at puberty, girls and rock stars go together like peanut butter and jelly."

"And you're an expert?"

"I was a teenage girl who had my fair share of boy-band crushes."

"You went to concerts?"

"Of course, I did."

"Without a chaperone?"

"Oh, yes."

"And just how old were you at your first without a parent?"

"Thirteen—Justin Timberlake. Probably wasn't the best decision my parents ever made, but Savannah and I made out okay with four of our friends."

CHAPTER 6

S carlett adjusted the air conditioning vent aimed in her direction. "She's growing up, Jake. You are going to have to face the fact that you can't keep her in protective custody forever."

"So, you think I should let her go to this concert without adult supervision?"

"Maybe not this one, but there will be a time when you have to allow her to venture out." She paused, glancing out the side window for a few seconds before turning back toward Jake. "I have an idea. I don't want to intrude but let me talk to her about this one."

He laughed. "Oh, you're not going to intrude—just take over? I get it, Harvard. Exactly what are you gonna say?"

"I'm working on a plan that might work for both of you."

A broad grin crossed Jake's face even though he did not look in her direction. "A plan? Kinda like the secret plan to leave your law practice and bully your way into Shepherd and Associates?"

"Well, not exactly that life changing. And for the record, I did not bully my way into Shepherd and Associates. Hiring me was your idea.

I simply asked to buy in as a partner, a position you continue to withhold."

"Only on the job."

"The job was what I wanted. Correction. The job *is* where I want to be as a partner. But we won't argue about that now. Let me suggest a plan to Sabrina."

He tipped his head, pointed to his temple, and then flicked the finger in her direction as though he had a revelation. "Oh, I get it. You want to negotiate the issue—use those mediation skills of yours."

"Make fun all you like, but they are better on a teenage girl than your take-no-prisoners approach. Sure, you can flex your 'I'm the parent; you're the child' authority, but she'll continue to believe you're wrong and harbor resentment. If my plan works, both of you get what you want."

***

When they reached the office the following morning, Jake let Scarlett and Kai out and then drove off to do his interviews.

"Good morning," Scarlett said to Liz as she followed Kai into the reception room.

"Where's Jake?"

"Remember, he's not coming in this morning. He's on his way to Central Detention to interview Phil's client. Can't help but wonder why he wasn't released on a bond if his wife is so wealthy. You think she cut him off?"

"Maybe, but more likely the judge wouldn't set a bond *because* of her wealth—flight risk."

"Right. And she wouldn't be covering his legal fees if she had a problem with him."

Liz glanced at the screen of her computer. "I've got about an hour's worth of work left on these transcripts, and then I'll start researching the Carden case for possible neighbors or associates around the time of Anna's birth."

"Thanks. I'm going to make calls to some of the names on the list Anna gave me. Maybe we can order lunch in because Jake expects to be out all day."

"Are you two singing at the club this weekend?"

"Not this weekend. This is Jake's weekend with Sabrina, and you know how protective he is. She likes to go for the two-step and line dancing, but he's not enthusiastic about it even though the bar area is off limits to minors. We only take her when we have another couple with us so she's never alone at the table. But, she is not happy with him at the moment."

Liz smiled as she took a dog treat out of a jar in a drawer of her desk and handed it to Kai. "She's a teenager. Giving parents a hard time is in the contract."

"Yeah. Barely fourteen but thinks she's twenty-five. Her current issue is she wants to attend a rock concert without a chaperone. You can guess how that went over when Jake thinks she's still his little girl."

"Don't get caught in the crossfire. Sabrina is strong-willed, and compromise is not in Jake's vocabulary."

Scarlett shifted the strap of her briefcase from one shoulder to the other. "As if I didn't know that, but it's too late. I talked him into letting me take her to the mall tomorrow for shopping, lunch, and a proposal for a possible solution. I think I have a plan that will work for both. Wish me luck."

***

After making a cup of tea, Scarlett settled down at her desk and began reviewing the list of names Anna provided. With a pen and fresh legal pad on the desk, she punched in the first number, the home of Anna's maternal aunt in Charleston, South Carolina. While the phone rang, Scarlett mentally rehearsed what she would say if the woman answered. After four rings, the call went to voice mail. *No surprise. No one answers these days if they don't recognize the name or number on their caller ID.*

"This message is for Mrs. Irene Jorgensen. My name is Scarlett Kavanagh. I'm a private investigator with Shepherd and Associates in Arlington, Virginia. I'm currently working for your niece, Anna Carden. I would appreciate it if you would give me a call." Scarlett left both her office number and her mobile.

After replacing the receiver on its base, Scarlett skimmed her list and decided to try the brother of Anna's father. As she paused, contemplating whether to speak with his wife if he was not available, she noticed her subject resided in Oregon and glanced at her watch. Can't call now. *It's barely six a.m. in Portland.* Taking a sip of tea, she again referred to the list. The third name to catch Scarlett's attention was categorized as a close friend of Nora Carden's in Virginia.

When a woman answered, Scarlett identified herself and asked to speak with Marilyn Sherwood.

"This is Marilyn. Why are you calling?"

"I appreciate your apprehension in these days of so many fraudulent telephone calls. Please feel free to authenticate me by looking up Shepherd and Associates on your computer. You'll see we are located in Arlington, Virginia. Check the phone numbers. You'll find that one will match the number on your caller ID right now. Take your time. If you like, we can hang up, and you can call me back."

For several seconds, the phone was silent. "That's not necessary. I believe you. I know Anna-Claire suspects she may have been adopted. She asked me about it. Is that what this is about?"

"It is." Scarlett put a check by the woman's name on her list and began taking notes on the conversation.

"Why can't she leave it alone? Poor Nora worshiped that girl to the day she died. What difference does it make?"

"That's a personal choice only an individual can make. I can tell you that Anna is adamant about learning the truth."

"It's ridiculous. If Anna-Claire were adopted, I know Nora would have mentioned it, considering how long we were friends and how much time we spent together on church projects and social interactions. My god. Nora and I were friends for over twenty years. We even had conversations about going through labor and giving birth. Her delivery was difficult. It's why she never had another child."

With a soft tone, Scarlett said, "I understand. However, Mrs. Sherwood, we have compelling evidence that Nora and Lawrence Carden are not Anna's biological parents, or at least one is not. It's important to Anna to know exactly who she is. I believe she deserves to know. With both parents deceased, there is no harm to be had by uncovering the truth. Wouldn't you agree?"

Again, the phone went silent for an even longer period. Scarlett waited. When Sherwood finally spoke, she said, "I see what you mean. But, honestly, Ms. Kavanagh—that's your name, right? Nora never said or suggested in any way that Anna-Claire was not her birth child. In fact, over the years, she described many things about her pregnancy and Anna's birth. She even compared traits and talents Anna had with Nora's mother and grandmother. She followed in her father's footsteps, becoming a doctor. It makes no sense that you're telling me Anna-Claire is not Nora's child. To even doubt it for a second makes me feel guilty—like I'm betraying my friend."

"I get it. But do you mind telling me how old Anna-Claire was when you met Nora?"

"I don't remember exactly. It was a long time ago, but I'd say about four, maybe five. She wasn't in school. The Cardens joined our church, and Anna-Claire was in the preschool Sunday school class that I co-taught."

"Do you know how long the Cardens had lived in Virginia at that time?"

"Not exactly. I know they had been here for a while, but when we met, they had just moved to a new home near our church."

"How would you describe Anna-Claire at that time?"

"I'm not sure I know what you mean, but she was a pretty little girl. I have all boys, so, I enjoyed having a girl to buy girlie things for at Christmas and birthdays."

"Was her hair dark?"

"Not then. She was blond, like Nora. But she had the darkest brown eyes. An unusual combination. Her hair did darken as you must know."

"True. She has lovely dark brown hair now. What about Nora and Dr. Carden? Can you describe the two of them?"

"Nora had green eyes. She used to say she was a green-eyed cat in another life. Larry's were blue. He was a bit more handsome, but Nora wasn't ugly. She didn't wear makeup. I think she would have been really pretty with makeup. Maybe I shouldn't have said that?"

"You're fine."

"Why is all this important? Can't you just trace Anna-Claire's birth records?"

Scarlett laid her pen on the pad. "We're working on that, but you never know what details might be important. If you think of anything that might be relevant, would you give me a call? I know Anna would appreciate it."

"Sure. Please tell her hello for me. I haven't seen her since Nora passed away."

"Absolutely."

After terminating the call, leaning forward with elbows on her desk and chin resting on her hands, Scarlett pondered the conversation. *Not much information, but definite confirmation about the green and blue eyes. Green and blue do not make brown. What the heck is going on here?*

CHAPTER 7

By lunchtime, Scarlett had made four additional calls to people on Anna's list. Two answered but provided no useful information. She left messages for the other two. While the time was finally acceptable to make the call to Oregon, she decided to have lunch first.

"Any luck?" Liz asked, taking a spinach salad out of a takeout bag and opening the container as Scarlett entered the breakroom.

"Your salad looks good. Maybe I should have ordered the same. No, not really any luck. But I'm not surprised. I haven't reached my primary targets—Joel Carden and Irene Jorgensen. I think relatives and friends from around the time Anna was born are the ones most likely to know about her birth. The aunt didn't answer, and I haven't called the uncle yet because of the time difference. How about you? Did you find any new names to contact?"

"Just one so far, but I've got leads on a couple more. Dr. Carden being in the military has created a barrier in the investigation. Like rentals, military housing doesn't identify the occupants of property on the government sites. I'm hoping city directories and census records will turn up more."

After Scarlett sat down at the table, she opened the container with her Cobb salad. "Although I didn't receive any new information, the woman I talked to described Anna's father as having blue eyes and her mother green—pretty much confirming she is not their child."

***

After clearing away lunch trash, Scarlett returned to her office and placed a call to Joel Carden's home in Oregon. According to Anna, her father's older brother was a retired CPA. When a male voice answered, Scarlett asked if the gentleman was in fact Joel Carden.

"Speaking. What is your business?"

"I am a private investigator in Arlington, Virginia, Mr. Carden. Your niece, Anna-Claire Carden, hired me to help her with exploring her family history. Do you mind if I ask you a couple of questions."

"I'm not an advocate of giving information to someone on the phone I don't know. How do I know Anna hired you?"

"You don't. Do you have a computer nearby? If so, look up Shepherd and Associates dot com in Arlington, Virginia. You'll see a phone number. Compare that number with the one on your caller ID right now.

A long pause ensued.

"Anna? What would Anna need a private investigator for? Is she in some kind of trouble?"

"No, no. Absolutely not. This is a rather complicated matter. Anna is trying to learn more about her background."

"And she needs a private investigator for that? I'm confused. Did she tell you to call me? Why didn't she just call me herself?"

"Like I said, it's a bit complicated. Were you close to your brother's family at the time of Anna's birth?"

"I'm not sure what you call close. We've been living in Oregon for close to forty years. Larry and his family were in the South. The military took him there; he met Nora, and they stayed on the East Coast."

"So, did you have any type of contact with your brother around the time Anna was born? Telephone? Visits?"

"Around that time. I don't know exactly when. We usually saw Larry and Nora during the Christmas or Thanksgiving holidays when they visited our parents. I'm afraid there wasn't much contact after Mother passed—just a card at Christmas and a basket of fruit or box of cheese."

"Do you recall visiting at any time during Nora Carden's pregnancy?"

"Not that I remember. Why is that relevant? I don't think I want to answer any more questions until I speak with Anna."

"Just one more. Have you or any of your children submitted your DNA to a genealogy database?"

"Why would you want to know that?" His tone grew hostile.

"Because Anna submitted hers, and the results were different from what she expected. We're just trying to check out if the lab people messed up."

"I have not and do not know of anyone in the family who has."

"Would you be willing to submit a sample to a database or give one to us to be analyzed?"

"I don't think so, Ms. Kavanagh. I have a problem with the personal nature of that request."

"I apologize. Investigations are often invasive. Let me ask you this. Were there ever any problems in your brother's marriage? I assume that being in the military, there were periods of separation."

"I thought you said one more question. Anna's birth was a *long* time ago. I was not in the habit of prying into my brother's affairs, and we weren't close enough for me to be his sounding board. My wife communicated with Nora once in a while. She might know, but she's not here right now."

Scarlett hesitated for a moment to complete writing notes. Taking a deep breath, she said, "Mr. Carden, is there any possibility that Anna was not your brother's biological child?"

"What are you implying? You think my sister-in-law cheated, and Anna is the product of an affair? Lady, you don't know the kind of woman Nora Carden was. Does this come from Anna?"

"I apologize if you took my question to mean I suspected marital infidelity. There are other possibilities—adoption, assisted contraception, sperm donors."

"I'm sorry, but I prefer to answer no more questions without speaking to Anna."

"Of course. That's your prerogative, but please keep my number and reach out if anything comes to mind. May I call back to speak with your wife?"

"I'll let her decide. I have your number."

"I understand. Thank you for your time." She rested the receiver back in its cradle.

Well, that went well. Scarlett made a note on her calendar to follow up with Mary Carden.

CHAPTER 8

Saturday morning, Scarlett woke a little before six a.m. The Karin Slaughter book she had been reading the night before lay between Casper and Ebony, her two Persians. Noticing Scarlett's eyes open, Casper, the white one, immediately rose, stretched, and proceeded to climb on her chest, purring.

"Can't slip out of bed on you, can I?" she said, scratching him under his chin as Ebony's eyes opened wide. Although both cats had copper eyes, Ebony's popped in contrast to his solid black fur. "I'll get your breakfast in just a minute."

***

By ten-thirty, Scarlett was in the car with Sabrina, heading to a popular mall. The plan included shopping for an hour or so, lunch, and a movie, leaving Jake free to meet with Phil Madison for the final report on his investigation of the arson matter.

Madison had a reputation for being one of the country's best and most expensive lawyers. His relationship with Jake began when Jake did a summer clerkship in his office before graduating from Yale. Over the years, Madison became Jake's friend, mentor, and supporter. When Jake left the FBI, Madison helped kickstart the P.I. firm with lucrative case assignments.

As Scarlett pulled her red MINI Convertible into a parking slot, Sabrina said, "I love this car. If you decide to get a new one, will you give me a chance to talk Mom or Dad into buying it for me?"

"Your dad hates that I have this car, despite the fact I know he likes to drive it. He doesn't think it's safe enough—wants me to trade it for an SUV."

"Sounds like him. Overprotective. He thinks nothing is safe enough. I'm surprised he doesn't want you to drive a Hummer."

Scarlett chuckled. "That's probably coming. Speaking of Jake's paranoia, I understand you have a concert you want to attend, and he's not giving the okay."

"Yeah." She looked down toward her lap. "I'm really pressed."

An expression of confusion arose on Scarlett's face. "You're what?"

"Pressed. You know—angry. He's ruining my life." She reached for the door handle and started out of the vehicle. "I think I'm adopted. No one would treat a real child like this."

"Wait. Wait a second. Let's talk about this before we go in. And you're not adopted. You know that."

Sabrina sat back in the seat but left the door open. "There's nothing to talk about. The mighty Jake Shepherd has spoken. I'm going to be the only one in my group of friends who misses the concert."

"Maybe not. Would you give me a chance to make a suggestion?"

The teen's head turned in Scarlett's direction, slightly cocked. "What can you do?"

"I have an idea. Not perfect, but it would get you to the concert."

With her hands in prayer position, Sabrina gazed at Scarlett. "Really?"

"What if Brenda and I get tickets near your group? We can make up a story about why we're going, take you, sit close by, and you can go home with the parent that picks up the others if you like. Don't say no before you think about it. Your friends don't know us, at least not Brenda, and I don't think they know me unless they've been on the Shepherd website. But even if they do, I work for your dad."

She fiddled with her purse for a minute or more before looking back toward Scarlett. "Sounds like I'll have babysitters."

"Absolutely not. More like a security detail, like a president's daughter has Secret Service."

"Will Jake the super cop go along with that idea?"

"I think your father will. Brenda works security and is ex law enforcement. I'm not stupid. He knows she's capable. He'll go along. We're not your parents, so no embarrassment there."

"Why can't I ride to the concert with my friends?"

"Don't push your luck. He will be more comfortable if he knows Brenda and I see that you get into the event safely and keep an eye on you during. If we see you to a parent's car after, we can believe you'll be safe to ride home."

After another pause, Sabrina's thumb went up, and a smile brightened her face. "You're pretty awesome."

"Thank you. You're pretty special as well. Let's go buy something fabulous, have a super lunch, and take in the show."

***

As they rode to the office on Monday morning, Scarlett turned the music down on the player and said to Jake, "Pretty good weekend, right?"

"Not complaining, but don't let your win with Sabrina go to your head. Time will come when even you can't get her to compromise."

"Correction, Sherlock. You're the one who fails parental compromise one-o-one."

After turning a corner, he said, "Wasn't on my Yale schedule, but Harvard must have given it priority. They also offered basket weaving and knitting classes, didn't they?"

She punched his shoulder causing a low growl to come from behind the seats. Scarlett turned around to face the German shepherd. "And you be quiet. You know I couldn't hurt him if I tried."

While Jake drove the SUV to a parking place behind the building, Scarlett and Kai went in to find Liz at her desk, even though it was only seven-thirty.

"You're here early."

The silver-haired analyst smiled. "Traffic was good. How was the weekend? The shopping trip?"

"All good. My plan was accepted, although Jake struggled a bit. Sabrina was easier than I expected, which means Brenda and I are going to a rock concert. Overall, Jake had a good weekend. He and Sabrina played tennis yesterday, plus he wrapped up the arson case and gave his report to Phil on Saturday."

"I didn't know he plays tennis."

"Well, he's not good at it—actually terrible. He doesn't know how to hit the ball with finesse. He slams it like he's trying to knock a baseball out of Yankee Stadium. He gets so mad that I half expect him to draw his Glock and kill the damn ball."

Liz laughed. "Jake does not like to lose. In fact, it's not in his catalog."

"He's met his match on the tennis court, but he looks good in his game shorts even though they are not his favorite attire. Sabrina loves winning, but I have to give Jake credit. As much as he hates to lose, he's a good loser with her."

"I gotta see that sometime."

"I'll let you know next time. As for Phil's case, looks like there may be a bonus in the mail."

"I like the sound of that. What was Jake's final take? It must have been good."

"It was an angry former employee. Kind of a cliche, but it got charges dropped and Phil's client released."

Kai circled the desk and sat, patiently waiting for his morning treat from Liz.

"I'm going to make a cup of tea and then dig into phone calls in the Carden case. Anna and her fiancé are coming in today. He wants to meet me."

"Umm. Should be interesting. Are you going to tell her all you've discovered?"

"Not sure. But they're not coming until four. I may have more info by then."

CHAPTER 9

B y midmorning, Scarlett's efforts to obtain information about Anna's birth from several more of Nora Carden's friends had failed to offer any information. Another attempt to reach Nora's sister failed.

Liz walked in as Scarlett rested her telephone receiver in the cradle. "Well, that's a big smile on your face. What's up?"

"I just got off the phone with an old friend who works in an FBI lab."

Scarlett's attention intensified. "And?"

"She says a rapid DNA test result could be compared with one done by popular database companies if performed by a professional in the field."

"Wow! That could reduce the time of proving whether Anna's original DNA profile is valid. But where do we find a qualified professional?"

"Marion gave me the names of several resources. She said we need a sample taken with a swab and carefully handled to protect the integrity. I'm thinking you might contact Anna and have her prepare the sample at her hospital. I'm sure they have the proper materials. I gave her all the kits I ordered. Maybe we should stock them."

"Liz, you are magic. What would we do without you? Jake needs to give you a raise."

The analyst beamed. "What else would I do with my time? Besides, I've always been fond of Jake, and having you here has just made it all that much better."

Before Liz finished speaking, Scarlett had her phone in hand, calling Anna. Looking at Liz, she pointed to the receiver and mouthed, "Voice mail," and then said, "Anna, this is Scarlett Kavanagh. I need you to do something before you come to the office. I believe you are working at the hospital until three o'clock. We need another DNA sample for rapid testing. I'm sure they have swabs at the hospital you can use to swab your inside cheek and protect it in a plastic bag."

As Scarlett ended the call, Liz started to leave but turned back. "One more thing, Marion said we need to have a specific release from the client for the testing and comparison of her DNA to relieve the testing company from any privacy concerns. I'll draft one up and have it ready."

"You're gold. Thanks. I hope Anna gets my message before she leaves the hospital."

***

As the clock on Scarlett's desk reached ten after four p.m., a low, guttural sound came from Kai, signaling the likelihood someone was arriving. Scarlett closed the file and straightened her desk seconds before receiving a ring from Liz.

"Dr. Carden and Dr. Larsen are here."

"Send them back."

As Scarlett stood, she noticed the fur on Kai's neck rise. "Kai. *Nein. In ordnung.*" The shepherd instantly responded to the German commands of "no" and "okay" but moved from his bed under the window to Scarlett's side as if to ensure he was ready if needed.

As the two doctors entered, dressed in hospital scrubs, Anna spoke, "Excuse us for being late and for our wardrobe. We both ran into overtime on our shifts and didn't have time to change. The hospital was crazy busy today."

"No apologies necessary. Just glad you made it." Scarlett extended a hand toward Anna's fiancé, an imposing figure some would call handsome. "I'm Scarlett Kavanagh."

"Dan Larsen," he said, shaking hands with Scarlett.

At six feet, two inches, Larsen's muscles challenged the bounds of his shirt sleeves. Scarlett resisted the temptation to mention how he looked more like an athlete than a physician.

Anna apparently read Scarlett's mind from her facial expression and said, "Dan's a former NFL player."

With a smile and a nod, Scarlett said, "Really. You left the pros for med school?"

"One injury too many. I decided I'd rather be the doctor than the patient."

"Fair enough. Please have a seat." As she sat in her chair, Scarlett glanced toward Anna. "Did you get my message?"

"I did. I brought two swabs, just to be safe."

"Good idea. I'm happy to say I don't think you need to send samples off to other databases. We'll have a rapid test done, and have the lab compare your original profile. If they match, then we have solid confirmation that the Cardens were not your biological parents." Feeling his harsh stare, Scarlett looked over to Dan Larsen. "Is there a problem, Dr. Larsen?"

"I just don't understand why this is so important to Anna, and why she won't set a date for our wedding."

"You know how I feel, Dan. How can I get married if I don't know who I am?"

"You are you. That's all that matters. I don't give a damn who your biological parents are or were."

Anna shook her head, tossing her long hair over her shoulder. "I think we are going to need to agree to disagree. But since you know exactly who your parents, grandparents, aunts and uncles are, I don't think you can understand."

Scarlett's eyes cut from one to the other. "If I might interject. I am not adopted—although sometimes I wish I were. But I understand. Many people feel a mystical draw to their heritage and wonder about things like did I inherit my love of cats, timid personality, or talent for writing from an ancestor? I am a twin, but my sister is a clone of our quintessential Southern Belle mother who loves social importance and having the right sterling silver fork by the porcelain plate, while I'm my father. We care more about the food than the fork and accomplishment more than position. But enough about me. As I said, with the DNA samples you brought today, I am going to send them to a prominent lab, along with your previous DNA profile. Their experts will compare the two. If they don't match, there could have been an error in the report you received. If they do match, even if only partially, we can assume you are not the Carden's child, but for absolute confirmation and a map of your ancestry, I suggest we submit to a few more databases."

"How long is that going to take," Larsen asked.

"The initial test and comparison with the results you received should take a week or less, but a comprehensive kit that provides a map of your ancestry with percentages and potential familial matches will take at least three weeks and with most companies from six to eight weeks. However, I will continue to do interviews with anyone who might have knowledge of Anna's birth." As Scarlett spoke, she opened the file and took out the release form for Anna to sign. "We have found a Georgia birth record for an Anna-Claire Carden but are not absolutely certain it is you, Anna."

"Really? Georgia? That's not me. I don't think my parents ever lived in Georgia."

"We'll see."

"So, are we done?" Larsen asked.

"For today," Scarlett rose as the other two followed. "I'll keep you informed on my progress."

"It needs to be ASAP," Larsen said, just as Jake passed by the open door on the way to his office. "I hope you don't drag it out to build your fees."

Jake stepped in. "Excuse me. I'm Jake Shepherd, and that's not the way we do things. Who the hell are you?"

Scarlett blinked an extended blink and sucked in a breath. *Oh, boy. Two alphas.* "Jake, you remember Dr. Carden. This is her fiancé Dr. Daniel Larsen. I'm sure he meant no offense."

The holster bearing Jake's weapon at his waist had caught Larsen's attention as he openly stared at it. Although a couple of inches taller, with the biceps of a body builder in contrast to Jake's shorter, leaner, toned body of a baseball player, the mere presence of the Glock leveled the playing field. Larsen immediately backed down.

"Apologies. She's right. I meant no offense. It's just that this quest has consumed Anna like a fire in pool of gasoline. I guess I'm jealous." Larsen's words bore more contrition than his tone.

Jake said nothing, just glared at Larsen for a second or two and then said to Scarlett. "I'm in my office if you need me." He left without another word, Kai following.

Scarlett breathed a silent sigh of relief as Anna appeared to do the same.

Shortly after the doctors exited the office, Liz appeared at Scarlett's door. "Did I hear Jake step in on your conference?"

"Oh, yes. A bit of tension for a moment. You know Larsen's a former NFL pro."

"I did not. Thank you for explaining why he looks more like Jimmy Garoppolo than Dr. Oz."

CHAPTER 10

"Well, you certainly gave Dr. Larsen a sample of your charming personality."

Jake snapped his head around to face Scarlett as he cranked the SUV. "The guy's a jerk."

"Maybe. But maybe he's just uptight about their wedding plans."

"I read a condescending, superior attitude, probably awarded along with his med school diploma, but it's your case."

Scarlett chuckled. "Look who's talking. But—there may be a lot more to this case than you think." She cut her eyes in his direction as if checking for a reaction.

After several minutes of silence, Jake said, "How so?"

A huge smile crossed Scarlett's face as she adjusted the air vents. "Got your attention, didn't I?"

He cocked an eyebrow and with a grin said, "You always have my attention, Harvard."

"Yeah, right. But this is . . . it's different. There's something going on. It's definitely not your ordinary track the-birth-parents case. Something crazy is going on."

"Tell me about it, Jessica Fletcher."

"Don't patronize me. Think about this. The birth certificate is an original, not a new issue after an adoption. It matches Anna to the Cardens, but her DNA does not match. Yet, even without the results of another DNA test, I know Anna is not the biological daughter of the couple who raised her. If nothing else, the eye color proves that."

"Whoa. Freaks of nature have happened. Recessive genes. And don't forget, the mom could be biological but paired with a brown-eyed sperm donor."

"Maybe. But the maternal aunt seems to be dodging my calls. I left several messages, identifying myself and my purpose, and no returns. I've called a dozen times at various parts of the day. I even called last night."

"Maybe she's away—a vacation, even out of the country."

"Possibly, but tomorrow, I'm going to call one of her children. Anna gave me a name and address, and Liz found a number."

"After you've been at this for a while, you're going to find a lot of people don't want to get involved with anything that sounds like an investigation."

"It's not like I'm investigating a crime. What would you think about me making a trip to South Carolina to interview witnesses?"

"Wrong person to ask. Ask your client how she feels about paying for your field trip. Dr. Doolittle may object. But you might want to wait until your tests come back and the investigation develops further."

***

Two days after the appointment with Anna and her fiancé, Scarlett's phone buzzed shortly after lunch. When she responded, Liz informed her Joel Carden was on line one.

"Really? Put him through." She grabbed a pen, a legal pad, and the Carden file.

"This is Scarlett," she said as anticipation spiked an adrenaline rush.

"Ms. Kavanagh, you asked me to call if anything came to mind about my brother's family around the time of Anna's birth."

"I did. Have you remembered something unusual?"

"I'm not really sure, but Mary, my wife, reminded me of an incident about that time. We were planning a trip east and wanted to stop by Augusta to see the new baby."

Augusta! "Do you mean Augusta or Alabama? Anna said she was born in Alabama."

"Augusta. Larry never lived in Alabama. He was stationed at an army base in Augusta at the time Anna was born."

"Did you get to see Anna when she was a baby?"

"No. That's the strange part. Well, maybe not strange. We were planning a trip south at the end of summer, before school reopened, and planned to include Augusta in the trip. Mary and Nora had been in contact during Nora's pregnancy, and we thought it would be a good opportunity to see our new niece. However, when I told Larry our plan, he said it wouldn't work as they were going to be out of town. We accepted his excuse but wondered a little why they would be traveling with such a young baby, and why they couldn't postpone it since we rarely got to visit in their area. It bothered Mary more than it did me."

"Did your brother say where they were going?"

"Not that I recall. I don't think it means anything, but Mary thought I should tell you. She also encouraged me to provide you with a DNA sample."

"I appreciate that. I'll have our assistant send you a kit. But, tell me, when did you first meet your niece?"

"Not for a couple of years, maybe three. They had moved to Virginia by that time, but they brought her to visit my parents on the Thanksgiving before our father passed away. He was in hospice, and we all knew he wouldn't live long."

"Did anyone in your family see Anna-Claire when she was an infant?"

The phone went silent for a minute. "Mr. Carden. Are you still there?"

"I'm sorry. I was thinking. I'm pretty sure my mother visited. Anna was her only granddaughter. Let me check with Mary—or better, she can talk to you. She had more contact with my mother than I did."

"Did your wife and Nora continue to have regular contact?"

"I don't remember. You'll have to ask her more about that. I think she liked Nora, but she can tell you more."

"Great. Please have her call me. I'll be here until at least five and all day tomorrow. I really appreciate your taking the time to contact me." As Scarlett ended the call, she looked up to see Liz at her door.

"This case is intriguing. Here's the DNA report." She handed Scarlett a printout of an email. "I had to come in to find out if Mr. Carden provided you with any new information."

"Hopefully. His wife is going to call me. At least he sounded a little more cooperative." She glanced down at the email. "So, the new test was a match to the test results Anna received from the database she used. I thought it would be." As she placed the paper in a manila folder on her desk, she said, "The uncle remembered some unusual behavior by his brother right after Anna was born but says his wife knows more. I hope she calls. Right now, I'd better give Anna a call and let her know about the match."

***

At five-thirty, Scarlett straightened her desk to leave for the day. Jake was on the phone in his office, and Liz had left early for a dental appointment. She placed the Carden file in a rack on her desk, thinking how disappointed she was to not have received a call from Mary Carden. "Maybe tomorrow," she said aloud. A ring of her phone caused her to flinch. Staring at it for several seconds, she debated whether to answer or let it go to voice mail because Jake would want to leave as soon as he completed his conversation. When it rang for the third time, Scarlett snatched the receiver. "Shepherd and Associates."

A soft voice said, "May I speak with Scarlett Kavanagh?"

Scarlett glanced at the caller ID screen, but it simply read, "Out of Area."

"This is Scarlett. How can I help you?"

"This is Mary Carden. Joel said you wanted me to call. I've been working at my church all day. I hope I'm not interrupting you."

"No, no. You're fine. I'm so glad you called."

"Larry said you want to know if there was anything unusual about my late sister-in-law, Nora, around the time of Anna's birth. Is that right?"

"It is. Did he tell you that Anna believes she was adopted?"

"Yes. But I think she's wrong. Nora and I talked at least twice a week during her pregnancy. I already had our two children, and she had so many questions about what to expect and what to do. She sent me a photo right before Anna was born. So, Anna's wrong. She's an only child, and I know that Nora had her."

Scarlett contemplated how to inform Mary that there was scientific proof Anna was not Nora's child. "Mrs. Carden, please forgive me if this sounds disrespectful, and trust me, I do believe you, but something isn't right. Anna has done DNA testing, and the results indicate her ancestors came from Italy, Greece, France, Spain, and Belgium."

"They must have mixed her DNA up."

"That's what I initially thought. However, we had another test run by one of the best labs and they came up with a matching profile. I don't think there is a mistake. Is there anything you remember that was strange or that changed after Anna was born? Your husband told me you had planned to visit to see the new baby, but Anna's dad nixed the idea."

The phone was silent for nearly a minute.

"Mrs. Carden? Are you still there?"

"Yes. Yes, I'm here. I don't know what to say. I just can't believe that Anna isn't Nora and Larry's child."

"Can you walk me through the contact you had after Anna's birth?"

"They called us from the hospital the night she was born, and Nora sent a photo of the three of them in the hospital. Anna was a pretty baby."

"Was the photo in color?"

"Yes."

"What was Anna's hair and eye color?"

"She was a beautiful blue-eyed blond. Chubby cheeks."

"Your husband said you saw Anna when his father was in hospice."

"Just briefly. Nora said she wasn't feeling well, and so she stayed at the hotel most of the time they were there."

"Were her eyes still blue?"

"They weren't. I noticed they had turned brown, and her hair was darker. But she was still a pretty little girl. I was a bit jealous with only boys. I never got to buy cute little dresses, fancy shoes, and dolls—you know—girly things."

"Did you receive other photos as she grew?"

"Only one more—her three-month photo."

"No more photos as she aged?"

"For some reason, Nora and I drifted apart. In fact, she seemed to avoid my calls, so I stopped calling. She never sent any more photos. I blamed the loss of contact on both of us being busy. I was active with my boys, their school, my teaching, and my church. We lived so far apart, which didn't help. But Anna has to be Nora's child unless the hospital got them mixed up. That was Joel's thought."

"I'm sure there's some explanation. But thank you so much for calling. If you think of anything more, please let me know."

CHAPTER 11

More than a month passed by as Scarlett waited for all the reports to come in from the DNA databases. As each arrived, it confirmed the original. Anna's heritage was clearly not Northern European as was the Cardens. While Scarlett immediately sent Anna an email with DNA information she received as it arrived, she did not share everything she had learned about the mysterious birth certificate and about the questions her interviews had produced. The anxious client called every day or so for updates.

While distributing their take-out dinner onto plates on Wednesday of the fifth week of representing Anna, Scarlett hesitated, as Jake approached the kitchen bar. "I need to make a trip to South Carolina," she said.

"Before or after dinner?"

"Cute. You know what I mean."

He grinned. "Your adoption mystery. I know. What makes you think you need to make a trip now? I can't get away. Trial in Lila's insurance fraud case is set for next week. And aren't you going to that concert with Sabrina?"

"The concert is over two months away, and I told you several weeks ago that I wanted to do some face-to-face interviews in Anna's case. All the DNA reports are in. All confirm she is not the biological child of the Cardens. She may not even be their legal child. We've found no record of an adoption. What's even stranger is no matches have come from the databases for Anna's maternal side and only a handful for her father's. But I've been told that potential matches come over a period of time. I've never been able to interview Nora Carden's sister. She doesn't return my calls. And Anna's paternal aunt confirmed the Cardens changed drastically when Anna was between four or five months old. She said Nora Carden began dodging phone calls, and they drifted apart after talking regularly during Nora's pregnancy. There are still major, unanswered questions."

"What have you told the client about the birth certificate?"

"No. I've been holding back, hoping to get more information."

"Probably a good call. I'll look at my case load tomorrow," Jake said, placing two glasses of tea on the table. "I'll let you know when I can get away."

After the food was all on the table, Scarlett slid into her chair and stared at Jake as he took a bite of his lasagna. "I'm perfectly capable of making the trip alone."

He took a swallow of tea, leaned back in his chair, looked at her, and said, "The training wheels aren't off the bike, yet."

"And what's that supposed to mean?"

"You know what it means. Yeah, you can get on a plane and certainly interview witnesses, even difficult ones, but you're not ready to fly solo when you don't know what you may be flying into. And, as I recall, I've had to get you out of a couple of dicey situations in the past."

"That's a cheap shot. Yeah, I defied you and took a big chance in Florida, but you got to be a hero. And I thought you considered this a simple case of find mommy and daddy."

"Yeah. And how many cops have been shot during simple traffic stops? You've told me often enough that this isn't a simple case. Hell, the mother may have miscarried and then bought a baby out of the back door at that doctor in Georgia's clinic."

"What?"

"You never heard about what's his name?"

"Are you talking about Thomas Hicks?"

"I don't know. Am I?"

"If you're talking about him, that was in the 1950s and '60s—way before Anna was born. Plus, they don't issue birth certificates for a miscarriage. And we've found no death record matching the birth record, which would have been recorded if the baby were born alive and died shortly thereafter. Finally, there's no record of the Cardens having a second child. Jake, it doesn't add up."

He put his fork down and looked at her, an eyebrow cocked. "And?"

"Everything is pointing toward the Cardens having a biological child," she continued. "But it was not my client. Nora sent Mary a picture of the baby with blue eyes and blond hair. The hair I can see turning, but I don't think Anna's eyes could have ever been blue. There's something we don't know."

"It does sound sketchy, which confirms my position that you are not going alone. You are telling me this is developing into more than a standard birth parent search. Although unlikely, you might be stepping into a firestorm. If it can't wait until I'm free, then take Brenda."

"Really, Jake. Take a babysitter?"

"I'm thinking more like a companion."

She put her fork down. "Companion my applesauce. Liz would be a companion. Brenda is a gun-carrying ex cop."

He took a swallow of tea. "If you don't like my terms, then let it go until I can make the trip. Nothing's going to change the facts in a couple of weeks."

"Nothing except it delays Anna learning who she is, easing her anxiety, and maybe saving her relationship with the hot fiancé. I didn't see patience in the stud's toolbox."

"Did I hear you say stud, hot fiancé?"

"Did you?"

With a quizzical look, he shook his head.

Although the subject of the Carden case was dropped, as Jake cleared the table while Scarlett put away the condiments, she said, "You win. I'll delay the trip, but I don't know how long I can stall giving Anna the information we've compiled. She's calling nearly every day."

CHAPTER 12

J ake dropped Scarlett and Kai at the office on Thursday morning on his way to meet with Phillip Madison. The attorney wanted to discuss several leads in a case Jake was working for him. Although it was nearly nine a.m., Liz was not at her desk as Scarlett and Kai entered. Kai immediately went to the reception desk.

"Sorry, old boy. You'll have to wait for your morning treat. Liz isn't here." The shepherd glanced over his shoulder as if he understood, sniffed Liz's chair as though she might be hiding in it, and then gave up, following Scarlett to her office. After making a cup of tea and giving the dog a treat from her supply, she settled into her chair and opened her computer. At nine-fifteen, the front door opened, bringing Kai to attention. Since he didn't bark or growl, Scarlett knew it was Liz arriving. As the shepherd proceeded to the reception area, he met Liz in the hallway, reversed himself, and followed her to Scarlett's desk.

"Hey. Sorry I'm late. I stayed up too late, binging on a Netflix series and slept through my alarm."

"No problem."

"I didn't see a vehicle in the drive. Is Jake here?"

"No. He let me out and went to Phil's office, and I think he's going to Lila's after he leaves Phil to go over his report in her case that's set for trial next week."

"What's on your calendar today?"

"Don't ask."

An expression of concern spread over Liz's face. "What's wrong?"

"I've got to bring Anna Carden in to explain all we've learned in her case, and for some reason, I'm dreading it."

"She knows she's not a Carden doesn't she?"

"She does, but the rest of it is so off the track. I'd rather Dr. know-it-all didn't come with her this time. He's not very helpful."

***

The office was quiet most of the morning with the phone ringing only two or three times. Shortly before lunch, Liz appeared at Scarlett's door, holding an email she had printed out.

"This just came in. It's the list of births at the hospital where Anna-Claire Carden was born." She handed the printout to Scarlett.

Opening the manila folder with Anna's name, she placed the document on top and glanced down at the list of about twelve entries. Each provided the name of parents, gender of baby, and date of birth. "Great! Maybe we will find the answer to our mystery in these records."

Liz shook her head in the negative. "The only answer on the list is that Anna was not switched in the hospital."

"What?" Scarlett's brow wrinkled, forming a frown, as she gave the document another look.

"Scarlett, it was apparently baby boy season in Georgia. There was only one female baby born in the entire period surrounding the date of birth on the Carden birth record. No way two families could take home wrong sex babies."

"Oh, my gosh, you're right. Well, we can check that off the list. I guess it's good because a switch would have made a mess of another family as well. Have you heard from Jake?"

"He texted that he won't be in until after lunch. What about I put in a delivery order for us?"

"Good idea. If you're ordering from that place we like, I'll have the chicken salad plate."

"Got it."

"I'm going to put in a call to Anna. Best to get it over with."

As Liz returned to her desk, Scarlett lifted the receiver of her phone. Checking the number on the inside of Anna's folder, she dialed. After only one ring, Anna answered.

"Is there news?"

"A little bit, but I do have some things we've learned that I need to bring you up to speed on. I know you're at work; however, I think it best you come in so we can go over everything."

"I can come when my shift is over at three if you don't mind working a little late. Would that be okay?"

Although she knew her afternoon was clear, Scarlett pulled up her calendar. "That will work. Look forward to seeing you."

"I am such a coward," she said to Kai who lay on the floor under the window by her desk. "I should have asked her to come alone. She'll probably bring him along."

CHAPTER 13

B y three-forty-five, Jake was in his office, reviewing footage from surveillance cameras in Phil Madison's case, when Anna Carden arrived, accompanied by Dan Larsen.

As the couple walked into Scarlett's office, both wearing scrubs, Anna in rose, her hair in a low ponytail, and Dan in teal, Anna said, "I hope you don't mind Dan sitting in."

If only you knew. "As long as you're comfortable, it is fine with me. Please have a seat. Can we get you anything? Coffee, tea, soft drink, water?"

"I'm fine," Anna said with Dan nodding.

"We just want to get to the heart of the matter. We've set the date for our wedding and have made reservations for a honeymoon in France, but Anna is still insisting she has to know her biological history. What have you learned?"

Scarlett swallowed the impulse to tell him it was Anna's case, not his. "Anna, as you are well aware, we have enough evidence to prove you are not the biological child of Nora and Lawrence Carden, but for absolute confirmation, I have asked your father's brother to volunteer a DNA sample. He agreed, but we haven't received it.

"Then you really don't know anything," Larsen said.

Again, stifling a sarcastic response, Scarlett said, "Not true. We have found a birth certificate, issued in Georgia, for a baby girl whose name was registered as Anna-Claire, born to Nora and Lawrence Carden on Anna's date of birth in Augusta—"

"Well, that answers the question. Anna was their child."

"Dr. Larsen, you did not allow me to finish. That baby was a blue-eyed blonde born to parents with blue and green eyes."

"So. Hair color changes and eyes can as well."

"I suppose there can be an aberration in any situation, but I've looked at a photo of a blue-eyed Anna-Claire Carden at three months." She withdrew an image from the folder and passed it over to the client. As Anna scanned the photo, Scarlett withdrew a second one, passing it to Anna as well. "I compared it with that one of Anna at seven months," she said, pointing to the last image provided.

"Oh no!" With the two photos in her hands, the color drained from Anna's face. Her response resonated through the building, bringing Kai to his feet and Jake to the door.

"Everything okay?"

Anna had buried her face in her hands while Larsen glared at Scarlett.

"Was it necessary to upset her like that?" he said in a vitriolic tone, reaching over to put a hand on Anna's shoulder.

"That baby is not me," Anna said, lifting her head with tears running down her face. "Who am I?" She pulled away from Larsen while Jake remained at the doorway.

"This was totally inappropriate," Larsen said as Jake moved into the room. "And where did you get that first photo? Did it ever occur to you it might not be Anna?"

"The first photo is a copy provided to me by Anna's paternal aunt, sent to her by Nora Carden. The second one, Anna gave me."

"It's a fake," Larsen said. "Let's go, Anna. You're being taken advantage of here." He reached for her hand.

"No, no, Dan. I've got to know the truth."

When Larsen continued his attempt to get her to stand, Jake stepped up, causing a knot to form in Scarlett's stomach.

"Back off, Dr. Larsen. I get that you're concerned, but Dr. Carden has a right to know what Scarlett has discovered. It's what she was hired to do."

"Don't give me orders."

"Dan, please."

I knew this wasn't going to go well. "It's okay, Jake. I can handle it."

"So you can, but I'm here, which means you don't have to. Dr. Larsen, your fiancée wants to know who her biological family is, and until she says she doesn't, she is in charge of what we do. We investigate. We don't create happy-ever-after-solutions. While I haven't been involved in this particular case, from what I have observed from the findings, something dicey happened about thirty-five years ago, and as of today, I'm on board."

Anna's gaze focused on Jake; her tear-drenched face sprung a smile as did Scarlett's. When Anna looked her way, Scarlett silently mouthed, "Told you so," and winked.

"Thank you, Mr. Shepherd." Anna turned to the agitated surgeon. "I love you, Dan. I do, but I can't marry you until I know who I am. If there is another Anna-Claire Carden out there, I can't go through a ceremony and say, 'I Anna-Claire take thee Daniel.' I may have another name. You have to know who you are marrying."

"I am marrying the woman, not the name. Change your name if it makes you happy." Turning toward Jake, with a contemptuous look, Larsen said, "Does that mean Anna is going to be paying for two investigators?"

As Jake crossed the room to take a place alongside Kai, he said, "Dr. Carden hired the firm. The rate remains the same no matter who or how many work the case. I believe now, the client has spoken. I suggest you give her your support."

Larsen eased back into the chair next to Anna's in front of Scarlett's desk. Jake remained standing. If looks were ammunition, Jake's body would have been perforated.

"Please tell me all you know, Scarlett," Anna said, wiping her face with a tissue from the box on Scarlett's desk.

"We've received reports from several of the databases we submitted your DNA samples to. Each corroborated your initial report. Your ancestors appear to have come from European countries, primarily on the Mediterranean with a few exceptions. None were found from Northern Europe or the UK. A few possible matches have been offered. I've submitted your DNA profile and what information we have to a company specializing in genetic genealogy analysis. They do a lot of work for law enforcement."

"That could take weeks. Our wedding is set for Labor Day Weekend."

"I can't give you a timeline. But to make sure we obtain reliable results, I have chosen one of the best companies. Choosing on the basis of cost or speed could be a big mistake." Scarlett turned to Anna. "I have spoken with your paternal uncle, his wife, and a close friend of your mother. Your paternal aunt feels something changed with

Nora when you were allegedly between four and six months old. As I've said, we located the Georgia birth certificate with your name and matching date of birth and parents' name. Although we considered an accidental baby switch in the hospital, the records indicate only one female baby born within weeks before and after your birth. We have found absolutely no record of an adoption."

"How the hell could that happen?" Larsen asked.

"We're asking the same question. We have explored a unique situation like one that occurred in Chicago when a baby was taken the day after birth. A couple of years later, an abandoned toddler was incorrectly assumed to be the missing baby and given to the parents. The child grew up, suspected something was not right, investigated, and ultimately discovered he was not the baby abducted. However, research has not produced a missing child who meets our criteria."

"So, what can we do next?" Anna asked.

"And how long will it take?" Larsen added.

Scarlett closed her file. "As I mentioned to you several weeks ago, I would like to travel to South Carolina to interview your aunt. I had a very brief telephone conversation with her daughter, Robin Sawyer. She was on her way out and didn't have time to answer my questions. I asked if she would be willing to give a DNA sample. She agreed to consider it, but we've not heard from her. It's not that far from Augusta. If we are able to locate any hospital personnel working at the time of your birth, I'd like to visit there as well. The idea would be to locate anyone who knew your parents around the time of your birth. It appears Dr. Carden was stationed at Fort Gordon but transferred to Fort Belvoir not far from here when you were still an infant."

"I feel so fake, like I don't exist. If there is another Anna-Claire Carden, I'm living her life? What happened to her? The name on my medical degree, on my license, belongs to someone else. And what about my date of birth? If the one I've always celebrated was hers, what is mine?" Tears again rolled down her cheeks.

"Anna, you're who you are. All that date of birth, name stuff means nothing. You are a brilliant, beautiful, flesh and blood woman. Every day, you save lives. Wasn't there a quote in Shakespeare about a name?" Larsen said.

"'A rose by any other name would smell as sweet,'" Scarlett said. "*Romeo and Juliet.*"

"That's it."

"It's more than that, Dan. I became a doctor, believing that medicine was in my blood. I was following in my father's footsteps. He wasn't my father. How could they do this to me?"

"They loved you, Anna," Scarlett said. "For whatever reason they did what they did, they wanted you, and they loved you. That is special."

"But if we have children, how can I tell them about their grandparents? I might have siblings—aunts and uncles to my children. I have to know. I need to know why my birth parents gave me away. Please understand."

Compassion filled Scarlett's heart as she saw the anguish in her client. *I want to know how they did it without leaving a record of any kind.*

Jake remained silent, a hand on Kai's head.

"Let me take you home. We can talk about it," Larsen said.

"No. I need to be alone." She took out her phone and touched the Uber icon. "I'll take a car home. You go home. I'll think this through and talk to you tomorrow." Turning to Scarlett, she said, "Please go to South Carolina and talk to whoever you can."

Jake spoke up, "I am testifying in a trial here next week, but we'll schedule the trip for the week after."

CHAPTER 14

As they settled into their seats on the plane to Charleston, Scarlett tucked the novel she bought in a terminal shop into the pocket behind the seat in front of her. Jake took a last glance at his cell before switching it to airplane mode. Delays caused the flight to be nearly five hours late leaving. While Scarlett had filled the time reading, Jake had spent part of it reviewing emails, including a report Liz provided in another client's case and the remainder walking around the terminal.

Settled in, Jake said, "You've done a good job on this case, Harvard."

She turned, crunching her eyebrows together. "Why, thank you. To what do I owe the honor?"

"I was a little dismissive in the beginning. But you picked up on something and ran with it."

"'A little dismissive? You wouldn't touch the case. But I don't deserve all the credit. Liz has been phenomenal." Before she could say more, the flight attendant began the routine spiel.

When the instructions were completed, Jake reached over and lifted Scarlett's book from the pocket. "Whatcha reading?"

"A new detective mystery."

"You don't get enough true crime on the job?"

"Sometimes fiction is just better. I don't recall seeing you read for pleasure. They did require reading at Yale, didn't they?"

"Very funny. I read occasionally, usually on a tablet or my phone."

"Changing the subject, what is our game plan now that we won't get there in time to interview anyone tonight?"

"Your call. This is your case."

"Really? I expected you to take first chair. If it's mine, then I think the cousin first. At least she took my call and seemed cooperative. Should we call ahead or just show up?"

"Probably show up. Didn't you say she is a stay-at-home mom?" As the plane taxied for the ascent, he stuffed a stick of gum in his mouth and offered her a piece. "It'll help with the popping in your ears."

"I'm good."

"You sure?"

"Yep. I'm an obnoxious gum chewer so best I restrict it to private times."

Jake chuckled. "Glad to see you have a flaw. I've been thinking you are perfect."

"Now, who's being funny?" She disengaged the bracelet she wore from the cuff of her sweater. "By the way. What really made you decide to work with me on this case? The facts or Dr. NFL?"

He grinned with a devilish twinkle in his eye and patted her leg. "You know that's classified, Harvard."

"That answers my question. Sure you don't want to take the lead and show him up?"

"I think you'll do just fine."

***

Soon after the plane touched down, Scarlett looked at her phone. There was only one notification, but it was from Liz.

> Check your email. A report came in from the genetic genealogy people. You'll want to see it.

Scarlett's heart beat faster. She considered opening the email on her phone but reconsidered, deciding to wait to read it on the larger screen of her iPad at the first available moment. As Jake unfastened his seatbelt, she put a hand on his shoulder, holding her cell up for him to see. "Jake, Liz says we have a DNA report. We might have identified a parent, or maybe both."

CHAPTER 15

After deboarding, they approached baggage claim, Jake turned toward Scarlett. "I'll take care of the luggage and rental vehicle. Find yourself a place where you can read your email. I know you're anxious to see what it says."

Scarlett smiled. "I think we've been together too long. You read me like a book." Her eyebrows rose. "Oh! Wait. I forgot. You read everyone."

He gave her an evil eye.

There was no seating near the baggage carousel, so, Scarlett went to a less populated area, set her tote bag down, and took out her tablet. Adrenaline coursed through her bloodstream as she opened Liz's email, skipping straight to the attachment. *This could have an answer.*

The form report read:

Mother: *Unknown.*

Father: Most likely candidate:

Victor (Vic) Anthony Lanza – Deceased
(shared 3390 cM)

DOB: April 4, 1953

DOD: July 14, 1990

Place of Birth: New York, New York, USA

Place of Death: Charleston, SC, USA

Methodology:

A. DNA Match Analysis

1. 21 DNA matches, analyzed

2.Top Matches:

a) Aunt/Uncle/Grandparent - Parent 2 – Veronica Lanza Salvadore (shared 1901 cM)

b) Aunt/Uncle/Grandparent – Parent 2 – Francesca Lanza Cardoza (shared 1790 cM)

c) 1st Cousin – Parent 2 – Phillip Salvadore (shared 798 cM)

d) 1st Cousin - Parent 2 – Maria Cardoza Burgess (shared 319 cM)

Public Records Search:

No birth, marriage, or property records located

News articles located referencing death of Lanza

Contact and Confirmation:

Contact was made with Maria Burgess. Little known information. Believes Vic Lanza moved to California where he built a career as an actor. She was aware through family legend that he purchased a historic home in South Carolina where he died in a fire as the result of a homicide.

Recommendation:

Obtain DNA sample from surviving siblings of probable match.

Scarlett stared at the screen, processing the data. *It all fits. Italian names, Charleston. Anna's father was Vic Lanza!*

"Hey, Harvard, let's go." Jake called out from about six feet away from her.

Startled, she looked up and beckoned him. "You're not going to believe this, Jake. Come look."

As he reached her, Jake parked her carry-on and his duffle bag next to her tote, took the tablet from her, and began reading the report.

"Anna's father was a famous actor," Scarlett said. "And he was murdered."

Jake looked up. "Well, that was unexpected. I remember Lanza's cop show. My mother was addicted. It was before we lost dad. He gave her a hard time about the authenticity of the procedure. That was a long time ago."

"I know it. I've watched reruns. It was a popular show. This should rule out any possibility of an invitro fertilization foul up. There's no way this guy would be a sperm donor."

He handed her the tablet and began to collect the luggage. "The guy could have been trying to make a baby with his partner, and the test tubes got mixed up."

"But did Nora Carden come to Charleston for IVF? Her sister lived here, but that would be a reach."

"Doesn't seem likely." Jake started for the exit. "Maybe we should look into the case while we're here. I remember that fire from TV news reports. I wonder if it destroyed the house."

"I can't believe who he was."

"Run him through Google later. Get the basics, and then let Liz pull the media coverage from newspaper sites on the Internet. For now, let's grab a car, get to our hotel, and check out a place for dinner."

As she tucked her tablet back into her bag, Scarlett paused. "Jake, do you think I should tell Anna?"

"I'd hold off. Try to get a sibling DNA sample to lock it down before telling her. Liz can work on tracking down Lanza's siblings." He glanced down at his watch. "Better idea. Let's pick up dinner and take it to the hotel. That barbecue restaurant Liz said is so good isn't that far."

She grinned. "I knew that would be the first thing you'd want to do here. But I get to choose at least once before we go back."

"You know I always give you your turn, Harvard."

CHAPTER 16

Charleston weather was sunny and warm on Monday morning as Jake and Scarlett drove toward the home of Anna's cousin. The Sawyer's residence was located in Mount Pleasant, a suburban town separated from the city of Charleston by the Cooper River.

"Maybe this is a pointless act. We have proof Anna is not a biological Carden." Scarlett brushed a stray section of hair off her forehead.

"I think you're looking for more than proof of that. You're also looking to solve the mystery of how she came to be raised by the Cardens, which might lead to the identification of her birth mother. If Lanza was her father, he can't tell you."

"True. The facts are just not stacking up right. But I feel a bit guilty about showing up at this woman's house without calling first," Scarlett said.

"Would you rather risk a refusal?"

"No."

"Southern manners and social protocol are left at home in this line of work, Harvard."

"I've been debating whether Lanza should be mentioned. Could Nora Carden have known him? Had an affair?"

"Like I said yesterday about telling the client, I think it is best kept under the radar until a reliable confirmation is made. You might ask if there is any known Masters' family ancestry matching Anna's. But keep in mind, a leak to the media about Lanza could create a frenzy. The guy was an A-list celebrity with a page-one demise."

It took nearly an hour to reach Sawyer's neighborhood from their hotel. However, the ride was smooth and the scenery attractive. As they neared their destination, manicured lawns, traditional southern architecture, and empty streets provided a peaceful ambiance. Parked in the driveways were Toyotas, Hondas, and Volvos all appearing to have just left the carwash. Only garbage receptacles awaiting a weekly pickup marred the perfection.

"Southern suburbia at its best," said Scarlett as Jake stopped the SUV in front of a two-story, moss-green clapboard dwelling with cream trim and columns, accented by faded-red shutters. "This house looks like a life-size replica of a doll house my sister and I had." She gave him a once over. "You clean up pretty good, Shepherd. I'm glad you went for the casual business look. Your usual jeans and cowboy hat would have probably had a neighborhood watch member dialing 911."

"I would venture to guess they still might have phones in hand, but your professional appearance should put their suspicions to rest."

Once in front of the double doors, Scarlett pushed the Ring doorbell. In less than a minute, a shadow, seen through the glass inserts, came forward.

"Can I help you?" a female voice said through the door.

Mrs. Sawyer, this is Scarlett Kavanagh with Jake Shepherd. I spoke with you recently regarding your cousin Anna-Claire Carden. Could we talk for a few minutes?"

The pause that ensued gave Scarlett a fear they would be rejected. But after what seemed like a half hour, the door opened, and a meticulously groomed and dressed woman in her late thirties smiled. "Come in. Yes, I remember the conversation. Anna-Claire actually emailed me and said you might visit."

"Thank you. As I said, this is Jake Shepherd. He is helping me with this."

"Nice to meet you," Sawyer said. "Anna-Claire mentioned you as well. May I offer the two of you something to drink? Coffee? Tea?"

"I'm fine," Scarlett said. Jake nodded in agreement.

Sawyer ushered the pair into a living room with period decor and motioned for them to sit.

"I have to say, Ms. Kavanagh, I'm a bit conflicted about your investigation. I know my aunt and uncle adored Anna. Why is she trying to prove she was not their child?"

"As I said in our conversation, she submitted her DNA sample to the popular platform, and the analysis indicated her heritage was not a match to your family. We've since gained confirmation."

"But I clearly remember Aunt Nora's pregnancy. She had suffered two miscarriages and was so excited to be having a baby. We went to see them about a month after Anna was born. I am sure your sources have made a mistake. Maybe Anna had a medical procedure that altered her DNA—a transfusion or something."

"That's only possible in rare cases, usually an organ transplant. Did you continue to have regular contact with your aunt's family?"

"Not as much after they moved to Virginia, but we did see them on holidays. I know Anna is their child."

"But she's not," Scarlett said.

"She has to be," Sawyer insisted.

"DNA doesn't lie," Jake said. "Multiple labs have confirmed her ancestry does not come from all that is known about both of the Cardens."

"I have to ask why you didn't return the DNA kit our office sent," Scarlett said. "When we spoke, you said you would be happy to provide a sample."

"I don't know. Maybe because my dad didn't think it was a good idea. He's a lawyer, and to him, everything has the potential to cause legal issues. I put it in a drawer, and to be honest, I forgot."

"Do you know why your mother won't take my calls?" Scarlett said.

"I do. My mother." Sawyer turned her head, wiping a tear from her face. "My mother has advanced stage ALS. It has affected her mentally. If you talked to her, she might not even remember she has a sister, much less remember Anna. Some days, it takes her a few minutes to know who I am."

"I am so sorry. I had no idea," Scarlett said.

"You don't have to apologize. You couldn't have known. I don't think Anna knows. We have little contact. Anna has been so busy getting through medical school and then working long hours as an intern. We just lost contact. When Aunt Nora passed away, Mom was still in the early stages and didn't want anyone to know. She didn't want to be pitied or treated differently."

"That's completely understandable. But I have to ask again. Would you be willing to give us a DNA sample today? I have a kit with me."

Sawyer stared at Scarlett with a look that suggested she was considering the request.

Jake spoke. "If you're right about Anna, having a sample from a blood member of one of the Cardens would be helpful in refuting the evidence Scarlett has collected."

Scarlett smiled at him.

"Sure. Why not? What can it hurt?"

"Thank you, so much," Scarlett said, reaching into her briefcase to extract kit. "Can I ask you another favor? Would you be willing to facilitate a meeting with your dad since your mom really can't be interviewed?"

"I can do that. He is trying to slow his caseload down, partly because of Mom and partly because he wants to retire in the next year or two." She accepted the kit Scarlett handed her.

"Just take a swab out, put it in your mouth, and rub a couple of times on the inside of your cheek. Then put the swab in the tube. I'll fill in the labels."

CHAPTER 17

When Sawyer contacted her father's office, his assistant said he was in Columbia, taking depositions. Glancing at Scarlett, Robin said, "He's out of the office today. Are you going to be in Charleston tomorrow?"

Scarlett nodded.

"Barb, I have someone here who wants to meet with him about a family matter. Can you fit them into his schedule tomorrow? They're here from Washington, DC." She looked toward Scarlett with raised eyebrows as if for confirmation. Scarlett gave a thumbs up sign.

Terminating the call, Sawyer said, "She is going to work you in at eleven tomorrow morning. He's in court earlier."

Scarlett and Jake both started to rise. "Thank you for your help. I know Anna-Claire appreciates it."

"I just hope you prove that it was all a big mix-up. But it was nice meeting both of you. Have a safe trip back to Washington."

✦✦✦

After leaving the home of Robin Sawyer, Jake spent the afternoon at the hotel, going over case files he had brought on the trip. Scarlett used the time preparing for her interview of Paul Jorgensen and comparing notes with Liz on the search for Vic Lanza's siblings. At four o'clock, Liz called to say she had found a Lanza sister, Veronica Salvadore, living in Connecticut. Scarlett immediately put in a call but failed to connect.

"Veronica Lanza Salvadore. That's about as Italian as it gets. Let's grab an early dinner, and you can try again when we get back," Jake said as Scarlett put her cell back in a pocket of her slacks.

"My choice, right?"

"Your choice."

"I choose The Post. Their menu looks fantastic, and the reviews are all excellent."

***

Although Scarlett tried the number Liz found for Veronica Salvadore, Vic Lanza's sister, the night before until close to nine o'clock, she only reached voicemail. After a late breakfast, they headed to the law office of Paul Jorgensen. As soon as Scarlett finished fastening her seatbelt, she took her cell from her purse and tapped in Salvadore's number. With a sigh, she said, "No one answers the phone today unless they recognize the name or number on caller ID. I'm probably wasting my time."

"Roll with it, Harvard. It's not fatal. Just a pin prick in your process. Her phone is probably a cell. Most people use them exclusively," Jake said as he put the SUV in reverse. "Try shooting a text with a graphic of your card. Can't hurt. Worse case, we make a trip to New England when we're done here. Track her down in person."

It took less than a half hour to reach Broad Street in Charleston, where the courthouse was located. A mixture of two- and three-story buildings lined the street on both sides. Jake parked on the street in front of the building next to Jorgensen's.

"We're here with fifteen minutes to spare. Shall we go in or wait five minutes or so?" Scarlett said.

"Go in. It's too hot to stay in the vehicle."

The first floor of the building held a storefront merchant. Jake and Scarlett entered the hall to the offices above via an independent door. "I guess this building has a Historic Preservation Act exemption to the ADA elevator requirement," Scarlett said gazing up the narrow staircase.

"The exercise will do you good, Harvard."

She gave him an evil eye.

At the top of the stairs, entry through a predominately glass door required electronic release of the lock. Jake hit the button for the intercom.

"At least security is twenty-first century," Scarlett said, "but the logo on the door is cliche." She referred to the Lady Justice holding scales and a sword. "I bet over half the lay people coming through the door have no idea what that image means."

"Don't expect me to argue with that."

Inside, a receptionist sat behind a desk on the right next to the opening for the hall leading to internal offices. The name plaque on her desk read "Penny Carpenter." She smiled. "You must be Mr. Shepherd and Ms. Kavanagh. Barbara told me to expect you. He's in but on the phone. As soon as he hangs up, I'll take you back to his office. Can I offer you coffee, or water?"

"We're fine," Scarlett said. "But thank you for offering."

"Please make yourself comfortable. It won't be long."

Scarlett nodded and took a seat on a plump, leather couch while Jake sat on a matching, barrel-back chair. A small coffee table held a spread of current magazines, including *Charleston*, *Sports Illustrated*, and *People*. After scanning the room, Scarlett considered picking up a magazine but changed her mind. Jake sat motionless as though he was thinking.

"He's off the phone. I'll take you back now," Penny said, her Southern drawl oozing out the words.

As Jake and Scarlett followed Penny down the hall, they passed several closed doors and a glass-walled conference room, similar to many Scarlett had seen in Atlanta law offices. Jorgenson's office was at the end and appeared to be as large as the conference room. Upon entering his office, Scarlett immediately assessed the decor, which was rich in tradition—Oriental rug, mahogany bookcases filled with law books, and the obligatory bronze Lady Justice at the corner of his massive executive desk. Jorgensen wore a starched, white dress shirt and red tie. *Got to wear a touch of the power color when going to court,* she thought.

He did not rise nor smile but motioned for the pair to take seats in the two chairs immediately in front of his desk. Scarlett sat, but Jake remained standing.

The attorney appeared to be in his late fifties, maybe early sixties. Clean shaven, his hair was predominately gray with only traces of its original brown remaining. Although he bore an inscrutable expression, his body language exposed his distaste for the intrusion.

"I'm Scarlett Kavanagh, Mr. Jorgensen, and this is Jake Shepherd." She considered offering to shake his hand across the desk but thought he might refuse, so she did not. Neither did Jake. "We're here because your niece hired us to research her ancestry."

"I don't know why you want to talk to me. I don't know anything about that. In fact, I don't know why Robin had you put on my calendar."

Jake's eyes bore down on Jorgensen, but he said nothing.

"We would just like to ask you a few questions about your knowledge of Anna-Claire Carden's birth."

"What makes you think I know anything about Anna's birth?"

"Maybe you don't, but maybe you know more than you realize."

"Ms. Kavanagh, at the risk of being rude, I am a busy man. I don't know anything, and I don't have time for this type of foolishness."

Sensing Jorgensen was not going to allow the meeting to last, Scarlett went right to the core. "Can you tell me if Nora Carden knew Vic Lanza?"

The pupils of Jorgensen's eyes constricted like a cat's eyes in sunlight. "Who?"

"Vic Lanza."

Pushing back in his chair, Jorgensen folded his arms across his chest. "Who is Vic Lanza? I never heard of him."

Before Scarlett could respond, Jake said, "You really expect us to believe that?"

Scarlett cringed.

"I beg your pardon. You have no right to come into *my* office and question my veracity."

"Then don't lie. What I'm trying to figure out is why you feel it necessary to be untruthful. It suggests to me you know something you don't want to admit."

"Who the hell do you think you are? You come in here . . . . What is this—an interrogation? I know you're former FBI." His tone flared, and his eyes bore into Jake's.

"If you know I'm former FBI, you should also know I was an HRT sniper. So, unless you think I'm going to shoot you, you might calm down and answer the question truthfully."

"What is HRT?"

"Surprised you don't know that either. Hostage Rescue Team."

"I've never dealt much with the FBI. I'm a civil lawyer."

"Then you and Scarlett should speak the same language. She worked civil. I prosecuted Federal crime."

"You're a lawyer?"

"Pretty sure I am. Have a piece of paper that says I am. But let's get back on topic. You damned well know who Lanza was. I'm sure his murder here in Charleston was a major story in the local media. It lit up the nationals. Why would you lie?"

Steam coming from Jorgensen was nearly visible. "You need to leave. I don't have to take this from you. And I don't have to answer any of your damn fool questions."

"You already have." Jake stood. "Let's go, Scarlett. We've gotten all we need from this guy."

***

When they were both in the Yukon, Scarlett said, "Well, that went well. Did you have to piss him off and shutdown the interview? We didn't get a thing out of him."

Jake turned his head to face her, cocked an eyebrow, and said, "Really, Harvard? Is your radar turned off?"

"Apparently the battery's dead. Enlighten me, Sherlock."

He turned back to face the steering wheel and inserted the ignition key. As the motor kicked on, he said, "The hostility when we walked into that office was thick enough to slice with a knife."

"I caught that."

"Why? Why would a couple of private dicks from D.C. rattle this guy's cage?"

"Good point."

"He dodged answering questions by asking one. Classic action when you're avoiding giving an answer. When you mentioned Lanza's name, his pupils retracted—a natural defense when you want to shut something out. And he pulled back with his arms crossed in a defensive position, distancing himself from us. I could see his body tighten, much as he tried to hide it. Don't forget. He's a lawyer, experienced in the art of controlling his body language so as not to reveal a negative reaction in a courtroom. And there is *no* way he didn't know who the dead guy was. You knew who he was, and you were just a kid when he died. I knew who he was, and I'm from Oklahoma. Everybody, residing and breathing, in this town at the time knows who he was."

"I still don't see how you think we got all we need, or was that a bluff?"

"Harvard, the son-of-a-bitch has something to hide, and it's a lot more than the fact your client was adopted." He reached across the console and put a hand on her thigh. "The bastard's got skin in the game. Don't know how just yet, but I'll figure it out." Removing his hand, he turned the ignition and prepared to pull out of the parking space. "Let's run by the library, dig into newspaper articles of the time. We're stuck here till tomorrow morning. It'll give us something to read on the plane tomorrow."

"Jake, we don't have any evidence to indicate Nora Carden was ever in Charleston when Vic Lanza was here. She was living in Augusta when Anna was conceived. And we don't even have positive confirmation that Lanza is Anna's biological father."

"And you don't know Nora Carden was Anna's mother. But I smell a connection of some sort to Paul Jorgensen."

"You don't think he's Anna's father?"

"Fooling around with your wife or girlfriend's sister? Now, who would do that?"

She gave him a dirty look.

CHAPTER 18

The afternoon passed by quickly with research into media records about Vic Lanza—his show, his career, and his death. Articles covering his murder revealed facts about the antebellum mansion, situated on a former cotton plantation known as the Marley Plantation. As Scarlett studied images of the mansion, she passed one across the library table to Jake. "My mother would kill to live in a place like that. She would see herself as Scarlett O'Hara."

"I've met your mother. I can certainly see either her or your twin being the grande dame of a place like that. What does the article say about the damage from the fire? Was it destroyed?"

"It wasn't. They restored it, and it's now a museum outside the city." She snapped a photo of the image when Jake returned it.

"Why don't we take a run out there? Gather more background on the actor. We've got time," he said.

***

Upon returning to the hotel after taking a drive to the museum and
finding it closed for the day, a quick glance at the parking lot revealed
no empty slots close to the entrance. "I'm starved," Jake said. "I'll drop
you off in front. Go on up to the suite and put in a room service order."
He swung the SUV around and pulled under the canopy sheltering
the hotel entry.

"Do you know what you want?" She unzipped the compartment on
her leather cell phone case. "I haven't looked at the menu. Have you?"

"Nope. But you know what I like. Surprise me."

She nodded, took the keycard out of the phone case, gathered her
belongings, and exited. As she passed through the lobby, several guests
stood in line at the desk, but no one waited at the bank of elevators.

When Scarlett reached their suite, she let herself in. With the heavy
drapes closed, the room was dark, and she stumbled over what turned
out to be Jake's gym bag. "Damn it, Jake," she muttered to herself.
"Did you leave it there?" Regaining her balance, she thought how out
of character it was for him to leave his bag in the living room. "The
housekeeper must have moved it." Satisfied with her explanation, she
crossed the area, dropped her briefcase on the floor next to the desk,
and tossed the keycard onto the desktop. As she was about to reach for
the switch on a nearby lamp when a voice came out of the dark.

"Freeze."

Scarlett's heart lurched with her ability to breathe paralyzed for a
few seconds.

The voice, unsteady but definitely female, came from the direction
of their bedrooms.

A cold chill raced through Scarlett as she eased a finger to the
Maps icon on her phone that still hung from a strap around her neck.
Thank, God, it hasn't shut down. As she slowly turned, an overhead
light suddenly illuminated the room, and Scarlett was face-to-face with

a Smith & Wesson semiautomatic. The woman holding the weapon wore black slacks, a white shirt, and appeared to be in her late thirties to early forties. Neither attractive, nor ugly, her face was forgettable. Almost as puzzled as frightened, Scarlett's mind raced, checking off possibilities of who the woman was and what she wanted. *Is she in the right room? Robbery? Drugs? Psycho?*

Taking a deep breath, and sucking up all the courage she could muster, Scarlett calmly asked, "What do you want? If this is a robbery, I can give you what cash I have—my watch, and this." She pointed to a diamond and emerald ring on her right hand.

"I don't want your money. This is not a robbery. I want you to go back to wherever you came from."

Scarlett detected a slight tremor in the woman's grip on the gun. "You want me to leave? Who do you think I am?"

"I know who you are. You're a private investigator."

"Okay. But why do you want me to leave Charleston? Who are you?" Scarlett's eyes grew large with a combination of confusion and borderline panic, which she told herself she would control.

"I want both of you to leave. Go back to Virginia or Washington, or wherever. Just leave us alone. Where is he?" The woman looked around as though she expected to see someone.

"Where's who?"

"Your partner. The other investigator, the man you came here with."

"He's not here. Why do you want us to leave? Who are you?"

"You don't need to know who I am."

"What are we doing that is so important to you that you broke into our rooms with a weapon? Why?" *This woman must have moved Jake's bag so whoever entered would make a noise and alert her.*

"The family has suffered enough. Where *is* your partner?" Although her voice retained a nervous quality, the volume increased. "Where is he?"

"If you're talking about Jake, he's running errands. We needed some things they don't sell in the hotel. Why don't you put that gun down?" Scarlett pointed to the weapon. "And we can talk about the problem—maybe find a solution." She stared straight into the woman's eyes. "I don't know who you are or what your problem is, but this is not going to help." She hesitated, waiting for a response. "Why can't you tell me who you are?" Scarlett stalled for time, praying Jake saw the notification she sent on his phone.

The woman ignored the questions. "When will he be back?"

Scarlett took a deep breath. "Your guess is as good as mine. Half hour, maybe." Her brows pinched, producing a look of confusion. "Do I know you? What's your name?"

"You don't need to know me. You just need to do what I say."

"You're pointing a gun at me. I think I have a right to know who you—" Before Scarlett could finish the sentence, her phone rang, causing her to flinch and the woman to brandish the semiautomatic in a menacing manner. In self-defense, Scarlett's hand went up. "Careful. It's just my phone."

"Leave it. Don't answer."

Scarlett glanced at the screen and saw the image of Kai. She blinked, a feeling of relief coursing through her body, which she tried not to show. "It's Jake. If I don't answer, he's going to think something is wrong. He's bringing dinner and probably has a question about it."

"I thought you said he was running errands."

"He's doing both."

Another ring pierced the space between the two women. Scarlett could see uncertainty on the assailant's face.

"You better let me answer, or he's going to freak out."

As the third ring sounded, the woman's gaze flicked from side to side. "All right. Answer it. But put it on speaker. Don't even try to warn him about me."

Scarlett nodded, swiped the telephone icon to the right, and said, "Jake, where are you? Have you picked up the food? Talk loud, you're on speaker because my hands are wet. I was washing my face."

The phone was silent for nearly ten seconds. "Not yet. I'm about to get to the restaurant. Do you want barbecue beef or pork?"

"Beef." She took a breath. "But be sure you ask for the hot sauce for mine." Staring at the intruder, she continued, "You know I hate that sweet stuff you soak your sandwiches in." As she spoke, Scarlett brought the phone to face level as though talking into it.

"Gotcha."

The woman made a hand gesture indicating she wanted the call terminated, not realizing Scarlett had just told Jake she was a hostage. Turkey was her barbecue of choice, never beef, and she never used hot sauce.

While lifting a finger to signal to her attacker she needed a little more time, she said to Jake, "Will you be more than thirty minutes?" She eased a finger to the camera icon.

"Maybe. I'll give you a call when I'm near the hotel."

"See you when you get here." As she responded, she tapped the camera icon and quickly forwarded the photo to Jake.

The woman's face displayed fury as she likely heard the click. She again brandished the gun, darts shooting from her eyes.

"Drive safe." Scarlett wanted to leave the line open but decided it would be too risky. She turned the screen toward her captor and hit the red button to terminate the call.

"You took my picture."

"I did not."

"Don't lie. I heard the click."

"If you heard a camera click, it was an accident."

"I don't believe you. Put that phone down on the desk and lay down on the floor on your stomach."

"You've got to be kidding." Jake's words echoed in Scarlett's mind—never give an attacker more control. The demand ignited a fire in Scarlett. "There's no way in hell I'm going to lay down on that nasty floor."

"I'm not kidding. Lay down on the floor, or I'll shoot."

Drawing on every inch of her being to stay calm, Scarlett glared at the female and said, "That's not going to happen. I am not allowing you to execute me with a bullet to the back of my head. If you're going to kill me, you're going to do it looking straight into my eyes." For emphasis, she pointed two fingers toward her eyes. "You've been watching too much TV. I don't know who you are or what your problem is, but it's nothing compared to what it will be if you pull that trigger."

"I don't think so."

"Really? You're in a hotel full of people, Myrtle. Security cameras are everywhere."

"Why did you call me that? Why did you call me Myrtle?"

"Well, I've got to call you something, and unless you tell me your name, it's going to be Myrtle. Do you really think you haven't been seen, Myrtle?"

"Stop calling me that."

"Then tell me who you are. I can tell you this. Your face is on a dozen video cameras. You shoot me, and those images will be on newspapers, TV, the Internet, and maybe wanted posters. I don't know what you are trying to accomplish, but is it worth spending the rest of your life in prison?" She hesitated for a moment, gathering her thoughts. "Why don't you just lower the gun and tell me why it's so important to you that Jake and I leave Charleston? I know you don't really want to shoot anyone. You're not a killer. Myrtles are not killers. Every problem has a solution. We can find one."

The woman's eyes were wild with a look that was half fear and half panic. "The only solution is for you to stop prying into people's lives. Leave Charleston. I don't want to kill you, but I will if I have to. You need to leave. I can't let you do what you and your partner are doing. You're ruining his life. You're ruining mine."

Scarlett's mind raced. *Ruining his life? Charleston? Jorgensen? She's got to be talking about Jorgensen. How are we ruining his life? Her life?*

CHAPTER 19

J ake had just pulled the vehicle into a parking space at the very back of the hotel lot when the message indicating Scarlett's location hit his phone. He knew exactly what it meant. Scarlett was in trouble. He backed out, tires screeching, and circled back around to the hotel entry as he hit Scarlett's number in his speed-dial list.

A parking valet approached and waited while Jake was on his phone. When he exited the SUV, the door nearly hitting the young man. Jake whipped out his ID, held it up, and shouted to a bellman standing near the hotel entry, "Emergency. Call 911. Say hostage situation in progress, may be armed, fourth floor, suite 416. Alert your security to meet me there."

With a startled look on his face, the bellman rushed inside to his station to do as ordered while Jake raced past him to the elevators.

Debating as to whether to wait for an elevator or take the stairs, Jake pushed the button and looked around for the stairs. Fortunately, doors to a car opened. It took him less than a second to decide that with four flights to climb, the elevator should be faster.

As he stepped in and pressed the number four button, Jake's phone pinged with an incoming text from Scarlett. It was the photo she had taken of her assailant. The face was not in sharp focus, but the barrel of a small, semiautomatic, clearly pointing toward the photographer grabbed his attention.

Jake had barely stepped into the fourth-floor hall, when another elevator opened. A tall, older man, wearing a jacket with "Security" on the back, exited.

"Are you the guy who says there's an emergency hostage situation in progress?"

Jake put a finger to his lips to quiet the man and held up his phone displaying the image of the assailant. In a hushed tone, he said, "Are you the only security on duty?"

The man nodded.

"You have a name?"

"Joe. And you?"

"Jake." He pointed to the image on his cell but noticed the man's eyes go to his gun. "I'm a PI. Former FBI." With his left hand, he reached in his shirt pocket, took out his ID, and held it up for Joe to see. "Are you carrying?"

Joe flipped his jacket back to reveal a Glock 16. "Who's the hostage?"

"My associate. She was able to send me a message and that photo. You need to evacuate the rooms around ours—quietly—and get people stationed at the stairs and elevators to keep bystanders clear. As a precaution, the entire area should be put on lockdown. Use your bellhops, maids, desk clerks, whoever. When guests begin exiting rooms on this hall, they are going to be asking questions. Point to the back of your jacket so they see you are security. If necessary, point your weapon up toward the ceiling, and give them a quiet signal with your other hand. A little talking won't be noticed, but a lot will." Jake drew his weapon and started down the hall toward the suite.

Trailing Jake, the man said, "Shouldn't we wait for backup? They are on the way."

"No time. If you look closely at that photo, the unsub's got a gun. Something could spook or trigger her at any minute. Her back is to the door, which is good. Call 911 and confirm the unsub is armed. Have them alert their people that the assailant is holding a gun on the hostage."

Joe's pupils enlarged as he appeared to freeze.

Damn rent-a-cop ran through Jake's mind. *But at least he's another body.*

"After you contact the PD, call your front desk and have them ring the phone in the room. Tell them not to stop ringing until you give the notice."

"Do you know what you're doing?"

"I hope so. I'm going in. You stay behind. I need that phone ringing to cover the sound of the lock opening when I use my keycard."

"When do I have the desk stop ringing?"

"When I'm in."

"Are you crazy, man? You storm in there like Superman, and some-one is going to die. That broad has a semiautomatic."

"Well, if you stay behind me, it will be me or Scarlett, and you can be the hero—maybe write the book."

"You're insane. Did you get kicked out of the FBI on a mental card?"

"You're wasting my time, but if it eases your mind, I was FBI Hostage Rescue Team for five years. I go in. You cover. Got it?"

"You're going to shoot a woman?"

"I hope *not*."

As they neared the suite, Jake stopped and turned to the security guy. "Keep your wits. We've got this."

"What?"

"Just use whatever training you have to not fall apart on me. When SWAT arrives, they are going to ask you what we've got." He handed his phone to Joe. "Show them the photo. Tell them who I am and to hold back unless they hear a round go off."

"Why would they listen to me? Won't they just bust in?"

"Not if they're any good. They're not going to breach the room until they know what's on the other side. Likely try negotiating if possible."

"How do you know they are even sending the SWAT team?"

"I don't. I'm assuming you have a competent agency down here. Hostage is a high-risk callout."

When Jake reached the door to their suite, he moved close and pressed his ear against it to listen for the phone.

CHAPTER 20

Three units to the right of Jake and Scarlett's suite, a door opened, and a family of four came out of their room. The adult male, most likely the father, started to call out to the two men. Responding as Jake instructed, Joe turned slightly, pointing to the printed word "SECURITY" on the back of his jacket, and shooed them toward the elevators.

His ear against the door, Jake listened for the ring. When the first one came, he positioned the keycard in the slot. With the second, he tripped the lock. On the third, he opened the door, slithering inside like a cat. As the phone continued to ring, frustrating the woman, he went unnoticed until he spoke.

"There's a nine-millimeter aimed straight for the back of your head. Put the gun down—easy."

The woman jumped, and then froze, seized with panic.

Scarlett froze as well, even though she had seen him enter and struggled to hide a sign of anything happening. The trace of relief on her face had not appeared to register with her captor.

"I would rather not hurt you," Jake said. "But if you don't put that gun down, I will have *no* choice. The result won't be pretty. Ask anyone, I don't fucking miss. . . . Turn around."

"No. I'm not taking my eyes off of her. My gun is pointed at her."

"I get it." He spoke slowly, lowering his tone significantly and emphasizing each word. "But pay close attention. You're in my wheelhouse—way out of yours. The second you discharge that gun, I'll fire mine. You're an amateur, lady. I'm a pro. You can't win this one."

The phone rang again, and the woman flinched, her hand shook, and the gun faltered, creating a risk of accidental discharge. To regain control, she grasped the weapon with both hands and in a tone suggesting she was talking to herself, said, "I don't want to kill anybody. I just want you people to leave." Becoming more assertive, she said, "Leave us alone." Although attempting to display strength, on the last word, her voice quivered and tears began streaming down her face. "Please say you'll leave. Please don't make me do something terrible."

"You shoulda put that in a text or an email. But I hear you." Softening his voice to a patronizing tone, he said, "Put down your gun easy before you *accidentally* do something you'll regret. We'll talk about it. See what we can work out."

"You can't fool me. I don't want to go to jail. If I put the gun down, you're going to call the police, and I'll go to jail."

"Maybe. Maybe not. We don't know that." Between making each statement, he eased forward, moving closer and closer to the woman. "Maybe you won't. But put the gun down before you do cause that to happen. If it's the police you're worried about, that race is on. They are on the way and may be in the hall right now."

Her head jerked around, but her body remained rigidly in place, thereby preventing her from having Jake in her view. "I don't believe you. How would anyone have known?" Her tears appeared to dry as she assumed a defiant tone. "She didn't tell you. I heard the whole conversation, and I don't hear anyone in the hall."

"You think they're going to blunder in like a stampede of buffalo? If they're not here now, they will be in minutes. And just to bring you up to speed, Scarlett told me everything I needed to know."

"You're lying." Her labored breathing was heavy enough to cause her shoulders to move. "I don't know what to do." With her eyes wild with confusion, she began to cry again. "This isn't how it was supposed to go."

As he inched closer to the woman, Jake looked beyond her to Scarlett, making eye contact. Using one hand, he gave the traditional sign for yapping, followed by a quick tip of his head. She caught the signal and began talking.

"You need to listen to him, Myrtle. He's absolutely right. You don't want to spend the rest of your life in prison or worse. Nothing I've seen about you suggests you're a criminal. I think you're a good person who has found herself in a bad situation. Don't make it worse. You *don't* want Jake to pull that trigger. He won't miss. He was an FBI sniper."

"Why did you people have to come down here and ruin our lives?" Her finger moved to the trigger. "You're confusing me. I just. . . want. . . want you to go back to Washington."

"I get it," Scarlett said, trying to use a soothing tone. "And maybe we will. But you're not in a position right now to dictate terms." Scarlett managed to keep her voice calm and compassionate. "You pull that trigger and injure or kill me, and I can promise you, with my hand on the Bible, Jake will fire. You will die. None of us want that to happen. You don't want that to happen."

With Scarlett's distracting the woman, Jake moved even closer, holstered his gun, and then signaled Scarlett to move to the right of where she stood. She responded, ducking down as well. Instantly, he sprang forward to the assailant's left. Using his body to compromise her balance, he simultaneously grabbed the gun in her hands, forcing the aim to her right. The semiautomatic discharged before he gained complete control, shattering a lamp as the bullet passed through and then pierced a wall. At the sound of the gunshot, a team of SWAT operatives breached the door in full armor.

With her leverage gone, the woman crumpled to the floor, her face in her hands.

"Welcome, boys," Jake said, holding the suspect's gun above his head. "Suspect neutralized. You can stand down. It's under control."

"Is anyone hurt?" the lead operative said.

"Not unless you count the lamp and the wall over there that took the round," Jake said as Scarlett stood up from where she had moved to dodge any fire.

Jake flipped the weapon around and, holding it by the barrel, handed the Smith & Wesson to the lead operative. Pulling back his jacket, he held his left hand up in a halt position and gingerly removed his weapon from its holster, using only two fingers, and passed the weapon to the operative. Once disarmed, he took his credentials out of his pocket and thrust them forward. "Before you get excited, I'm legal. I'm a licensed PI, and you can see my LEOSA card there."

"Former law enforcement authorization to carry, huh. What was your agency?"

"Joe didn't tell you? FBI. Hostage Rescue and Violent Crimes."

"Well, that experience sure came in handy for everyone tonight."

"Yeah. Kinda did."

Taking a deep breath and steadying herself, Scarlett walked over to Jake, who put an arm around her shoulders and jerked her close.

"This is my associate, Scarlett Kavanagh," Jake said to the cop. "You okay, Harvard?"

"Now that it's over, I'm fine. What took you so long?"

Jake smiled. "I didn't see any reason to rush. I knew you could handle it." He gave her shoulder a pat. "Can't leave you alone for five minutes. But *you* might say, 'Thank you, Jake, for saving my lovely as. . . sets—again.' How many times does this make?"

She turned to face him, pointing a finger at his chest. "It's your job. Read the contract. But one thing I noticed. For the tough guy who doesn't negotiate, you're slipping, Shepherd. Tired of channeling Bruce Willis?"

"Touche," he said, giving her shoulders a squeeze.

"I assume you guys are kidding," the cop said.

Scarlett turned toward him. "Of course we are. I was darned lucky Jake got and read the signals I sent."

"Ma'am, maybe you should let our medic check you out. You have been through a trauma."

"I'm fine."

"She's a lot tougher than she looks but sometimes gets herself in some pretty tight corners," Jake said.

Two of the operatives had handed off their weapons and quickly moved forward to handcuff and take control of the assailant, who was crying hysterically. Once secured, they pulled her to her feet and started out of the room.

"I'm fine," Scarlett said. "She never touched me. I don't think she would have intentionally. She just wanted to scare me."

Both Jake and Scarlett moved out of the way as the officers escorted the suspect out. She kept her head bowed, staring at the floor,

"That may have been her intent, but pointing a loaded gun at someone, especially when you're not trained on it, is grounds for serious injury, whether intentional or not," the cop said as he returned

Jake's credentials. "I see you're from DC. What are you doing in Charleston?"

"What was supposed to be a simple track-down-birth-parents case is turning into a traffic stop gone wrong," Jake said.

"Do you know her?" He pointed toward the hall, visible through the open door.

Jake shook his head. "I do not. Not a clue. But I'd like to know how the hell she got into our rooms." He turned his focus to Scarlett. "Did you let her in?"

"No. She was already in the suite when I got here. I think she was hiding in one of the bedrooms when I came in."

The SWAT leader shifted his focus to Scarlett. "What about you, ma'am? Do you know your assailant?"

"No. I don't. She wouldn't tell me her name or what she believed we were doing to mess up her life. She just kept saying Jake and I need to leave Charleston. We are ruining someone's life—a man. She didn't give his name either. She said we were ruining his life and hers."

Jake looked at her quizzically. "I thought I heard you call her Myrtle."

"She wouldn't tell me her name, so I called her Myrtle."

Jake chuckled. "Nice touch."

"I need to add one thing," Scarlett said, looking down and then up at the cop. "From things she said, I believe the woman is somehow connected to our case."

"What makes you think that?" Jake said.

"Well, we were definitely her target, and we haven't had any other business in Charleston. She kept mentioning a man. She might have been talking about Jorgensen?" She turned toward Jake. "You thought he was lying "

"Jorgensen? What's his first name?" the cop asked."

"Paul," Scarlett said.

"I thought you might be talking about him. He's a pretty well-known lawyer here. What makes you think she's connected to him?"

"He's the only man we have interacted with here. She knew we were from the Virginia-DC area. How would she know that unless she knows Robin Sawyer or Paul Jorgensen? I don't see it being someone in Robin's life, and we were in his office today. I didn't see this woman, but we only saw his receptionist and him. She's definitely not his wife, but maybe a sister, a lover, an employee. But I don't understand how we could be ruining his life."

"I think I can answer that," Jake said. "I told you the guy was hiding something, and he has skin in the game. I read guilt all over his face. That would make some kind of sense to connect her to him, but I doubt an employee would risk going to prison to protect the employer."

"Could be an office romance."

Jake gave her a look. "Oh, you've heard of office romances?"

Scarlett glared at him. "Don't go there."

"Oh. I forgot." He grinned. "That's off limits."

As Jake finished his comment, a tall man in a suit and tie entered the room.

The SWAT team leader gestured toward the newcomer, "The detectives are here. We'll let them take over."

"Roy, what have we got?" the detective said.

"No bodies, no blood tonight. Pretty simple assault with a deadly—maybe intent to kill, false imprisonment, trespass, plus a few other minors. I'll let the victim and her hero fill you in on the rest. Shepherd, the PI"—he pointed to Jake—"is former FBI HRT and Ms. Kavanagh is the victim. Shepherd neutralized the suspect before we entered. Do you want to talk to the suspect here at the scene or want us to transport her to booking?"

"Read her the rights and take her in. And try to find out who she is. One of your guys says she won't give her name. Jerry and I will see her after she calms down a bit. I assume you have custody of the weapon?"

"Yep. We'll log it in. It's an old Smith & Wesson, Semi, nine-mil, probably second generation."

As the SWAT leader left, the detective handed Jake a business card that read, Detective Gregory Lester. Jake glanced at the card and said, "I know you need to get our statements, but before we get started, do you mind if we put in a room service order? I'm starving."

"You just took down an armed perp, holding a hostage, and food is your main concern? Was this just another day in the life for you?"

"No. But it wasn't my first rodeo either, and I'm damned hungry." He looked around. "Did you talk to Joe?"

"Who?"

"Joe, hotel security—my wingman. I hope he didn't have to go change his trousers. This assault was ten levels above the pay grade of a guy who wears a Glock as a fashion accessory."

"If you're talking about the guy wearing the jacket with security on the back, he's with my partner. Right now, I want to hear how you pulled off this rescue without anybody getting hurt. Was it skill or sheer luck?"

Jake grinned. "As soon as food is ordered, I'll draw you a map."

After a noticeable pause, in which Lester studied Jake, he said, "You're serious, aren't you?"

"You're damned right, I'm serious. Be sure Joe has his people pull all the CCTV video that might show how the woman got into our suite, how she got to the hotel, whether anyone else was with her, and he can probably push a food order through faster."

CHAPTER 21

While Jake spoke with the detective, Scarlett had moved to the small dinette table and sat on one of four chairs, watching. When Lester left the room to give instructions to his partner, Jake picked up the hotel booklet to place a food order. Looking down at Scarlett, he said, "What would you like?"

"I'm not hungry."

"Okay. I'll order you a turkey sandwich."

"I said, I'm not hungry."

"You will be."

***

As Jake completed the order, Lester, along with his partner, returned to the suite. This time closing the door.

"Where's Ms. Kavanagh?" Lester asked.

"She's in the bedroom. Did you get what you needed from Joe?"

"He gave my partner"—Lester used a hitchhiker's style thumb motion to gesture toward the other detective—"a description of what happened from his vantage point. He's gone to work on obtaining the surveillance videos for us." Again, indicating his partner, he said, "This is Detective Gerald Cannady. Jerry, meet former FBI Special Agent Jake Shepherd."

The two shook hands.

"I hear you've got steel in your Jockey's," Cannady said. "Congrats on taking the perp down with no bloodshed."

"Some days, you trap the fox. Some days, the trap gets you. Today was a good one. Where do you guys want to start?"

"If you don't mind trading places with Ms. Kavanagh, we'd like to take her statement first. I think that table will make a good place to talk. Don't worry, when your food arrives, we'll let you know and take a break."

Jake grinned. "I'll get her and make myself comfortable in a bedroom while you do your thing."

In a bit more than a minute, Scarlett returned to the suite's sitting room. After preliminary exchanges, the trio sat down at the small table.

"Just for clarification, what is your role here, Ms. Kavanagh?" Lester asked. "Are you a member of Shepherd's staff or here as—"

Sensing where the question was headed, with a stern expression on her face, Scarlett said, "I am an employee of Shepherd & Associates."

Lester gave a quick glance around the room as if to note the intimacy of Jake and Scarlett's accommodations. Returning his focus to her, he smiled. "And your job title?"

"Associate. I am a licensed private investigator but still gaining experience. I practiced law in Atlanta for approximately ten years before deciding to change careers."

"Lawyer?" Lester said. "No background in law enforcement?"

"None. Jake and I are both lawyers. He was an Assistant U.S. Attorney before joining the FBI."

Lester turned to Cannady and made a what-do-you-think-of-that expression, before continuing the interview.

"Are you and Shepherd both staying in this suite?" Cannady asked.

Scarlett nodded but gave him a look of why ask that? "We are. I think you knew that. If you noticed, there are two bedrooms. One is mine; one is Jake's."

The detective acknowledged her statement with a tip of his head. "Can you give me a brief account of what brought you and Mr. Shepherd to Charleston?"

"A case. Several months ago, a young, professional woman came to our office wanting to hire an investigator. She believed she was adopted by the couple who raised her and wanted confirmation. If true, she wanted to locate her birth parents. Jake doesn't take domestic cases but was fine with me taking it. I liked her and could see the situation was causing her a great deal of stress. She was almost desperate—like on fire—to learn the truth about her heritage. My research produced some rather odd information, which I think may be protected by attorney-client privilege at this point. It's not that I do not want to share the information, but I am a licensed attorney and that privilege may have attached."

"Yeah. I'm quite familiar with attorney-client privilege. But can you tell us how the incident tonight ties into Paul Jorgensen?"

Scarlett shook her head. "I cannot. I may be able to obtain a release from the client. But right now, I don't feel free to provide facts about the case. I believe the client will consent. With what happened tonight, we are looking at a serious investigation and could need your help. Give me until tomorrow."

"Fine. Not a problem. Shepherd has my card. Putting that on hold, let's get back to what happened," Lester said. "Starting with your arrival, can you give us a complete description of how this incident took place? I believe you've said you arrived at the room—the suite—and the suspect was already inside. Are you sure she didn't come in behind you?"

"Positive. First of all, I would have noticed someone in the hall. Second, if someone were close enough to get in the door behind me, I can't imagine I wouldn't see, hear, even feel them. And finally, I turned around to consider fastening the inside locks out of habit, but since Jake was parking the SUV, I knew he would be coming up shortly. So, I didn't. That turned out to be a very good thing. She came from the small hall that leads to the bedrooms. It was dark because those drapes were closed and no lights were on. Either the woman or housekeeping closed the drapes. We left them open."

"What about your keycards? Are they all accounted for? Could either of you have lost one?"

"We had only two. I used mine to enter the room, and Jake used his when he slipped in."

"Since there is only one means of entry, hotel surveillance cameras will hopefully show how she got in," Cannady said. "So, give me the step-by-step sequence of what happened, starting from the time she revealed herself to when Shepherd disarmed her."

***

After giving a thorough account of the incident, Scarlett said, "I definitely believe there is a connection between this situation and our case but am shocked that it could be so serious as to take the action this woman took."

"I have to say, you and Shepherd did a remarkable job in keeping it from becoming a tragedy. Not many could stay as cool as you apparently did," Lester said.

"I recognized pretty quickly that she did not know what she was doing."

"How did you do that?"

"She was nervous, almost frightened. I saw her shake. But the main thing I noticed was her grip on the gun. She held it wrong. At one point, I told her that if she kept her finger on the trigger, she might fire accidentally, which was my biggest fear. She actually listened to me. I don't think she had ever held a gun before."

"That was extremely sharp of you to recognize. Do you have firearms training?"

"My father and I went to a gun range frequently when I was a teenager. He had done a lot of competitions and taught me everything I know. It was something special we shared. So, yes, I know quite a bit about guns. Jake and I frequently go to a gun range to practice. He believes in staying in shape physically and with his firearms. He's required to requalify his LEOSA license every year. But he was an FBI sniper and accustomed to practicing his skill a lot more often. I go with him most of the time."

"Is it possible that this woman could be part of another case you and Shepherd worked or are working—maybe she followed you here?"

Scarlett tipped her head toward her shoulder with a slight squint of one eye. "I suppose anything is possible, but I don't—"

A knock at the door interrupted Scarlett. "That must be the food Jake ordered."

Lester stood. "We'll take a break and allow you and Shepherd time to enjoy your food."

CHAPTER 22

After he sent Scarlett out to interview with the detectives, Jake placed a call to Pete Cooper, his partner in the security agency.

"What's your calendar like?" Jake said when Cooper answered.

"Pretty average. Have you got something you need?"

"I do. If things up there can run themselves for a day or two, I could use you to do me a favor. Scarlett and I are in Charleston, and I need Kai and backup. Can Sonny handle the shop?"

"Without a doubt. What have you gotten yourself into now?"

"I wish I knew. Right now, two detectives are interviewing Scarlett. A woman with a Smith & Wesson broke into our suite tonight and held Harvard hostage."

"Damn. Is she okay?"

"Shaken but tough. She handled it like a pro."

"Scarlett's a class act. I take it you took the perp down?"

"Yeah. She's in custody. But the question is: What the hell is going on? We're down here on a search for birth parents. Why would someone commit a felony to block an adoption investigation?"

"I take it you're sure this wasn't a random act?"

"Definitely not. Apparently, the woman's plan included us both, but I had let Harvard out and gone to park the truck. She managed to send me a signal."

"Damn." Cooper cleared his throat. "You want me to leave tonight?"

"Tomorrow morning should be soon enough. I'll give Liz the heads up that you'll be picking Kai up at the office. At this point, I don't want Scarlett alone, particularly after this woman is released. We suspect she's somehow connected to a pretty prominent lawyer here in Charleston, which means he's likely to have her out after her first appearance. And since Scarlett isn't licensed to carry here. I don't want to take any chances until we put some of these pieces together. Are you sure Sonny can handle your commitments up there?"

"No problem. If he needs extra help, Randy's got a friend who just retired from the Capitol crew and wants to pick up a job every now and then. I checked him out, and he's good police. Listen, Jake. If you and Scarlett are in jeopardy, Sonny and I will both come. Brenda and Randy can keep balls in the air up here."

"Not yet. I may be overreacting reaching out to you."

***

Jake had barely finished his call to Liz when a knock came at the door. "It's unlocked," he called out from the chair on the far side of the room.

Detective Cannady stuck his head in the room. "Your dinner is here. We're headed downstairs for a cup of coffee while you two eat. See you in thirty."

Jake stuffed his cell in a pocket of his shirt and went into the bathroom to wash his hands.

When he reached the living room of the suite, Scarlett was on the loveseat, sipping a glass of tea that came with the room service order.

Aren't you going to join me for dinner?" Jake asked as he took the metal warming lid off one of the plates.

"I told you I wasn't hungry."

He stopped what he was doing, staring at her for several seconds before speaking. "Would you like something stronger than that tea?"

She shook her head. "I'm fine. It's not like it's the first time I've had a gun pointed at me since I met you. I should be getting used to it."

He walked over, sat down beside her, put an arm around her shoulders, and pulled her close. "You don't get used to having your life threatened. Don't let anyone tell you differently. This is a risky business. Sometimes, the most benign cases can take an unexpected turn. You don't have to do it. I'm sure you could go back to family law."

Her head snapped around. "No way. I love this work."

He started laughing. "And why am I not surprised?" He gave her a squeeze, stood, and returned to the table. "I called Pete. He's bringing Kai down tomorrow."

She gave him a puzzled look.

"Until we know how deep the crap is we've stepped in, I am not taking any chances. After I'm done with the detectives, I'm having the desk clerk change our suite, or else we're moving to another hotel."

***

True to their word, the detectives returned thirty minutes after departing. Jake opened the door and let them in.

Glancing around the room, Lester asked, "Where's Ms. Kavanagh?"

"It's been a long day. She's gone to her room. If you have any more questions for her, she'll get back with you tomorrow."

"No problem. We're good for now. How long are you planning to stay in Charleston?"

"We were scheduled to leave tomorrow, but it's on hold after this. We will be changing rooms. I thought about changing hotels, but this one is large enough that changing rooms should be sufficient, plus I have backup coming tomorrow."

"What kind of a hornet's nest do you think you're in the middle of?"

"You've got me on that one. But I'll find out."

Lester and Cannady took seats at the table, while Jake took a Pepsi out of the refrigerator and unscrewed the cap. After taking a drink, he sat across the table from the pair.

Lester began. "I have to say, what happened here and how it was handled was . . . was. I'm not sure how to describe it. According to Ms. Kavanagh, she used the 'Send My Location' app on her phone to signal you there was a problem and then was able to send you a photo of the perp aiming the S and W at her. What made you think you could enter this room under those circumstances?"

"No voodoo. I could see the psycho was an amateur, maybe unhinged, but also careless. The photo Scarlett managed to send me showed her back was to the door, which gave me an edge. Of course, there was always a possibility she changed position, but my gut told me she probably didn't. I could also see she didn't know how to handle a firearm. The scene would have played a lot differently had Scarlett not been able to snap that picture."

"You were that confident?" Lester's brow wrinkled in a frown. "You two must be an extraordinary team."

"I was trained to be confident. If you don't believe you can do the job, you're going to fail." Jake took another drink of the Pepsi. "My worst fear was she would accidentally shoot Scarlett. The longer they were in there, the greater the risk."

"Sounds reasonable." Lester flipped a page of the small notepad he had been taking notes on. "I know you're a former Fed but don't know exactly what area you worked in."

"Hostage rescue and violent crimes."

There was no mistaking Jake's response took Lester by surprise. "That explains a lot. How long have you been in the private sector?"

"What you really want to know is why I left but didn't want to ask, right?"

Lester took a breath. "I was that transparent?"

"You and just about everyone who learns I am an ex-agent. It wasn't because I wanted to leave. I liked having a badge, although there are a few perks to not having one. I left because it was the only way I could be a parent to my daughter after her mother married the ASAC."

Lester's face registered surprise, as did Cannady's. After a minute of silence, Lester said, "Got it." He closed the pad and his pen. "That's probably enough for tonight. Since you're hanging around, we'll probably be running into one another. You have my card. I'll touch base tomorrow morning."

As all three men stood, Jake took out his wallet and handed Lester his card. "I'd appreciate it if you could keep this out of the media if at all possible—or at least don't reveal our names. I'd like to see if Jorgensen shows up. And if you can include us to the extent possible in the investigation, I'll keep you informed of what I uncover. I'm willing to share and hope you'll be willing to do the same."

Lester turned toward his partner for a second, and they exchanged looks before he turned back to Jake. "I'm sure we can make something like that work, and for the record, we don't release victim names here."

Jake reached out and shook hands with both detectives. "Good. Let me know what you find on the tapes and Myrtle's identity. My gut tells me I want to have another chat with Attorney Jorgensen, but I'll wait to hear something from you first."

CHAPTER 23

With the detectives gone, Jake went to Scarlett's room, tapped on the door and opened it without waiting for an invitation. She sat on her bed with her computer in her lap, still wearing the same clothes.

"I'm going down to the front desk to see about switching suites. Are you up to moving tonight?"

"Can we do it tomorrow? She's in custody." Scarlett's state of exhaustion was clear from the pale shade of her complexion and the look in her eyes.

He studied her face for several seconds. "It's all catching up with you, isn't it?"

"I am tired."

"With no sign of an accomplice, I think we can wait, but I'm going to leave the Glock here while I'm gone. Come lock the deadbolt behind me? I'll text you when I'm back at the door."

After seeing him out, she closed her computer and prepared to take a shower.

***

Jake was gone about thirty minutes. He returned with key cards for another suite and for the room beside their new suite, which he reserved for Pete Cooper. Scarlett met him at the door wearing a gown and robe. The dishes from dinner remained on the kitchenette counter.

"Hmmm. You smell nice he said as he passed by, dropping the key cards on the dinette table. "Want to talk, watch TV, or go to bed?" He glanced at the kitchen clutter. "I can take care of the dinner remains."

She forced a slight smile. "If you don't mind, I'll probably just go to bed. We'll likely have a busy day tomorrow trying to figure this all out. Maybe I can reach that sister of Victor Lanza."

"Not a problem. I get it. I'll close down for the night in here. You go on to bed." As she walked toward the bedrooms, he called out, "I'm going to skip my workout tomorrow, so let me know when you're ready to go down for breakfast."

***

At midnight, a light knock came on Jake's bedroom door. His TV was still on and was the sole illumination of the room. Wearing only black boxer briefs and a tee shirt, he slid off the bed, crossed the room, and opened the door to find Scarlett looking like a sad puppy.

"I don't want to be alone."

He took her hand and pulled her against his chest. "You're not going to be."

CHAPTER 24

The next morning, Jake decided they should not have breakfast at the hotel. "There's a Cracker Barrel about fifteen minutes from here according to my phone. Let's pack up the room for the bellhop to move our stuff while we're gone." When Jake had met with the night manager to arrange for the relocation, the man eagerly volunteered his staff to take care of transferring their luggage to the new suite and assured Jake the location would be kept strictly confidential.

"Are we taking our computers and files or leaving them for the hotel people to move?"

"Taking."

"That's what I thought."

***

From their corner table in the busy restaurant, Jake and Scarlett were almost finished eating when his cell buzzed. Glancing at the caller ID, he said, "It's our detective." Resting his fork on the plate, he answered, "Hey, Lester, what's up? Any news?"

Scarlett watched intently as Jake jotted notes on a small pad he kept in his shirt pocket. As the conversation progressed, she could tell Lester had made progress in the case.

When Jake terminated the call, he put the cell back on the table. With a slight nod, he flicked a pointed finger at her. "You nailed it. Myrtle's name is Barbara Malone. She's forty-nine, single, no record—and she's on Jorgensen's staff. He's already shown up, but no one is talking."

"I knew it. Do they have any idea what she meant about our ruining his life and hers?"

"That is yet to be discovered. They're digging deeper into her personal life, family, etc."

Without warning, Scarlett's eyebrows pinched together. "Wait a second. I heard Robin call the person she talked to at her father's office Barb. That must be Myrtle."

"Sounds like it."

"Did they learn how she managed to gain entry to our rooms?"

"According to the hotel cameras, she approached a housekeeper, apparently claiming to be you, and succeeded in convincing the maid to let her into the suite. The woman is off today, but there's a plan to question her. Malone's car was still in the hotel parking lot where they found her purse and ID."

"Did he say how they knew which car was hers?"

"Her keys. They were in her pocket. They just walked through the lot, pressing the fob until a car answered."

Scarlett chuckled. "I've done that when I drove a white SUV. But don't have to with red MINI. Did Jorgensen say *anything*?"

"Zip. The judge levied a fifty-thousand-dollar bond on her at first appearance, which hasn't been posted, yet. My money says Jorgensen will get her out. If he's involved, he doesn't want her talking."

"He'll probably have to find someone to actually arrange the bail. I don't know about South Carolina, but Georgia does not permit attorneys to post bail or act as a surety for a client."

"As I recall, most states don't. Since I was a prosecutor, it never came up, but if I recall my ethics class, D.C. frowned upon it. But I bet he figures out a way to make it work."

"Oh!" She held a hand to stop him. "I've got a text from Liz."

"And?"

"She says Pete and Kai left at six, and she's found an email address for Lanza's sister. She thinks I might have better luck introducing myself by way of the Internet." She watched him take the final bite of his pancakes. "Do you have any idea how long it will take Pete to drive down?"

He swallowed the food and followed it with a swig of coffee. "Somewhere in the neighborhood of eight hours. If he got away at six, he should arrive somewhere around two. That gives us time to meet with Lester. You heard me say we wanted to meet with him this morning. He's got us down for eleven-thirty." He took a quick look at his watch. "We should have enough time to go back by the hotel, get our rooms organized, and grab a quick lunch before Pete arrives."

Scarlett drained the last bit of tea from her cup as Jake took a credit card out of his wallet to pay the check. As he keyed in the payment, she typed an email to Veronica Salvadore, Vic Lanza's sister.

As Jake held the restaurant door for her to exit a few minutes later, Scarlett asked, "Why exactly did you want Pete and Kai here in Charleston? Are you that afraid of Myrtle?"

He laughed, "You mean Barbara, don't you?"

"You knew who I meant."

"No. I'm not afraid of Myrtle. What scares me is what we don't know. I can guard against danger I know, but the unknown—not so well. Pete's got good instincts. He spent twenty-six years with the Bureau, plus I want you covered any time you leave the hotel until we sort this out."

"Where are you going to be?"

"Most of the time with you, but it's a good idea to have backup."

CHAPTER 25

"Well, this is unusual. The police department is located inside City Hall," Jake said as he parked the SUV.

"True. But it's a beautiful building. We're about ten minutes early. Should we kill a few minutes before going in?"

"We should be fine."

As they entered the building, Scarlett scanned the pristine lobby and its atrium. "This is impressive."

"Yeah. According to Lester, we check in with our ID and give his name. Someone will escort us to his department."

After passing through security and following the procedure, a uniformed police officer led them to the second-floor detective division.

Lester met them at the elevator and took them to a small interview room. "Did you have any trouble finding us?" he asked, motioning them to take a seat.

"Not a bit," Jake said. "Have you guys turned up any more info on Ms. Malone?"

"Not a lot. She owns a small house and appears to live alone. She's divorced, no children."

"Is she still in custody?" Scarlett asked.

"So far. According to the CO on her unit, she refused breakfast and has spent most of the time here crying. She made one call to Jorgensen."

"You seemed to be familiar with him. Can you tell me what you know?" Jake said.

"He's one of those TV lawyers with billboards around town. You know the type—MVAs, slip and falls."

"Gotcha. Ambulance chasers. I'm going to go off the boards a bit here, but are you familiar with Vic Lanza?"

"The actor? The one who died in a fire at the old Marley Plantation?"

"So, you are familiar with him."

"What's he got to do with Malone and Jorgensen? The guy's been dead over thirty years." Lester squinted, giving a perplexed expression.

"My guess is you were just a kid when that fire happened, but you knew about it."

"Everyone knows about that. The place is a museum now. But why are you asking?"

"He may have something to do with the case we're working. We aren't sure, but when I asked Jorgensen if he was familiar with the guy, he claimed he never heard of him."

"That's pretty strange. Him, the fire, the plantation—they are legendary around here."

"Would the investigation have been done by your agency?"

"No, not likely. That place is not in our jurisdiction. It's an unincorporated area that would fall under the county boys. The Charleston County Sheriff's Office would have handled it."

Jake made a note on the small pad he carried. "Do you have any contacts I might connect with in that agency?"

"I don't, but my partner does. His uncle is the undersheriff over there. Let me get him in here."

He took out his phone and typed a text. "While we're waiting for Jerry, can I get you a coffee, water, soft drink?"

"I'm fine," Scarlett said.

"I could use a cup of coffee—black."

"You've got it. I'll be right back."

It took Lester less than five minutes to return with a coffee for Jake and one for himself. As he handed Jake the Styrofoam cup, he said, "Getting back to where we were, what can you tell me about what you're working on and how Jorgensen fits in? Someone said you're here to trace a client's birth parents."

"That's the way it started. In fact, the case was Scarlett's, and I didn't get involved until she began uncovering some rather bizarre facts."

"Have you identified the birth parents?"

"Nope. We have one possibility, but it is not confirmed."

"So, why are you here in the Charleston area?"

"The sister of the adopted mother lives here. She's Jorgensen's wife," Scarlett said.

"Oh, that makes sense."

"We came down hoping to talk to her about our client, but it seems she's chronically ill. We met with her daughter—Jorgensen's daughter, and she set us up with her dad. He was not very receptive, and as Jake said, denied knowing who Vic Lanza was." An insect flew by her face, causing her to wave it away. "It's a strange set of facts. According to all our information, the client was born in Augusta with a birth certificate matching her adoptive parents, but her DNA does not seem to support that. It's making no sense at all."

"How does Lanza fit it?"

"We aren't sure, but the DNA has matched our client with some of his family. Obviously, we don't have his DNA so we're running it down by trying to reach one of his siblings. It just seems to be a strange coincidence that our client shares DNA with Lanza or a member of his family, and the client has adoptive relatives in the area where he lived and died."

"I have to agree. I don't believe in coincidences," Lester said. "There must be a tie-in."

A knock came and the door opened. Detective Gerald Cannady stepped in. "You wanted something?"

"Jerry, you remember Ms. Kavanagh and Mr. Shepherd from the callout last night."

Cannady nodded.

"They are interested in background on the Marley Plantation fire and the murder of that actor. You think your uncle could help them out?"

"What is it you want to know? There was a lot of press. You could probably get anything you need from the newspaper archives."

"We've done a cursory look but will definitely be digging deeper. I was hoping the investigating agency might still have some of the files, the murder book, or even some of the evidence in storage. Detective Lester, here, says your uncle might be of help."

Cannady glanced toward Lester and back to Jake. "Yeah. Undersheriff Rowland over there is married to my mother's sister."

"Could we trouble you to give us an intro so we might have a look at the old file if it's still around?"

He appeared to ponder the request for several seconds before responding. "Yeah. I can do that." He reached in his pocket, took out a card, and handed it to Jake. "Best time to get him is afternoon, say three-thirty or four. Give me your number. I'll set it up and text you the confirmation."

"Appreciate it."

CHAPTER 26

After meeting with the detectives, Scarlett and Jake returned to the hotel and found their luggage had been relocated to the new suite. "This is an upgrade," Scarlett said as they entered the new accommodations.

"I'm sure they don't have guests taken hostage every day, and the fact that their employee helped the assailant gain entry puts them in a precarious position."

Scarlett grabbed her things and proceeded to move them to the bedroom farthest from the door. Once in her room, she unpacked and organized everything while Jake simply took his suitcase to his room and left it unopened, choosing instead to open his computer to check email and to touch base with Liz as to any activity arising in his other pending cases.

Once Scarlett had everything unpacked and put in its proper place, she sat down on her bed with her laptop and checked her email. A response from Veronica Salvadore immediately caught her attention.

Ms Kavanagh,

In reply to your message, I would certainly like to learn more. I checked your website as you suggested.

I am unaware of my brother having any children, but we are Italian. Italians love family. If Vic had a daughter, I want to know.

Please give me a call at your convenience. I am available all day today at the number below.

Veronica Salvadore.

A smile crossed Scarlett's face. *Nice.* She took her phone from the bedside table and tapped in the number Salvadore provided. It rang only three times.

"Ms. Salvadore, this is Scarlett Kavanagh. Thank you so much for your response to my email."

"Well, it came as a surprise but gave me a chill to think Vic may have had a child. Tell me everything."

"We are in the investigation stage and can't be sure, yet. However, A genetic genealogy check of our client's DNA profile produced your name and the name of a potential first cousin. His name is Phillip Salvadore."

"That's my son—or at least, it's his name. I know his wife persuaded him to do the DNA test after I did mine."

"Do the names Francesca Cardoza and Maria Burgess mean anything to you?"

"They do. They are my older sister and her daughter. These names came up as related to your client?"

"They did, along with yours."

"Who is your client?"

"Before I release her name, I would like to confirm that you are related. But I can tell you, she is a lovely person and holds an advanced, professional degree and an impressive job. If she is related to your family, you would be proud."

"How did this all come about? Who is her mother? Vic was never married."

"At this point, we have no idea. What I can tell you is she was raised by a loving couple but never knew she was adopted. For lack of a better name, I'll call her A.C. It was only after the parents who raised her passed away, and she did a DNA test with one of the leading companies that it all started to suggest she was not their biological child. If you would be so kind as to allow us to test your DNA, it will be so helpful. Are you willing to do that?"

There was a momentary pause, during which Scarlett held her breath.

"I can do that, but how? Do I send it in to one of those companies?"

"No, no. We can send you a kit with a couple of swabs. Just follow the instructions. We'll provide a prepaid envelope with overnight delivery. I'll let you know the minute we receive results. We have two major labs that already have A.C.'s profile."

"This is really giving me a tingling feeling. Losing Vic was hard, but it was so long ago. He had left New York for California years before he died. But he always remembered to send gifts at Christmas. Our mother was still alive when he died. If he had a child, how she would have loved to have known it. Is she possibly the daughter of the woman who killed Vic? We were told he was dating that woman."

"We don't know."

"They never told us much about her or the extent of their relationship. They did ask the family about her having a plea deal without a trial. The family was okay with it when they said she would be in prison for the rest of her life, and we wouldn't have to go through a trial. But if your client is Vic's daughter, I want to meet her."

"Do you know of any other relationships Vic might have had?"

"No. I don't know. Vic and I weren't in regular contact. He checked in with our mother and had her visit him on the set, but she never mentioned any relationships. He was totally focused on his career. We brought Vic back up for his funeral and burial. It was all arranged without any of the family going down to Charleston. His agent handled the details."

"Do you know anything about the woman? Why she did it?"

"No. All I know is she was French and worked on the set as a makeup . . . no, wardrobe person. I don't think she spoke English very well. I was pregnant with Phillip at the time. My husband tried to shield me because he was afraid the shock would create problems for my pregnancy."

"What about his estate? As successful as he was, there must have been a sizeable estate."

"Vic left Mom a nice nest egg, which we all ultimately shared when she passed away. He also left that mansion to the acting school he attended. I think they sold it to the State of South Carolina for a museum. It was built before the Civil War. Since he wasn't married, and had no children, there was really no heir to leave it to."

"I really appreciate your helping us out. Do you mind if I contact you again as questions may arise? And I will certainly update you with what the DNA test reveals."

"Certainly. Ms. Kavanagh, if it turns out that your client is Vic's child, I would really like to meet her. Will you help us do that?"

"Of course. I'm sure she will want to meet you as well."

After terminating the call, Scarlett sent Liz a message to take care of getting the DNA kits to Salvadore, using Amazon as quickest way to get delivery of kits in New York the next day. Once finished, she went to Jake's room to fill him in.

"Looks like you're making progress, Harvard." He glanced at his watch. "Pete should be rolling up in about an hour. I'm sure he will be hungry, so, let's wait to eat until he gets here. I'm going to call for an appointment with that guy at the Charleston County Sheriff's Office. I hope he'll cooperate with us."

"I can wait. But I'm going to make a cup of tea right now. Do you want anything?"

"I'm good. By the way, I got a message from Lester that Myrtle was released. Jorgensen must have found someone to take out the bond, but I'd bet a day's billables he fronted the money."

"Does Lester think there's any danger of her making another attempt to contact us?"

"Not if she's smart. The order on her first appearance includes a no-contact with victims and witnesses."

***

Pete Cooper and Kai arrived at ten minutes past two. From the lobby, he called Jake who gave him their suite number.

Kai ran to Jake and then to Scarlett the minute the door opened.

"Hey, buddy. Good to see you." Looking up at Pete Cooper, he said, "Any problems on the ride?"

"All clear. We made one stop. Traffic was light." He turned toward Scarlett. "Hey, pretty lady. This guy treating you right?"

Scarlett opened her arms and gave him a hug. "About the usual, but with you here, he'll have to behave. Thanks for coming."

Cooper smiled and then focused on Jake. "So, what have you gotten yourself into?"

"We're trying to unravel it. We've got a dicey lawyer whose paralegal was the assailant who held Scarlett at gunpoint for about an hour last night. She's out on bond now."

"Are you worried she might try again?"

"Not a huge risk, but I never saw last night coming."

"Tell me again. What is this case about?"

"Believe it or not, it's a track down birth parents. But it's one for the books. Our client may be the daughter of an A-list celebrity who was murdered about thirty-five years ago here in Charleston. No evidence yet as to who her mother was or is, but we do have a suspect."

"Leave it to you to pull down unique cases. So, you're thinking there's a connection between the case and what happened last night."

"We both are, Pete," Scarlett said. "There's so much about this case that we haven't pieced together, yet."

"Let's get some lunch, and we'll give you the high points. Scarlett and I have an appointment later this afternoon to meet with the undersheriff of Charleston County, the agency that handled the murder of the potential father of Scarlett's client. The incident last night was handled by the North Charleston Police Department."

Chapter 27

Undersheriff Lex Rowland met Scarlett and Jake in the lobby of the Charleston County Sheriff's Office. Pete Cooper had stayed behind at the hotel with Kai. A tall, imposing man, Rowland shook Jake's hand and gave a polite nod toward Scarlett. "I understand you want to see what we have on the Vic Lanza homicide," Rowland said. "Are you writing a book or looking to do a TV show or something?"

Jake smiled. "Never been accused of that before. No book. No TV. We're doing background on a case. It may be irrelevant, but since we're here, I thought we should dig into it," Jake said.

"I don't know how much help we can be, but let's go to my office where we can talk." He turned and walked down the hallway with Jake and Scarlett following.

Once the trio was seated in his office, Rowland cleared the files on his desk and took out a legal pad and pen. "Jerry said you're former FBI. What was your area?"

"Primarily violent crime. If you know the drill, I started in bank robbery, moved to HRT, and ended up in violent crimes."

Scarlett glanced around the room at the plaques and trophies. Most were related to the job but several represented Rowland's coaching of a Little League team.

"HRT. Impressive. How is the private sector working for you?"

Jake made a facial gesture with one eye squinting. "Some better, some worse. I miss the badge, but sometimes, it works better that I don't have one. I'm not required to read anyone their rights."

Rowland chuckled. "I get that. I'm closing in on retirement and wondering what next? Thought about the P.I. role but not sure."

"Word of advice?"

Rowland nodded.

"Hook up with a good lawyer. Best way to build a bread-and-butter client base."

"Sounds reasonable. Thanks. Back to your goal. If I understand you right, you want to review the Lanza file, if we still have it. You're making an FOIA request? That was a mighty long time ago. I had barely put on the uniform."

"We're hoping that it's gathering dust somewhere in your archives. Do you know if anyone who worked the case is still around?"

"The names are in the file. You'll have to check. I'll have my people see what we have in storage. It has been a long time, but considering the victim's fame, I suspect it's been preserved. I'm surprised that true crime TV hasn't dug it up and made a documentary. I'll let you know what we find. How long are you in town?"

"Right now, it's open ended. But I'll keep you posted. By the way, what do you know about a lawyer named Paul Jorgensen?"

"He does a lot of annoying advertising—billboards, TV. Other than that, nothing. Why do you ask?"

"He's connected to the case we're working. Scarlett and I met with him yesterday, and he came across as squirrely. Has there ever been any scandal involving him that you are aware of?"

Rowland shook his head. "No. When I was a rookie, he was a PD. You know we always have an attitude towards those boys who get the perps off who we work so hard to take down."

"Public Defender—huh!" Jake turned to Scarlett. "That's the first we've heard of him dancing in the criminal courts."

Rowland slapped a hand on his desk. "Wait. I just remembered. He was the P.D. who defended the French woman who killed that actor."

Scarlett's hand went to cover her mouth as she reacted.

"No, shit. You just upped the game. The son-of-a-bitch said yesterday he did not know who Vic Lanza was, which I knew was a lie but—"

"He defended the woman convicted of killing Vic Lanza?" Scarlett interrupted, her eyes projecting her astonishment.

"Now, I'm convinced he did something dicey in the case," Jake said. "His paralegal, who held Scarlett hostage last night, kept saying our investigation was ruining his life. Apparently, there *is* something to uncover."

Rowland looked from Scarlett to Jake. "You've got my attention, now. But what could he have done? Surely he wasn't covering something up in order to throw the case? What are you thinking?"

"Right now. I haven't got a fucking clue. But the case is gaining more and more traction. Let us know as soon as you find the file."

Grabbing the pen, Rowland made a note and circled it with a flourish. "I'll assign one of my detectives to work with you on it."

When the undersheriff laid his pen down, Jake stood, reached across the desk, and shook his hand. "Thanks. Appreciate your Southern hospitality."

"Glad to oblige. Let us know if you uncover anything you believe would be of interest to us."

***

"How did it go with the locals?" Pete said as he and Kai joined Scarlett and Jake in their suite.

"I think it went better than we expected," Scarlett said, reaching over to scratch Kai behind his ear.

"It looks like we can rely on cooperation. The undersheriff we met with is assigning a detective to work with us. Let's get everything together and look at what we've got and what we're missing."

As Scarlett spread files on the suite's dinette table, Jake took cold drinks out of the minibar for all three and grabbed the room service menu. Returning to the table, he plopped the menu down. "Take a look and then tell me what you want for dinner. I think we need to eat here while we work on a plan."

Pete picked up the menu. "I'm good with that. So, finish bringing me up to speed. How long have you guys been working this case?"

Scarlett looked down and counted out the time on her fingers. "It's been at least six weeks—maybe eight. As we told you, the client came to the office to hire Jake. She had read about him in that magazine article."

"Oh, yeah. Poster boy P.I.," Pete said, grinning.

"No wisecracks. That damn piece wasn't my idea."

Ignoring him, Scarlett continued, "Sherlock turned his nose up at the case, but I could see how important it was to her, so, with his permission, I took the case."

"How did you get Shepherd onboard?"

"We found evidence that the couple who raised Anna, the client, had a biological baby with the same name born the same day Anna was born, but the DNA disputed the known ethnic heritage of both parents."

"Sounds like a textbook, switched at birth case. They took the wrong baby home from the hospital. Couldn't you run a check on the other families?"

"Not possible," Scarlett said. "There weren't any other female babies born at that hospital during the time Anna's mother was a patient."

Pete leaned back in his chair. "That's a wrinkle."

"Isn't it?"

"Any scientific possibility for a DNA mix-up?"

"No. We have run the profile with several different sources, and all produce the same."

"Wow! You do have a puzzle. And you say you believe the birth father was a celebrity?"

"The genetic genealogy research suggests it," Jake said. "Scarlett talked with his sister earlier today, and she is cooperating. Liz is sending her a couple of DNA kits. We should have something within a week. If it proves he is the father, he died here in Charleston before she was born. Murdered. A big deal."

"You haven't mentioned his name."

"Vic Lanza. Heard of him?"

"Heard of him? Hell, yes. He was on one of the hottest TV shows back in the what? The 1980s? You think your client is his child?"

"Maybe."

"Who's the mother?"

"We don't have any idea, yet. There have been no DNA matches turn up for the maternal side of Anna's family."

"Apparently a woman was convicted of the homicide, and we found out this afternoon that she was represented by a lawyer who just happens to be an uncle of the client and the employer of the woman who broke into our rooms and held a gun on Scarlett."

"Damn. You've got a ticking bomb. I assume you're going to talk to the woman."

"Step one is to finalize the DNA connection with Lanza. Talking to the inmate may take both legal acrobatics and social finesse."

"If social finesse is a requirement, you better send Scarlett in. You are no good at that," Pete said.

Scarlett laughed.

"Never said I was. But the fact is, a little help from the locals would go a long way. Do you have any connections with the field office down here?"

"Not that comes to mind, but I'll check. If I don't, Sonny or Deke may. Want me to handle that?"

"Yeah. That would work. Cross your fingers that the sheriff's office finds the file."

"Jake. AI just found a possible name for her. It's Marielle Devereau."

"Sounds very French," Pete said.

"That could account for why no DNA matches have surfaced," Jake said.

Pete looked confused. "What makes you say that?"

"France does not allow their people to submit to the genealogy companies."

"I didn't know you were an expert on DNA," Pete said.

"I know things." Jake grinned.

"Jake, she must be Anna's birth mother. We need to get her DNA," Scarlett said.

"First, we have to get to her. But if Lanza isn't the father, we would be wasting a lot of time and effort. I think we have to sit tight a few more days."

"Oh, no." Scarlett's brow wrinkled.

"What's the problem?" Jake said.

"I've got an email from Anna. She wants to know what we've found. What should I tell her?"

He tapped his pen on the pad in front of him. "Nothing right now."

"Come on. We've got to do better than nothing. She hasn't heard from us since we got here. She's not going to like not hearing something, Jake. But I can't tell her we think her mother might be a murderer."

"Tell her we're closing in on a possibility and don't want to get her hopes up until we nail it down."

"Her boyfriend is going to say we're just running up the tab."

"Her boyfriend can go to hell as far as I'm concerned."

Pete looked from Scarlett to Jake and back. "Something I don't know here?"

"Jake and Anna's boyfriend didn't hit it off so well."

"Pompous asshole."

Pete broke out laughing. "Classic Shepherd attitude. What's your problem with him?"

"He's a surgeon and a former NFL football player," Scarlett said. "I have to admit, he's pretty full of his self-importance. They are engaged, and Anna refuses to set a date for the wedding until she learns who she is. I kinda understand."

"Two alphas. I get it. Getting back to the plan," Pete said. "I suggest we get every bit of information we can dig up from media archives. Ferret out any names and start the research for who we can talk to.

Was this French woman pregnant? Surely there's a record. If so, what happened to her baby?"

CHAPTER 28

After breakfast the next morning, a trip to a dog walk for Kai, and an agreement on dividing the research, Scarlett, Jake, and Pete returned to the hotel suite to research deeper on the Lanza murder. Scarlett focused on local media, Jake covered national, and Pete looked into coverage by the entertainment community.

By noon, Scarlett stood, stretched, and said, "I'm ready for a break. How about you guys?"

Pete hit save and closed his laptop. "I'm with you on that, and if you guys don't mind, I'm going to hop over to my room and touch base with Sonny to be sure all is cool in D.C."

Jake looked up at Pete and said, "You go ahead. When you're done, we'll head out for a bite to eat. I'm getting cabin fever."

"Let me guess. You want barbecue for lunch?" Scarlett said.

He grinned. "What would you like, Harvard?"

She glanced toward Pete. "Let's let Pete choose. He's neutral."

"Barbecue is fine with me, or a good hamburger."

Jake took out a coin. "Heads it's hamburgers—tails barbecue." He flipped the coin and held it out for Scarlett to make the call."

"Barbecue. Let me see the other side of that coin. Knowing you, it's a trick coin."

Jake laughed and turned it over.

***

Once their drinks were served and orders taken, Jake said, "What has everyone learned about Lanza?"

"He got a hell of a lot of press," Pete said. "But probably to be expected. Most of the industry wrote long tributes to how talented he was, how good he was to work with, and how much was lost with his death."

"The local papers carried a little of that," Scarlett said. "But they focused on the fire at the historic plantation and the woman arrested for his homicide."

"Did either of you find any scandals or articles suggesting he had enemies, professional disputes, broken relationships?"

Both Scarlett and Pete shook their heads.

"How long did it take for the papers to name his killer?" Jake asked.

"Pretty much the day after. It seems like she was at the house all day. It was a Sunday, and his security team only worked until three p.m. There were two on duty that morning. One testified that Marielle Devereau, a wardrobe mistress on the TV show, was staying at the mansion. The other one said Devereau and Lanza were fighting early in the day."

"Was there any mention of her giving a statement?"

"Not much. The papers said she was distraught, but her English was so poor, no one knew what she said."

"Was Jorgensen mentioned?"

"Oh, yeah. He did the usual 'no comment' to all media questions."

"What about the national news. What did you learn, Jake?"

"A lot of duplication. They did talk a little about Marielle's background. According to the *Times*, the show was her first job in the states. She came to study fashion design and met someone from the series. It seems they had lost a member of the wardrobe team, and she fell into the job."

"What about her family?"

"She apparently had no one in the U.S."

"Did they mention a motive?"

"Nope. None was given. The speculation was a lover's quarrel. One of the makeup women said she thought they were having an affair." Scarlett looked down at her phone. "Liz is calling." As she answered the cell, she stood, signaled the men she was stepping outside to take the call.

"Hey, Liz. What's up?"

"It's Anna Carden. She says she needs to talk to you. What do you want me to do?"

"I emailed her that we were working on something and should be able to give her an update soon."

"Apparently, soon isn't good enough."

"Okay. I'll give her a call on my disposable. I'm afraid to give her this number. Did she give you a time I can reach her?"

"She did. She said she is off today, so, you can call any time."

"Thanks. I'll make the call right now."

"Are you guys making any progress?"

"We're doing research right now and waiting to hear from a detective about the police file on the death of Vic Lanza. We know so much but so little is confirmed. Have you heard if his sister received the DNA kits?"

"She did. Hopefully, she sent them out to the labs. I've alerted them to put a priority on the analysis. You'll hear the minute I do."

Scarlett returned to the table.

"What was Liz needing?" Jake asked.

"It's Anna. She's restless—"

Before she could say more, the waitress appeared with their orders.

"I'll call her on the other phone after I eat."

"I would still hold back."

"Don't worry. I'll stall."

Jake barely took a bite of his sandwich when his phone buzzed. Picking up the cell, he gulped down the food.

"Shepherd here."

"Detective Blackwell. I was hoping to hear from you." Jake took a quick sip of water.

"Great! You can send it to the email address on my card. Appreciate it. I'm sure I'll be in touch."

Terminating the call, he said, "They found the file. Blackwell, the detective Rowland assigned, is emailing the documents to me."

***

Once back at the hotel, Jake immediately opened his inbox. The Lanza murder file had arrived. He looked up at Scarlett and Pete and said, "I'm forwarding a copy to both of you and to Liz. This should give us a better perspective. You guys start reviewing it while I take Kai for a walk."

Scarlett immediately took her computer out of the safe while Pete went to retrieve his from his room.

***

The room was silent for most of the afternoon. All three studied the Lanza file intently. At three-fifty, Jake leaned back in his chair, and said, "We've got to interview this woman. This file doesn't convince me she killed him."

"That may not be easy," Pete said. "I did a little research on prisoner visitation down here. You need to be on her list. Otherwise, your best bet is to get someone in law enforcement to schedule a visit and take you along."

"We've gotten cooperation from the local teams, but that might be pushing the envelope. Have you thought of anyone we know in the local office of the Bureau?"

"The one here is a Satellite. Likely small staff."

"One of us has got to know someone here." Jake whipped out his cell and began typing.

"What are you doing?"

"Texting Liz to get a list of all Feds in the area. One of us might know someone."

"Even if you find someone willing to work with you on this, you're going to need a reason for law enforcement to make the visit."

"Well, looking at this file, I'm not seeing that a significant amount of work was done identifying the killer. Seems like they took the easy way out. We can say we're working a cold case or we're working with something like the Innocence Project. It's almost true. You've reviewed the file. They didn't even look at anyone else. First suspect, a naive young woman who didn't speak the language and didn't offer much resistance. And I'm smelling spoiled meat with this guy Jorgensen. He didn't attempt to put up a defense."

"That's the Shepherd I know and love. Never go with the obvious," Pete said.

"And guys," Scarlett said. "Where would a nineteen-year-old, French immigrant get a Smith & Wesson revolver? The file said the murder weapon was likely an S & W, Model 10. That was an old gun."

Pete gave Scarlett a look of surprise. "I'm impressed, pretty lady. You know your guns."

"Forgot to tell you." Jake pointed toward Scarlett. "Harvard gives me a run at the range."

"Good to know," Pete said.

"Not true. He lets me win so I won't become discouraged." They all chuckled.

"You made a good point about the woman acquiring that type gun, Harvard. I'm sure there was a lot of heat on the detectives to clear this one—high profile celebrity. All eyes on the cops to bring it home. And what the hell was Jorgensen's role? How much investigation did he do to eliminate his client as a suspect? Did he phone it in? Was he lazy, have an ulterior motive?"

"Jake, I don't see anywhere that the defendant, Marielle, was pregnant. All I see is that witnesses saw them arguing, no one saw her leave, and she didn't offer an alibi. She was only nineteen, didn't speak the language, and had no one in this country that I can see to support her."

"From what I've read so far, Madison would have blown this one out of the water before lunch," Pete said. "Where's the direct evidence? No murder weapon. No witness. No forensics. It's all circumstantial. And interesting to note that the fire was deemed accidental by the State Marshal. No sign of arson, so, it wasn't purposely set as a coverup."

"But what I'm seeing from the autopsy report is a likelihood the victim knew the assailant. I think I want to have a little chat with Jorgensen, the man with memory loss."

"He's not going to talk to you, Jake," Scarlett said. "I'm not even sure it's ethical with the hostage issue pending."

"You know, we might have this all wrong about Myrtle being a nut job. Jorgensen might have been the mastermind—orchestrated the whole thing," Jake said.

Scarlett stared at him for several seconds. "Why would he—"

"He's a smart lawyer. He's told Myrtle something or she's found something out that can cause him to be asked some serious questions, and he doesn't want her spilling his secret. He sets her up to commit a felony, acts as her attorney, and we have a two-way gag. She can't talk because it incriminates her. He can't talk because of attorney-client privilege. He's bought himself an insurance policy."

"Well, that's a theory," Pete said.

"Harvard, we need to meet with the prosecutor assigned to handle Myrtle's case. Get him to connect with us."

"That can be your entrée to the prison. You believe the incident is connected to the prisoner," Scarlett said.

"She's right, Jake. That should bring the local detectives on board if you get the attention of the prosecutor."

A phone rang from across the room. All three had their cells on the table.

"Where's that coming from?" Pete said.

"It's my second phone. It's probably Anna." Scarlett looked at Jake. "I've got to tell her something, Jake."

"Do what you need to do."

After retrieving the phone and answering, Scarlett went into her bedroom to talk.

"Scarlett, have you found anything out? We cancelled the original wedding plan and honeymoon. Now, Dan and his mother are driving me crazy about setting another wedding date."

"I wish I could tell you that we have identified your parents, but I can tell you we're moving closer and closer. The genetic genealogy report provided a name for a man who may have been your father. Unfortunately, he is deceased. But we were able to track down his sister. She's agreed to provide DNA samples, and we've expedited kits to her with prepaid envelopes to submit the samples to the two labs we're using. If it turns out you share enough centimorgans, I think we will have your father identified."

"What about my mother? And what about where I was born?"

"That's a work in progress. We met with your cousin, Robin, and she gave us a DNA sample. It's at the lab as well."

"What about my Aunt Irene?"

"I'm sorry, Anna, but we can't talk to her. She has ALS, Lou Gehrig's disease, which your cousin says is advanced and affecting her brain."

"Oh, my gosh. I didn't know. Did you talk to Uncle Paul?"

"Briefly. He seemed busy, but we may have another meeting. Right now, we're hoping to lock down your father. As soon as I know, I'll contact you."

After ending the call, Scarlett sat down on the bed to gather her thoughts. *At least I was honest. If this woman, Marielle, is her mother, that's going to be hard to tell her.*

CHAPTER 29

Friday morning, Scarlett woke with a piercing headache. When she staggered into the common area of the suite, Jake had already taken Kai out and worked out in the hotel gym with Pete. The smell of coffee emanated from the Keurig. He took one look at her and said, "What's wrong? Are you okay?"

"Headache. I've got a sinus headache."

"You want an aspirin?"

"It won't help. I need something with an antihistamine, and I didn't bring any."

"Here. Sit down. Let me grab a sip of my coffee, and I'll run downstairs to the sundry shop. What should I get?"

She made it to the small desk, took a piece of hotel stationery from the drawer, and wrote down the names of several over-the-counter sinus meds. As she handed it to him, she said, "Jake, I don't think I can go with you and Pete to the museum this morning. If you don't mind, I'll stay here with Kai. If you can find one of those meds, I should be over it by the time you get back."

He rubbed her shoulder while he talked. "Not a problem. We've got it covered. I'm sure it won't be the last time we make the trip. You stay here and take care of yourself. Don't leave the room or open the door for anyone. I'll put the 'Do not disturb' sign on the door and leave my weapon in the drawer by my bed."

"After the other night, you don't have to remind me twice."

***

When Jake and Pete arrived at the museum, it was just opening and only two other visitors were in line to enter. After purchasing tickets, they embarked on an unescorted tour.

"I have to note," Pete said. "This is my first visit to a thirty-some-thing-year-old crime scene." He reached into a nearby rack and took a museum brochure. "What are you looking for?"

"To paraphrase a Supreme Court Justice," Jake said, taking a small notepad out of his pocket. "I'll know it when I see it." As he spoke, Jake pulled out a drawing from the portfolio he carried. Pointing to the sketch, he said, "It looks like the original floor plan of the building has survived, but a big chunk of the property was sold for that tract of houses we passed."

Pete gazed around the area. "I'm thinking the killer had to be familiar with the house in order to navigate this place. It's the size of a hotel." He glanced down at the pamphlet. "This brochure says it has thirty-five rooms, but when they rebuilt the area on the top floor damaged by the fire, they redesigned it to create a restaurant and a gift shop. What did a single guy need with that many rooms?"

"Got me there. Whoever the killer was, he or she had to be known to the victim because there was no sign of forced entry, according to the file."

"I noticed that, but you're assuming a thorough check was done. Couldn't the fire have destroyed evidence of a break in?"

"The fire was believed to have started on the second floor and spread partially to the third. Fire typically rises. This floor, which is obviously where sources of entry are, escaped damage. The body was found here in the entry hall at the bottom of those stairs on this marble floor." Jake pointed to the left.

Pete gazed upward at the mezzanine overlooking the massive entry hall and accessed via a pair of semi-circular staircases. "According to one of the crime-scene photos, there was a trail of blood that indicated Lanza was shot upstairs and then stumbled down, bleeding out, presumably trying to escape."

"I noticed on one of the reports that a passing motorist called it in. Somewhat curious that anyone was traveling out this way at night since there were no homes in the area back then."

"I assume a mobile was used. Interesting, since mobile phones were not common back then. Maybe the caller was the killer. Did the records indicate whether the 911 call came from a male or female?"

"Male."

As they walked up the staircase on the right, Pete said, "Shepherd, according to this brochure, the top floor was originally servants' quarters and storage. With the restoration, a restaurant, gift shop, and a room dedicated to Vic Lanza took over the floor. The Lanza room might be worth checking out."

"Copy that." When they reached the landing at the top of the staircase, Jake paused. "You studied the arson report. Refresh my memory. Where did it say the fire originated?"

"The opinion was a lit candle fell into a chair here in this sitting area. It would have been over there," Pete pointed to the right where a pair of occasional chairs with plump upholstery flanked a Chippendale tea table holding a cup and saucer and a trio of staggered-height candlesticks. "Looks like they created a duplicate setting to the one destroyed by the fire."

"The fire was probably accidental and not a coverup," Jake said as he walked closer to the table and tipped a candlestick toward the chair. "I'd say the fire was accidental but the bullet intentional. The candle was likely knocked over in whatever skirmish preceded the fatal shot."

Jake turned, faced Pete, and put his hand to his chest. "I'm Lanza. The first round hits me in the chest; I stagger back and hit the table, knocking the candle off. The second round hits me in the gut, and the perp flees." Jake staggers toward the stairs, clutching his torso, grabs the railing and stops. "I go down the stairs, half walking, and half falling until I collapse on the marble and poof. It's over."

The other pair of visitors had come up the left stairs and stared at Jake with confusion written on their faces.

Pete caught sight of the man and woman. "Don't mind him. He didn't take his meds this morning." They quickly turned to walk down the hallway to the left.

Ignoring the couple, Jake continued his assessment. "And no one sees or hears anything out here in the middle of nowhere at the time. Why didn't he maintain security full time?"

"Not everyone can be Jake Shepherd. But in all fairness, this place is built like a fortress with thick walls and heavy shutters. He probably felt safe inside the building."

"And just how tight was the security when they were on duty? Did they check that all who went in came out?"

"The security guys' statements said that the guest lists were kept in the guard station at the gate, but no one could find any after the fire," Pete said.

"That sounds like someone with intimate knowledge knew how to eliminate potential evidence."

"I've been thinking about what Scarlett said about the gun, Jake. I agree about the mystery of a young immigrant having a weapon of that kind, but I also feel that isn't a woman's typical gun. Maybe the murder weapon belonged to the victim."

***

After touring the second floor and finding nothing of interest, Jake and Pete went up to the third level.

"Refresh my memory, if all of the relevant actions took place on the two floors below, why are we up here?" Pete asked. "I don't see how we will learn anything about the death or the fire in the restaurant or gift shop."

"Over there." Jake pointed to a door with a plaque overhead indicating it was the Victor Lanza room.

"Oh, yeah. Wonder what they have in there."

"One way to find out." Jake walked across and opened the door. Inside, film and TV posters lined the walls. Glass display cases bearing memorabilia were scattered around. Scripts, programs, letters, invitations, and photos filled the cases. In the center of the room, a tall, slender display case held seven Emmy statuettes.

"Interesting," Jake said. "I guess it makes sense to have a room displaying his achievements since he was the last owner and a celebrity with a significant fan base. A double draw for tourists."

Pete ambled around the room while Jake stood, reading inscriptions on the Emmys.

"Jake. Over here. You need to see this." Pete pointed to an item in a counter-height glass case.

Crossing the room, Jake glared down at the object Pete pointed out. His body tensed with the thrill of discovery as he assessed the item.

"Our killer is in that book."

CHAPTER 30

"Maybe," Pete said. "Considering the card describes it as Lanza's address book, it would sure be worth a look if you could get to it. I wonder why it wasn't kept in police custody as evidence in the case."

"They had their suspect, or so they thought; therefore, no need to run down more."

"Considering they turned the book over to the museum, the information inside may have been redacted."

Jake nodded. "It could have been, but I'd like to see. Maybe any redactions would have been limited to phone numbers and addresses. The names could have been impressive and worth preserving."

"Question is, how are you going to get access to it? I don't think a docent is going to unlock this case and hand it to you."

"Good question. An FOIA request should produce access, unless South Carolina doesn't have an FOIA law. This is a state owned and funded property." He whipped out his phone and typed the question into the perplexity.ai app. "Yep. They've got a freedom of information statute. Let's find the office for this place, and I'll file an application."

"I've got a feeling the staff here won't know what you're talking about. How often would a demand for information be made to a museum? Maybe you should hold off. Let Scarlett present it with her charming manner and legal expertise. You go in there with your King Kong, alpha male attitude, and you'll piss these little old Southern ladies off. Who knows what else you might need in this place? We can come back tomorrow."

Jake gave him a look of displeasure that quickly dissolved into recognition of the plausibility of Pete's suggestion. "You think I can't be charming?"

"Yeah. About as charming as a starved pit bull with a piece of raw meat."

***

As they drove back to the hotel, Pete said, "What if this woman in prison isn't the mother of your client? Are you going to keep working the case to prove she's innocent? You've opened a Pandora's box."

"I've thought of that. But there are a couple of things going on here. We've pretty much gotten credible evidence that the victim was the client's father, so who killed him would likely be important to the client. But if not, then I turn the evidence over to an innocence project. You know me. I can't walk away from a person rotting in prison for something they did not do or accept the fact that a killer appears to have gotten away with murder."

"Did it ever occur to you that the woman may have actually been guilty? Just because their evidence is pathetic doesn't mean she is innocent."

"Good point. But my gut tells me, she's innocent."

"Oh. Okay. I'd say something snarky, but I've been around you too long to doubt you."

The car was silent for nearly five minutes while Pete gazed out the window as they passed through a picturesque tunnel of oak tree limbs from both sides, crossing overhead on the two-lane road. Jake appeared consumed in thought but broke the silence first.

"This case is like a box full of pieces for multiple puzzles. Sorting out the ones that fit is the challenge. We start out looking for the biological parents of a client—simple case of follow the yellow-brick paper trail and maybe throw in the DNA. And we find official records of the adoptive parents having a baby on the client's alleged birth date and with her name, but the client doesn't genetically match. DNA science says the birth father was an A-list celebrity who was murdered here in South Carolina. A woman, who could be the mother, is in prison for killing him, but there's no DNA on file connected to the mother." Jake pumped the brakes to slow as a rabbit scampered across the road. Turning back to Pete, he said, "Then add a key witness, who was the alleged killer's defense attorney, who lies about the obvious and may have sent an armed woman to intimidate me and Scarlett into abandoning our investigation."

"The math isn't working. You think that lawyer sent the woman who held Scarlett hostage rather than her acting alone?"

"Maybe." Jake glanced down at his watch. "He's hiding something, and it must be pretty big. Putting her in the position of a criminal might be his way of keeping what she knows from being revealed. She's an accomplice after the fact so she won't rat him out, and he's got attorney-client privilege in his pocket to seal his lips about her. He's not stupid. The guy's got a dog *and* a pony in this show. But what could he have done to switch babies if the client is the French woman's child? I can see him taking her baby for placement, but that doesn't explain the missing one. Why no paperwork? Why was his defense of her so pathetic? What would make him stick his neck out, maybe risk losing his license, to foster an illegal adoption?"

"Love or money. It's usually one or the other, my friend. How long were you in law enforcement?"

"Long enough. But who would pay him? Probably the adoptive parents. On the other hand, whose love would we be talking about? Did he have an affair with his client? From her photos, she was a beautiful young woman. That would certainly be a no-no in any jurisdiction. Were they having an affair before the fire, and he was jealous of Lanza? Maybe he was the killer? No. I think that's a journey too far. There's no evidence that he could have known her before he was assigned to defend her."

"But he could have had an affair while representing her and is the father of her child, in which case your client is not her child."

"In that scenario, I would definitely contact an innocence project, but right now, I'm starved. Want to eat at the hotel or pick something up on the way?"

"What about Scarlett?"

"I'll give her a call. I think I need a trip back to visit our friend at the Charleston Sheriff's Office, but it'll probably have to wait until Monday. Getting that book might be easier through him than confusing the little old ladies with an FOIA request. I'll try to set it up now."

CHAPTER 31

Although Scarlett's headache had cleared by the time Jake and Pete returned to the hotel after visiting the museum on Friday, a storm had come up shortly before their arrival. Upon making a call to the Charleston County Sheriff's Office in hopes of making an appointment to meet with Lex Rowland again, he learned the undersheriff was out of the office for the duration of the weekend. Between the inclement weather and inability to meet with Rowland, the trio had discussed options for the weekend and agreed returning to Virginia for two days would not be cost effective. Setting the case aside, they had assumed the role of tourists, visiting sites around Charleston and taking a drive down the coastline on Sunday.

On Monday morning, as the three sat in Cracker Barrel waiting for their breakfast orders to arrive, Jake said, "As much as I am hesitant to leave you alone at the hotel, Harvard, I think taking Pete on this call may serve us better."

Pete cut his eyes back and forth between the two with a dubious look. "You're not going all male chauvinist on us, are you, Shepherd?" He focused his gaze on Scarlett and winked.

"Of course not. But this is an old school cop who I believe will pay more attention to other cops than to lawyers."

Scarlett grinned. "I'm okay with staying behind. It will give me a chance to review everything again and sort out what to tell Anna. She's off today and her fiancé is out of town for a conference. I promised I would call her for a more detailed discussion."

***

Jake and Pete arrived at the Charleston County Sheriff's Office five minutes before the ten-thirty appointment time. A clerk took their credentials and then directed a nearby deputy to escort them to the undersheriff.

Rowland stood as the two entered. His expression indicated he had not expected Pete. "Where's your lovely partner—Ms. Kavanagh?"

"She's doing some work back at the hotel. Undersheriff, this is my partner in our security company, Peter Cooper, retired FBI. I brought Pete along since he is working with us on the case."

Rowland reached across the desk to shake hands with Pete. "So, what brings you gentlemen here today? My people did get you some documents in the Lanza case, didn't they?"

"Absolutely, and I appreciate your help with that," Jake said. "I've got a list of the deputies and detectives who worked the case, which I'll leave with you. Maybe someone here knows if any are still around. In reviewing what you had, we were a bit surprised to find no direct evidence implicating the woman convicted of killing him."

"Really? It happened long before I came into the department, and to be honest, I've never reviewed the file," Rowland said as they all took seats.

"Understandable. Why would you? But now that we've gone over it, Pete, Scarlett, and I are convinced a jury would not have returned a guilty verdict based on the evidence in the file. Frankly, I'm surprised a prosecutor would have charged her without more. Even more surprised that Jorgensen allowed her to agree to the plea."

"Again, no ability to comment."

"And we don't expect you—"

A voice came over an instrument on the desk. "Undersheriff, we've got a problem."

"Excus—"

Jake motioned for him to go ahead.

"What kind of problem?"

"An active shooter over at that big daycare center close to the city limits."

"How bad?"

"All available uniforms are en route, and we alerted SWAT but need your directions. The shooter has a worker captive at gunpoint. We don't know any more."

"Do we have anyone on the scene?"

"We do. Two cars. Oh, no." The dispatcher's voice shook. "There's an officer down."

"Patch me through to anyone on the scene." Rowland's face projected the gravity of the situation.

A voice came over the phone. "Sir, this is John Green. I'm on the scene. We have one deputy down, but thankfully, it doesn't look like a life-threatening shot."

"Give me an assessment."

"The assailant has a young, female employee—teacher I believe—held hostage with a gun at her head. The students and teachers are in a large playroom in the center of the building. The shooter and hostage are believed to be in the lobby."

Jake and Pete stared intensely at Rowland, totally absorbed in the information coming through.

"Undersheriff," Green said, "We need SWAT, a good marksman, and a negotiator."

"Copy that." His face tensed with stress over the gravity of the situation. "I'll issue the orders and am on the way."

As he terminated the transmission, he hit a button and issued the promised orders, including a command to not engage unless fired upon or by his instructions. He then looked toward Jake and Pete. "Sorry, guys. You heard."

"We did," Jake said as he and Pete both stood.

"The real problem is, I don't have my best marksman. He is with the sheriff at a conference. Not good."

"You've got the best you could have standing in front of you," Pete said.

Rowland's brow pinched, and he shook his head. "Enlighten me. What do you mean?"

"Shepherd was a sniper with HRT. He can shoot the wings off a mosquito at a hundred yards."

Rowland paused for a second and then looked toward Jake. "Is that true?"

With a snap of his head, Jake said, "I don't miss."

"Excuse his lack of humility. It's exceeded only by his skill. All that said, if I'm ever in a firefight again, I want him standing next to me." Pete tipped his chin, raising his eyebrows to indicate confirmation of his assertion.

The undersheriff remained silent for nearly a minute, appearing to process Pete's declarations. He looked down at his desk for a few seconds and then made eye contact with Pete. "My nephew told me about the hostage situation he shut down the other night."

"You can talk to me," Jake said. "I'm right here."

"This is damn unorthodox." He turned toward Jake. "Are you even willing to get involved?"

Jake gave a short nod. "I can give it a shot—no pun intended."

Obviously conflicted, he again gazed down at his desk. "I can't just put a civilian out there, no matter how good you are." After several seconds, he looked back up at Jake. "I don't have the budget or authority to compensate you."

"You're the acting sheriff, right?" Pete said. "I suspect you have the authority to deputize both of us."

Rowland leaned forward, palms on his desk. "You're an FBI sniper, too?"

"Nope. Retired FBI crisis negotiator." Pete reached into his pocket, took out his wallet, and produced his official credentials as a retired agent. "As a member of the FBI Crisis Negotiation Unit, I deployed on many of the same incidents that Jake's HRT unit handled back in the day. I can help your guy or gal with the negotiating. Jake and I have both been in numerous hostage situations, but It's your call."

"I might add," Jake said. "If you're worried about compensation, you need a favor. I need a couple as well. *Quid pro quo.*"

Without asking what favor Jake wanted, Rowland pushed a button on his phone system. "Lou, get me two badges out of Sheriff Abbott's cabinet and body armor for two." He then reached into a side drawer of his desk and took out a small booklet. "Raise your right hands and repeat after me."

"I do solemnly swear (or affirm) that I am duly qualified, according to the Constitution of this state, to exercise the duties of the office to which I have been appointed; and that I will, to the best of my ability, discharge the duties thereof, and preserve, protect, and defend the Constitution of this state and the United States.

"I further solemnly swear (or affirm) that during my term of office as Deputy Sheriff, I will study the act prescribing my duties, will be alert and vigilant to enforce the criminal laws of the state and to detect and bring to punishment every violator of these laws, will conduct myself at all times with due consideration to all persons, and will not be influenced in any matter on account of personal bias or prejudice."

Pete and Jake both repeated the oath.

As he read the last words, Rowland picked up the badges his secretary had brought in during the swearing in and pinned one on both Jake and Pete. He then handed each one body armor. "Do you need weapons?"

"No. We both have our own in the vehicle," Jake said.

"I suspected as much. Let's roll." Turning around to a coat rack behind his desk, Rowland grabbed his vest and hat. "Don't make me regret this."

CHAPTER 32

With lights and siren in a marked SUV driven by a deputy, they arrived on the scene in less than ten minutes. Law enforcement surrounded the area and warded off onlookers. Recognizing the undersheriff, they immediately cleared a path for them to enter where a captain greeted Rowland.

"What do we know, Arnie?"

Captain Arnold Stern looked at Jake and Pete with obvious uncertainty. Apparently, noticing his reaction, Rowland said, "I've deputized these two. They are both former FBI with impressive credentials. Shepherd is a sniper—Cooper a negotiator. Who do we have negotiating right now?"

"Marilyn Foster, and she's not getting anywhere. Can't get him to respond."

"Again, what do we know? How many children and staff are in there? Have any hostages gotten out? Do we have an identity? A demand? Was this a targeted hostage or one of convenience?"

"It looks like it could be a domestic. Probably targeted. We don't know his name yet. The assailant appears to maybe know the hostage he is physically holding, but we aren't sure. One teacher was able to talk to dispatch before he confiscated all the phones. Otherwise, we wouldn't know anything. He might have a thing about women or maybe this one. According to the license for this operation, the facility is licensed for fifty children—all ages, with some infants."

"Damn. And adults?"

"Including kitchen staff, about nine or ten—all women. No one has come out. He locked all the rooms that have exits to the back and sides. We think, from what the one hostage was able to tell dispatch, before he took her phone, he has most everyone locked in a large play area in the middle of the building, he's in the lobby area, holding a gun to the head of an adult hostage."

"And we know he's a lone wolf?"

"Yes sir. There's been no sign of an accomplice."

"Has Foster gotten him to say anything? Give his name?"

"Nada. Another problem. The crowd is growing. Most of them are parents. They're causing a distraction and seem to disregard the danger they could be in if this turns into a firefight."

Rowland glanced around the area. "That building across the street." He pointed to a seven-story office building. "Get them over there, inside. If they refuse, tell them you'll have to arrest them. I get that they are panicked, worried about their kids, but we can't let them get in the way or get hurt. Block any more who show up from getting anywhere close."

Rowland turned toward Pete and Jake. "Do you have any suggestions?"

Pete spoke first. "You need to know who this guy is. Does he have a history of mental health issues, violence? Does he have kids, a wife, a girlfriend, a mother, even a pet? Get anyone or anything he loves out here as quickly as poss—"

"Chief," a uniformed deputy called out as he rushed forward. "We've got a name." Coming to a stop in front of the undersheriff, he said, "Ray Brantley."

"What do we know about Ray Brantley?"

"Not much."

"Call it in for a SCDMV check for his residence and do a background. Have uniforms start canvasing the parents as soon as you get them across the street for any information about this guy. Someone might know more about him. And Blackwell, see that everyone else vacates the area, including press."

"Roger."

"How'd you get the name?"

"Parents in the crowd. A couple recognized him from the photo Lieutenant Brantley was able to get from surveillance video recorded on the school cameras. He was able to reach the company furnishing security through the registration of the alarm system. He contacted the company, and they pulled it from the cloud. Three of our guys took it through that group on the chance someone would recognize him. They said he was the school, I mean daycare, handyman, aka janitor, not too smart, and was fired last week."

Pete took in every word in silence as Jake visually surveyed the area, walking a few feet away.

"Shepherd, you're former hostage rescue, what strategy do you think best?"

"Give a Pete a go at talking him down, which probably won't work, but it is always best to try. It also stalls for time. If Pete sees it's not going to work or the guy is growing more agitated, then your people can help me get in. I can take him down."

"You go in there? You can't do that."

"Have you got a better idea?"

"No. But going in there could be suicidal. Why would you take that risk? You're not even on the payroll."

"I don't need to be on your payroll. You'll compensate me."

"Not sure I want to ask about that now."

Jake grinned. "Nothing illegal or immoral."

"Do you think you can take him down without bloodshed?"

"Regardless of what you've heard, HRT operatives are trained to save lives, not take them. I'll need a layout of the building, which I hope your property appraiser or building and zoning people can produce. I need it ASAP. Plus, I need a couple of your guys to get me through to the back side of the building from the road parallel to this one with a ladder for scaling the fence. As for equipment, I'll also need a pair of athletic shoes, preferably size 12 D. These boots weren't made for jumping fences or tiptoeing quietly on hard surfaces." He looked down at Pete's shoes, a pair of dark brown leather Skechers with thick rubber soles. "What size?" Jake said, pointing toward Pete's feet.

"Twelve medium."

"Nix the shoes. I'll swap with him, but I'll need a lock picking kit, a glass cutter, a pair of heavy gloves, a couple of rags, a pair of handcuffs to restrain the bastard if I'm successful, a bag to hold all of the above and my weapon, plus enough rope to lower the bag to the ground from the top of the fence."

"What about a radio for communication?" Rowland said.

"My plan depends on this guy not knowing I'm in the building, so, I probably can't be verbal, but give me one just in case, but I'll probably have it off. Can't have your transmissions giving me away if I go in."

"Gotcha. I'm also adding a body cam to your list. Any issues with that?"

"Nope. None at all."

As Jake and Pete exchanged footwear, Rowland said, "This plan could get you killed."

Jake grinned. "It's been tried, but I'm freakin' invincible."

Rowland looked toward Pete with a dubious expression.

"He can do it. He knows what he's doing."

"If this goes wrong, there'll be hell to pay. But if it goes right, Charleston County has a job waiting."

"Keep your job," Jake said. "But there are couple of things you can do for me." He turned toward Pete, "While we're waiting for the equipment, do your thing and buy us some time."

"Every second counts," Rowland said.

Pete slapped palms with Jake and turned toward Rowland. "Give your negotiator the heads-up, and I'm on it."

Jake adjusted his holster and handed his Stetson to Rowland. "Hold on to this for me. I'll go with Pete until my gear arrives. I'd like to know as much as possible about the guy we're dealing with."

As they were about to move, a deputy rushed up. "Undersheriff, we found out the perp lives with his invalid mother and a dog. No other known family."

"Get his mother and the dog out here ASAP," Pete said. "Most of these guys don't want people they care about to see them kill or be killed. He sounds like a loner and probably cares a lot about that dog."

"The dog?" Rowland said.

"The dog."

Rowland frowned and shook his head but said, "You heard him. Get them. Send a patrol with siren and lights." He then radioed the negotiator the message she was being relieved as Jake and Pete walked to where she was set up with a microphone, phone, and a headset. A look of relief crossed her face as she handed her equipment to Pete. He nodded in response.

Once situated, Pete spoke into the microphone, "Ray, we need to communicate. Ray, can you hear me? Is everyone in there okay? My name is Pete." Pete's tone was calm and compassionate. "I'm a retired FBI negotiator who just happened to be down here in Charleston, and I thought I might be able to help. . . . I've helped a lot of people like you. I've helped people in pain avoid making that pain worse. No one's dead. Yes, you injured someone, but I've been told it's not life threatening and that's a good thing." Pete paused, waiting for a response. "Ray, it would help if you could give me a sign that you're hearing me. How about you giving me a call." Pete called out the number on the phone provided by the prior negotiator.

Silence absorbed the air as no sound came from the building, nor from the surrounding law enforcement, despite SWAT operatives taking positions. "Ray, I hope you can hear me. Nobody here wants to hurt you. It doesn't have to end badly. I know you're upset. You lost your job. I get it. It stinks. But it isn't worth dying over. Hey. We've all had losses. I'm here to help. But you've got to tell me what you want."

Pete paused, hoping for a response as Jake stood motionless but turning his head back to Rowland for a sign the equipment had arrived.

"You've made your point, Ray. Now is the time to let it go. Come out with your hands in the air and we can talk—try to figure something out." Pete paused again, giving the assailant time to respond. "Release your hostages, Ray. Don't make more trouble for yourself. Don't risk innocent children being hurt. Again, call me." Pete repeated the number of the phone he held. "I know you have a phone or easy access to one. I cannot help you if you don't talk to me. Look out a window. There are dozens of armed lawmen surrounding the building. The one standing next to me can put a bullet exactly where he wants it to go. If you doubt it, look out the window at that No

Parking sign beside the drive. He can put a hole through the middle of the 'o' in the word 'No' with one shot." Pete turned to Jake. "Do it." He then raised a hand, waving to Rowland and pointing to Jake with his other hand as a warning that Jake was shooting.

Jake gave him an "are-you-crazy" look but drew his weapon and fired, accomplishing exactly what Pete predicted.

At the sound of a gunshot, the surrounding police tensed, weapons drawn. They were ready to fire.

"Easy team, stand down. Not an attack. Shepherd just killed a road sign for demonstration purposes," Rowland said, speaking into his radio.

"That's called a kill shot, Ray. Think of that letter 'o' as being a spot between your eyes. If they have to come into the building, you are going to be hurt. Not one person out here wants that to happen."

When there was still no response, Pete said, "Answer me one question, Ray. The first step in helping you is knowing your end game. Was it your goal to commit suicide by cop? That's the thing I absolutely need to know. Just one answer—yes or no."

Pete's phone finally rang. Grabbing it he said, "Ray. Is that you?"

A hoarse sounding voice responded, "Yes."

"Good. Thanks for making the call." Pete put the phone on speaker and laid it on the folding table set up for the negotiations. "Tell me your story, Ray. What can I do for you?"

"I want my job back. I want them to stop telling lies about me. If they don't, then I want to die."

"Wow, Ray. That's heavy. What lies are they telling about you?"

"They said I was inappropriate with one of the girls."

"Inappropriate how?"

"I don't know. They just said I was inappropriate and couldn't work here any longer. I have to have this job. I have to take care of my mom. She can't take care of herself."

"Ray. . . . You can't take care of your mom if you get yourself killed out here."

"I got insurance. It will give her a lot of money so she can pay for someone to take care of her."

Pete leaned his head forward, putting a hand to his forehead, shaking it slightly. After a second or two, he dropped his hand, raised his head, and looked toward Jake. They exchanged looks of recognition. Turning back to the phone, Pete said, "Ray. Your mom is on her way here right now. Your mom and your dog. You don't want to leave either of them. They need you. If you're gone, your mom may go into a home, and your dog could go to a shelter. Think about that."

"No, no. I don't want her here. I don't got a job. I'm no good for her. The people need to tell the truth. My mom shouldn't have to think her son did something bad."

Before Pete could respond, a call came out from Lex Rowland. "Shepherd."

As Jake turned, Rowland pointed to a bag he was holding and motioned for Jake to come. Before leaving Pete, Jake nudged him, held up his cell, and mouthed, "Keep yours close," while pointing first to Pete and then to the palm of his hand. Pete gave him a thumbs up.

CHAPTER 33

After Jake claimed the bag of requested items, the undersheriff directed him to a pair of deputies who were waiting with an F-150 pickup truck. Two ladders—one an eight-foot step ladder, the other an extension ladder—were loaded in the bed. Tossing the bag in the back seat, Jake got in behind it and clipped the body cam to his protective vest. When done, he took his phone out of his hip pocket. As they drove, Jake studied an email on his phone containing the floor plan of the building. It took only minutes to circle the block and stop in front of a residence directly behind the daycare building.

Once the driver parked the vehicle on the street and killed the engine, the three exited and convened on the sidewalk. "I'll take the explaining to the tenant or homeowner if someone is home," the driver said. The other turned back to face Jake and said, "I'll carry the ladder and spot you going over. You're one badass for taking this risk. You sure you don't want some of our SWAT team to back you up? We don't know for certain if there is more than one shooter in there."

"I don't. A team storms in on this guy, and I promise you there will be bloodshed. From what I can tell, he's a simple-minded guy in a desperate state of mind. Anything can spook him. Believe it or not, I know how to be cautious. I have no death wish. Take a look at the sky." Jake pointed upward where dark clouds were moving in.

"Just what we need right now." The deputy's tone was sarcastic. "Rain will just muddy things up." Focusing on Jake, he said, "Which ladder do you want? Or do you want to take both?" He went to the tailgate of the vehicle and lowered it as the other deputy approached the front door of the home whose yard would be used for access.

Jake followed to the back of the truck. After glancing at both ladders, he pointed to one and said, "The step ladder should work. No way to know how old and how strong that fence is. It may not support the other, especially when my weight is added." He peeled off his jacket, exposing his weapon, took the jacket back to the cab, and tossed it in the backseat.

Glancing down to Jake's waist, the deputy said, "You going to jump that fence wearing a gun?"

"Not a chance. I'd prefer not to get shot or have a wild discharge. It's going in the bag to be lowered gently. Show me how to turn this thing on." He pointed to the camera and then rolled up the sleeves of his shirt.

"Let me check which model he gave you." The deputy tipped his head forward to get a better look at the camera. "See the button on the side. Tap it twice."

Once Jake and the deputy assisting him reached the fence surrounding the back grounds of the target building, Jake drew his gun, checked it out, and slid it into the bag. "I'll go up the ladder first to learn the layout and where best to breach the fence."

The deputy didn't ask but his expression indicated a lack of understanding.

"I'm guessing there's playground equipment that could be in the way. Once I see the best place to drop the equipment and where I need the ladder placed for my going over the fence, I'll take the equipment up and drop it. I'll then need the ladder moved a foot or so away from where the equipment lands."

Again, the deputy gave him a puzzled look.

"I need to make sure I don't accidentally land on the bag. When I make the jump, it would be helpful if you took a grip of the ladder and held it steady for me."

"Got it. Should we wait for my partner to get permission to enter the property?"

"No. He's giving notice, not asking permission. This is exigent circumstances. We're going in regardless of how the resident feels about it, so, there's no point in wasting time."

***

Gaining access to the backyard of the center caused Jake no problem. Once on the ground, he immediately removed his semiautomatic from the bag and holstered it. Gaining entry to the building was not as easy. Compromising the glass of the awning style windows would not produce enough space for entry. Kicking in the door would provide the assailant with notice. Picking the lock on the backdoor appeared the best option but took longer since it was not Jake's strong suit.

Once in, Jake encountered a hallway that circled the building with a large, indoor room for play in the center. Based on intelligence he received, the children, teachers, and staff were thought to be confined in that room with the exception of the teacher Ray held hostage. Ray and his captive were believed to be on the front side of the building in the reception area, which was bordered by the office, the playroom, and a small cafeteria. The back entry was in the center of the building and out of visual sight of Ray's location.

Upon entry, Jake activated the body cam, drew his weapon, and moved carefully up the left side of the hall, hoping to hear some conversation enabling him to learn the assailant's position. The building was silent except for faint, indistinguishable sounds of Ray's voice. Once at the entry to the lobby, Jake pressed himself against the wall, out of the line of any possible sight by Ray. He holstered his gun for long enough to send a text to Pete.

> Distract. Draw him forward!

Outside, Pete read Jake's text and knew Jake was in position and needed to have the assailant's full attention directed to the front. The patrol car had just arrived with Ray's mother, a short, frail woman using a walker, and his dog, a beagle mix.

"Ray," Pete called out on the phone. "Your mom and your dog are here. What's your dog's name?" Pete leaned over and began petting the animal. "He's a friendly guy. Look out the window, and you can see him. I bet if we turn him loose, he'll find you."

"Don't do that. Don't you do that. I told you not to bring my mom here."

"I know you did. But I'm trying to help you. Your mom wants to talk to you."

"No. Take her home. You send mom and Sam home."

Ray's last words were given in a near shout that Jake could understand from his location in the hall. He carefully looked around the corner of the wall and saw Ray standing beside a desk in the lobby where his phone, on speaker, was lying on the surface. His left arm was around his hostage; his right hand held what Jake could tell was a revolver. From his position, there was no clear shot to Ray. He retreated slightly down the hall and once again texted Pete.

> **Need time.**

After reading the new text, Pete cupped his hand over the phone to block sound and looked over at the white-haired woman with tears pouring down her face. "Mrs. Brantley, you've got to talk to your son. This is critical."

Visceral fear shown in her faded blue eyes as her body trembled hard enough to rattle the walker she gripped with white knuckles. "Please don't kill him." Her voice shook. "He's not a bad person. Please."

Using a gentle tone, Pete said, "That's the last thing we want to happen, Mrs. Brantley, but right now, I need your help to save him. Can you help me?"

She wiped her face and nodded.

Inside, Jake quickly retraced his steps, following the hall around the building to the other side of the lobby. He stopped about ten feet from the entry to listen. *Keep this bastard's attention, Pete. If he looks around, I'm screwed.* Jake eased forward, with his back against the wall. Holding his breath, he peeked around the corner. *Bastard's back toward me. Good.* He pulled back to prepare for a move. *He's got to cock the revolver. I've got an extra second.*

Ray Brantley continued to hold the woman. From his new position, Jake could see her hands were bound with duct tape. Although Ray held his gun, it was not pointed at the hostage.

With the agility of a cat, Jake swung around the corner. "Police. Drop the gun. Drop it now."

Instead of dropping the gun, Ray raised his arm, pointing his gun at the head of the hostage.

Jake fired.

The hostage screamed, and the captor emitted a piercing screech as his gun fell to the floor. He grabbed his right arm with his left and virtually jumped up and down in reaction to the pain.

Rushing forward and kicking the gun across the room, Jake shouted into the radio, "Assailant neutralized. Send medics." He grabbed Ray and slapped a handcuff on his uninjured wrist.

Jake's shot had sent excruciating pain throughout Ray's entire arm and hand, producing severe damage to nerves, bone, and blood vessels causing a loss of function and inability to grip the weapon.

A bevy of deputies swarmed the building, immediately taking control of the assailant and retrieving the revolver while Jake turned to the hostage who had fallen to her knees in hysteria and helped her to stand.

"It's over. You're safe."

Once to her feet, she threw her arms around him and clung for several seconds without uttering a word. Her body continued to tremble.

"It's all over. Let's go into the office where you can sit."

Paramedics came rushing in, followed by Rowland.

Outside, Ray's mother was screaming. "They killed him."

Pete grabbed her arm. "No, Mrs. Brantley. He's not dead. Maybe injured, but not dead. The medics will take care of him."

CHAPTER 34

"Glad that's over. I'll admit, you delivered as promised, Shepherd," Rowland said as he, along with Jake and Pete, walked into his office. It had taken over an hour for the chaos to settle enough for them to leave the scene. "I don't know much about you, Shepherd, or why you left the FBI, but with your ability, you should be wearing a badge."

"All you need to know about Shepherd is if attitude, arrogance, and aptitude were Olympic sports, he'd sweep the gold," Pete said. "But if patience and diplomacy were required, he wouldn't make the team. But I can say without hesitation, if I were in trouble, he is the first person I would call."

"There's no question but that both of you knew what you were doing. I'm looking forward to seeing the footage from your body cam, Shepherd—see exactly how you managed to pull it off."

"About that footage," Jake said. "I'd appreciate you doing what you can to keep it from the media."

"Why? It's got to make you look good. If it shows what I suspect, it would probably go viral."

"I'm not your viral kinda guy. I prefer to stay low key. Give it to your internal affairs or whoever has to give a look at an officer-involved shooting, if this could be classified as one, but just try to keep it away from the papers and TV."

"As you wish. But in any case, we owe you," Rowland said as Jake and Pete each took a seat in his office.

"Yeah," Jake said as he unfastened the badge from his waist and handed it over to Rowland. "Can we talk about that now?"

"Absolutely, but first, I've got to ask how the hell you knew a bullet to the elbow would cause him to drop the gun before he could fire?"

"Simple. Ever hit your elbow on something hard? The pain shoots down the arm into the palm of your hand. Baseball pitchers who suffer from the elbow injury called the 'Tommy John' lose grip strength in the hand."

"And you could make the shot hit exactly where it needed to."

"Most of the time. Now let's talk about why I made the appointment with you and what we need."

"Shoot."

"Two things. First, we came here to work on locating the biological parents of our client. We now suspect that the woman convicted of murdering Vic Lanza is likely her mother. Therefore, I'd like someone on our team to talk with her, probably my female associate."

Rowland listened intently.

"We understand that visitors are not allowed at Leath Correctional, where she is currently housed, unless they are on the inmate's guest list. Obviously, we aren't since she knows nothing of us. However, law enforcement can arrange for a visit. You just submit a request to the warden as I understand it."

"You want me to set that up?"

"Ten-four. Second, I want full access to the Marley Museum, meaning all public and private areas and access to all artifacts for purposes of review and photographing."

"Wow! Tall order. Why do you need all that?"

"If I knew, I might not need it. When Pete and I were there a few days ago, we noticed something we think might be relevant to Lanza's murder. Maybe not, but Marley was the murder scene. The item that caught our attention is in a locked case. I'll sign whatever is necessary guaranteeing that we will neither take nor damage anything. One of their people can supervise. I'll also need to take my K-9 at some point. Maybe not on the first look."

"You're going to take a dog to the museum? What's with you guys and dogs? Cooper insisted on bringing Brantley's dog to the scene." He turned toward Pete. "By the way, I never asked you why that was important with the Brantley negotiation."

"Ray needed to recognize that something or someone he cared about needed him alive. He had a worthless mindset at the moment. Sometimes it works. If Jake hadn't neutralized him, it might have been a key to getting him to surrender. Never underestimate what pets mean to people." He pointed to Jake. "I would be afraid of what Shepherd would do if anyone messed with his dog."

Jake chuckled. "*I'd* be afraid of what I would do."

Rowland grabbed a pen and card from a holder on his desk. "I'm making a note of that to share with our people. You guys had the best in training."

"Yep," Pete said. "We left the job but took the training with us."

"So, what's the answer? Can you help us?" Jake said, growing impatient.

"I'd be an SOB if I didn't. You risked your life to help us, the least we can do is repay the favor. He picked up the handset to the phone on his desk and pressed a button. "Lou, submit a request to the warden at Leath Correctional Facility for a visit to an inmate by the name of," he turned to Jake and waved a finger seeking the name.

"Marielle."

"Marielle Devereau. List Deputy Gloria Romero and . . ."

"Scarlett Kavanagh," Jake said.

"Scarlett Kavanagh as who will be conducting the interview for purposes of an active investigation. Thank you. Let me know when you get the clearance."

"Active investigation. A bit of a stretch there, but thank you," Jake said.

"I didn't say whose investigation. Who knows, you might uncover something we would be interested in. The museum is going to take a little more research, but I'm pretty sure we can make it happen. I have your contact info, don't I?"

Jake took out his pocket pad, containing his business cards. "Just in case you've misplaced it." He dashed off the name of their hotel and suite number on the pad, tore it off, and handed it to Rowland together with his card. "If you ever need me and can't get in touch, you can reach my assistant at that number, and she always knows how to find me."

***

As Jake and Pete pulled out of the parking lot of the Sheriff's Office, Jake said, "Harvard's been burning up my phone. Sent her a text telling her we were helping out with a little matter for Rowland, but I think I've pushed the train over the abyss."

"Well, we did leave her with the idea we were headed to a simple appointment at eleven. It's now after five—six hours and counting. I take it, you didn't let her know where we were."

Jake scowled. "Why would I worry her?"

"I don't know. You walking into an active crime scene with an armed, crazy guy. Why would you let your partner know you were doing that?"

"She's my employee, not my partner."

"Oh, I think she's a lot more than your employee, but then I'll shut up."

"Good idea."

***

When they entered the hotel suite, Scarlett was sitting in the living room with her computer in her lap. The TV was on. "My gosh, Jake. Where have you guys been?"

Pete cut his eyes toward Jake as if expecting him to answer.

"Just working out the details of what Rowland can do for us," Jake said. "Ready to go find din—"

The TV caught his eye. A news show displayed an image of the daycare scene with a line of text scrolling across the bottom.

Scarlett followed his gaze as a voice-over said, "Hostages held at a daycare facility just outside city limits today by an armed assailant were dramatically rescued unharmed by the acts of two former FBI agents. One, a former FBI negotiator, engaged the assailant in verbal exchange while the other, a former FBI sniper, disarmed the man. The assailant is in custody at a local hospital—"

Jake grabbed the remote off the table next to Scarlett and clicked it off.

She stared at him with a look of shock on her face. "Is that where you were—working out details?"

Pete stifled a grin as Jake squinted one eye. "Near there."

"Oh, don't, Shepherd. Don't even try to cover it up. How many former FBI snipers and negotiators would be in Charleston today? It was *you*."

"Close up the computer, and let's go out. I'm starved, aren't you, Pete?"

"I'm not going anywhere," Scarlett said, "until you tell me what that was all about."

Jake looked toward Pete, who shrugged. "Better get on with it, Shepherd. She's not going to let it drop."

"Bottom line. We got you an appointment to visit Marielle Devereau in the prison. Rowland put in a request—"

"Jake, how were you involved in that situation at the daycare we just saw on the news?"

"Don't make a big deal of that, Harvard. Pete and I were in Rowland's office when the call came in. He needed a sniper. Pete volunteered me, and the rest is history. Now, you're making the trip with a female deputy tomorrow. I think her name is Romero."

With her face pinched in a frown, Scarlett ignored his comment about the prison visit. "You shot the guy holding hostages?"

"I didn't kill him. . . . He's going to be fine. I just nicked his elbow."

"Okay. Play your usual coy game. I'll get the whole story later—and *you* know it. It'll be on the Internet." With a flourish, she closed her computer. Placing the laptop on the table, she stood. "I'll go freshen up before going to dinner, but I'm choosing where we go."

"Employee? Right," Pete said with a smirk.

***

Thirty minutes later, the trio, along with Kai, were settled at a side-walk table of an Italian restaurant. Once the waitress had their orders, Scarlett tucked her napkin across her lap and said, "You haven't asked if anything special happened with me today."

"Gee, Harvard, I haven't. You're right. Fill us in on your day."

"Thank you. I had a long conversation with Anna." She turned toward Pete. "Anna is our client. We talked today, and I told her *almost* everything we've learned. I didn't tell her that the woman we suspect to be her mother is in prison—just that we are sure we know who her father was but to confirm it, we're waiting on the DNA results from the woman we believe is his sister. As for her mother, we are working on it and expect to either confirm the candidate soon, or we have to start from scratch."

"Sounds reasonable," Jake said.

"Yeah. But here's the problem. She's coming to Charleston—this weekend."

Jake didn't bother to hide his displeasure. "Did you try to talk her out of it?"

"Of course, I did. But she insisted that it would give her a chance to see her aunt, uncle, and cousin. What was I going to say to that?"

He leaned back in his chair. "Don't tell me—"

"Yep. Dr. NFL is coming."

"Damn!" Jake said and sat his water glass down on the table so hard the contents splashed out.

Pete looked at Jake, shook his head, and said, "You guys have lost me. Who is Dr. NFL?"

"Our client's fiancé. He's a former NFL player with an attitude."

"An attitude bigger than Shepherd's?"

"About equal."

"He's an effing jerk," Jake said, "and that is jerk spelled with a capital A."

"This should be fun."

Jake glared at him.

"Pete, maybe you can mediate between the two alphas," Scarlett said. "The good thing is they are not coming until Saturday. Since I'm going to the prison tomorrow, maybe I'll have something solid to tell Anna. Crossing my fingers that my visit with Marielle goes well."

CHAPTER 35

As Scarlett drove toward the visitor parking lot of the Leath Correctional Institution, on Tuesday, the fencing topped with coiled, razor barbed wire reminded her of the prisons she and Jake visited when searching for Faith Johnson. *They all look alike.*

Gloria Romero, a young deputy from the Charleston County Sheriff's Office, sat in the passenger seat, wearing the uniform of her agency and her sidearm.

"Ever been to a prison before?" Romero asked.

"I have. Not the most pleasant of places to visit."

"It's not something I've done all that many times myself. Maybe if more potential offenders paid a visit, they might think twice before breaking the law."

"For sure."

***

Upon entry, Romero checked her weapon, and both left a driver's license with an officer behind a window. Once through registration and security, they were provided identification badges. A corrections officer then led the pair to a small attorney interview room and said, "I'll be right outside. Just signal when you're ready to leave or if you need anything."

Scarlett took a seat at the small table, while Romero moved a chair near the door. "I'll stay out of your way. My sitting at the table might intimidate your subject."

"Why are these rooms always so dimly lit?" Scarlett said. "Even in Atlanta, the interview rooms were dreary."

"You work a lot of cases that take you to prisons?"

Scarlett turned to face Romero. "Not a lot, but Jake and I visited a couple in Florida on a case. I didn't go to prisons as a family law attorney. But if a client got into trouble on a misdemeanor, I would cover it, which meant I had to do interviews in the pretrial detention facility."

"So, you're a lawyer? I didn't know that. I was told you're a private investigator."

"I don't practice law any longer. In Atlanta, I did family law for nearly ten years before joining Jake in the P.I. firm. I kept my Georgia license and took the bar exam in Virginia to get a license there as well."

"Why would you work as a P.I. if you're a lawyer?"

"It's a long story. The simple answer is I was tired of domestic dysfunction—the bickering over minutia. Investigative work was always my favorite part of the job." Scarlett brushed a stray strand of hair away from her eye. "What made you decide to join law enforcement?"

"My dad and brother are cops in Columbia. I always wanted to be one but didn't want to work in the same agency, so here I am. My goal was to join the FBI, but the clock is ticking."

"Well, talk to Jake and Pete. They might can give you some help with that."

Romeo perked up. "No way. How?"

"They're both former FBI. Pete is retired, and Jake left for personal reasons. Jake spent time on the Hostage Rescue Team."

"Dang. What would cause Jake to leave?"

"It's complicated, but the simple answer is his daughter's stepfather was his supervisor at the Bureau."

Twirling a finger as though making an analysis, Romeo muttered under her breath, "Daughter's stepfather, former supervisor." Looking toward Scarlett, she said, "Oh. I get it."

Scarlett smiled. "We really appreciate your helping us make this visit possible."

"Not a problem. My boss didn't tell me exactly what the visit is about, but he said you would be doing the interview. I guess I'm window dressing."

Scarlett started to speak but a door opened and a petite woman, wearing a blue, two-piece prison uniform entered. Even without makeup, it was obvious she had been a pretty woman. Her dark hair was streaked with gray and slicked back in a neat ponytail.

"Ms. Devereau?" Scarlett said, standing to greet her. "Did I pronounce that correctly?"

"*Oui.* Yes. You're a detective?"

"Private detective. I'm Scarlett Kavanagh." She gestured to her side. "This is Deputy Romero from the Charleston County Sheriff's Office."

Devereau frowned. "I don't understand. Why are you here? What do you want?"

"As I said, I'm a private investigator. Deputy Romero's supervisor was kind enough to arrange this visit. It's not easy gaining access."

Devereau shook her head. "But why? I don't know you."

"I know you don't." Scarlett motioned for her to take a seat. "I'm here, hoping to find answers to some questions that a client of mine has."

With an expression of confusion on her face, Devereau said, "How could I have answers? I have been here for over thirty years. Is your client someone who knows me from here or the other prison?"

"Neither. Who I represent is someone from your past but not a former inmate."

Marielle stared at Scarlett for a minute. "I don't understand. Someone from America or France?"

"Someone from America."

"What questions can you have for me?"

"Ms. Devereau, I know you are here because you entered into a plea agreement concerning the death of Vic Lanza."

The nervous woman looked away. Almost under her breath, she said, "I can't talk about that."

After waiting for Devereau to again face her way, Scarlett said, "My partner and I reviewed the file on your case, and we feel it had issues. In fact, my partner thinks the evidence was insufficient to even bring charges against you, but if they did, a jury would likely have acquitted you."

With her eyebrows pinched together in a frown, Devereau again stared at Scarlett, not speaking.

"Marielle, is it okay if I call you Marielle? And please call me Scarlett."

She nodded.

"We think you may not have committed the act you're in this facility for."

"My lawyer said I didn't have an alibi. He said, no one would believe me because there was a witness who heard me arguing with Vic. It doesn't matter. It's too late to talk about now."

"Not necessarily. Look me in the eye."

Marielle did as Scarlett asked.

"Did you have anything to do with Vic Lanza's death?"

Upon the word death, Marielle froze.

"You didn't. Right?"

"Why are you coming here saying that? I've accepted that this is my life. I don't have any money for a lawyer. I don't have a way to support myself if they released me. And I don't want to hope for something and be disappointed. I've accepted this. I have a life here."

Scarlett stared at her for nearly a minute before speaking. "I understand. Please hear me out. I have another question, and it may be an even harder one for you to deal with."

Again, Devereau shook her head but did not comment.

"Marielle, you gave birth to a baby after you were convicted, didn't you?"

Devereau's pupils enlarged and her body tensed. She stood up and turned as if she intended to leave the room. But stopped and turned back around. "Why do you ask me a question like that?"

"I'm asking you that question because I think your daughter is my client."

Marielle's pupils expanded and she stood silent for a minute. "No. No. I don't have a daughter. You should leave."

Scarlett raised her hand in a low halt position. "Please, don't ask me to go. The woman I believe is your daughter desperately wants to know who her mother is. She is paying our firm a lot of money to discover who her parents really are. I believe you are her mother, and Vic Lanza was her father."

Devereau continued shaking her head and once again turned as if to leave.

"Marielle, please don't go. Please hear me out. Anna is a lovely woman. She wants to know who you are and to meet you. She only received the shock of learning a few weeks ago that the people who raised her were not her biological parents."

"They must have been. I have no child."

Scarlett's eyes followed her every move. *Her words say one thing. Her eyes say the opposite.* "I believe you do. Anna is your child."

Devereau stayed by the door but made no attempt to leave. "I don't have a child. Prisoners cannot have children."

"They can give birth. Did you hold her?"

"No."

Although she continued to deny Scarlett's statements, there appeared to be a softening in her attitude with a shred of curiosity. Suddenly, she returned to the table.

"I don't have a child, but if I had a child, what is she like?"

Scarlett took a deep breath. "First of all, she's beautiful. I can see traces of her in your face. But even more, she is very accomplished. She's a doctor, Marielle. So, she must be very smart."

In the background, Romero's expression projected approval as Devereau weakened her defense.

"A doctor? What kind of doctor?"

"She is a doctor, a pediatrician, in a hospital in Washington, D.C. She's engaged to another doctor, but she doesn't want to get married until she knows who she really is."

Devereau's eyes became glassy as tears emerged and threatened to stream down her face. She quickly wiped them away.

"Would you like to see a photo of Anna?"

"Her name is Anna?"

"Anna-Claire."

Again, the woman stood, walked toward the exit, and stopped. Although her back was to Scarlett and the deputy, they could see her put a hand to her face and suspected she again wiped away tears.

Scarlett took out her portfolio and pulled out a photo. "Marielle, Anna would love to see you, talk to you. Look. Look at this." She held the image up.

Devereau stood frozen for over a minute. No one moved, and the room remained eerily quiet. As she placed a hand on the door, Scarlett shivered with disappointment. *She's going to leave. I've missed my one chance.*

Suddenly, she turned, hesitating for several seconds before moving back to the table.

Without a word, Scarlett slid the photo across the table for the woman to see. While she didn't attempt to touch it, Devereau's eyes locked on the image, and she whispered, "Lara."

She named her Lara. She wants to acknowledge Anna.

Devereau looked up. "No. Never. If I had a daughter, do you think I would want her to come to this place? Want her to see a mother who is a prisoner? I could ruin her life. The doctor would not want to marry the daughter of a murderer. Don't tell her who I am. Don't let her know she is the child of a killer."

"Killer or innocent prisoner? You said you didn't kill him."

"I didn't. But everyone believes that I did. It doesn't keep me from being called a murderer—*tueuse.*"

"I read that you didn't speak English. You seem to speak it well now."

"How could I not? I've been in jail or prison for thirty-four years, ten months, and nine days."

"Of course." Scarlett turned toward Romero. "Do you have children?"

She nodded. "Two boys."

"Wouldn't you want to know your child?"

"Of course."

"Marielle, my partner is one of the best detectives in the country. If he believes you're innocent, he'll prove it. Would you talk to him if I brought him here?"

"Why should he believe me? It's too late."

"Because he already suspects you were wrongfully convicted—just from reading the record. And Jake has an incredible ability to read people. It's never too late. Your attorney back when it happened was Paul Jorgensen, right?"

She looked at Scarlett with surprise. "You know Monsieur Jorgensen? He sent you?"

"I've met him, but no, he did not tell me to come here. In fact, we believe he would like to stop us from pursuing you. Anna was raised by the sister of Jorgensen's wife and her husband. Did he have anything to do with arranging the placement of your baby? She was born December 9th of 1990, right?"

Devereau's face contorted into a frown, and she took a deep breath. "I don't have a child. I did not have a child on December 9th."

Scarlett could tell that the date of Anna's alleged birth had struck a dissonant chord. *Her baby wasn't born on December 9th.*

"Monsieur Jorgensen is a nice man. He tried to help me. If someone had a baby they could not keep, he would have taken care of finding the baby a good home."

Scarlett studied the woman for several seconds. "Why did you accept the plea agreement if you were innocent?"

"I had to. Mr. Jorgensen told me that he would not be able to convince the jury that I was innocent, and I could get a death sentence. I was terrified."

"I thought it might be something like that."

"He told me I might be eligible for parole, but I never apply. What would I do if they let me out? I have no job. I have no way of taking care of myself. I couldn't go back to France. My sister is all that is left, and I couldn't be a burden to her. I tried to learn to work a computer, but I'm not good at it. I'm used to being here."

"There could be a much better life for you, Marielle. Talk to Jake. Don't be shy. He is a bit abrasive, but he can help you."

"I think you should listen to her, Ms. Devereau. It sounds like you have something very important waiting for you on the outside," Romero said, to Scarlett's pleasant surprise.

Turning to face the deputy, Scarlett smiled her appreciation.

"But Anna, you said her name is Anna, she would be ashamed of me. She couldn't introduce me to her husband to be—his family."

"Why don't you give her a chance to make that decision. Let me arrange for you to meet, but first, meet with Jake. Then meet with Anna. Give her a chance. Don't shut her out. She is a determined young woman—almost on fire with her desire to know you. There could be grandchildren in your future."

The room went silent. Scarlett glanced back and forth between Devereau and the deputy.

"I will think about it. I have to go now, or I will miss my lunch."

"Will you at least see Jake? Whether you ever meet Anna, wouldn't you like a chance to be cleared? You can't want to die in this place."

Again, the room was silent. Devereau stood again. "What would I do if I were released? I have no money, no way to support myself, but I will see your Jake. What is the rest of his name?"

"Shepherd. Jake Shepherd." Scarlett took out her card and her small notepad. After writing Jake's name on the pad, along with the name of their hotel, she tore off the sheet and handed it with her card to Marielle. "Jake and I are both attorneys as well as private investigators. Would you be willing to accept a visit with us to discuss legal matters? It would make access a lot easier."

As she looked over Scarlett's card, she said, "I haven't had any visitors in over thirty-four years. It would be nice to have my name called for a visitor, even if just for legal reasons."

Although Marielle's tone lacked despair, her words tugged at Scarlett's heart. *Over thirty-four years with no visitors!*

CHAPTER 36

"Why didn't you call to let me know so one of us could have met you when you dropped the deputy off?" Jake said as Scarlett entered the suite. He was on a sofa in the living room, watching a movie on TV with Kai on the floor next to his stocking feet. His boots stood watch nearby.

"Because I didn't need you. I had a police escort," Scarlett said as she put her purse on a chair and slipped off her shoes. "Deputy Romero followed me back to the door of the hotel in her marked car."

"Good to know. Well, how did your interview go?"

"It started out shaky, but overall, I would say it went well. I like Marielle. She has agreed to talk to you, but she won't admit she has a daughter."

"Maybe she doesn't."

"Oh, yes she does."

He gave her a puzzled look.

"Anna looks a lot like her, Jake. And you should have seen her face when I showed her a photo of Anna."

"What's the plan for me to meet her? Are we going to need a deputy?"

"Actually, we're not. She is putting us on her visitor list, but if we identify ourselves as attorneys, we would not be restricted to standard visitation times."

He laughed. "Way to go, Harvard. You're thinking like a P.I. now. A bit devious but there's a bit of truth in it."

"You do have a bar card with you, don't you?"

"I do. But if she won't admit she has a child, how are you going to get a DNA sample from her?"

"I'm working on it. You take care of the exoneration angle. I'll work on the motherhood angle. But there's one thing you need to know. That woman never killed anyone."

"You're sure about that?" he said, laying the TV remote on a table.

"Positive. Jake, she is fragile and passive. Absolutely nothing about her suggests she could have the ability to take a gun and kill someone. She's been in prison over thirty-four years for something she didn't do—virtually lost her adult life. But she is resistant to the idea of being released. She feels there is no life for her outside the prison. She's never applied for parole. My god, Jake, I understand. She was so young, from another country, alone here. She has no one in the United States to help her reenter society if she is released. No job. You think she could come out and be hired to work on a movie or TV set? Not hardly. She's right. She wouldn't be able to support herself."

He leaned back on the sofa and stretched his arms in the air. "I wouldn't worry too much about that. Do you know how much she could collect from the state for wrongful incarceration? There would be a line of personal injury attorneys waiting at the prison gate. Probably get a book deal. Lanza was big. Money will not be a problem. But have you thought about the fact that she might be depor—"

A knock interrupted Jake. Kai sprang to his feet on full alert.

Scarlett went to the door. After checking the viewfinder, she said, "It's Pete," and let him in.

As he stepped inside the suite, Pete said, "Hey, pretty lady. How was your trip to the prison?"

"On a scale of one to ten, I'd give it an eight. A little rough at first, but I think I made progress. I liked the woman, and I'm positive she is Anna's birth mom. But Jake just brought up another issue. You were about to say she might be deported if released, right?"

"Yep. She was likely here on a student visa or maybe work visa, but she wasn't here long enough to become a citizen. Green card? Maybe but I doubt it. Commission of a felony without citizenship. That could make her a candidate for deportation unless she is completely exonerated. She might know that and not want to go back, so, staying in prison keeps her here."

"She did say she has a sister in France. Maybe she would be happy to go back. But I doubt it. When she admits she's Anna's mother, she will want to stay here."

"Anything specific about her that convinced you she's the mother?" Pete asked.

"The physical similarities are obvious. Anna has the same eyes and the same hair, even though Marielle's is streaked with gray." She looked toward Jake. "I'm going to leave you guys while I change into comfortable clothes and check my email." She picked up her shoes, grabbed her purse, and left the room.

Once in her room, Scarlett quickly changed to jeans and athletic shoes and sat down with her laptop to scan her inbox. After deleting dozens of emails without opening, she reached one from Liz. A quick scan of the contents brought her to her feet and sent her back to the living room.

"It's confirmed," Scarlett said in an excited tone, holding her laptop. Liz got the DNA reports back from samples of Joel Carden, Robin Sawyer, and Veronica Salvadore." Both men directed their full attention to her, as Jake pressed mute on the TV remote. "She shares two thousand one hundred ten centimorgans with Veronica which unequivocally indicates a full aunt. Anna does not share any centimorgans with Joel Carden or Robin Sawyer—no relation."

A smile crept across Jake's face. "You did it, Harvard. Congratulations."

"Catch me up. Who are Veronica, Joel, and Robin?" Pete said.

"Veronica Salvadore is the late Vic Lanza's sister. Joel and Robin are blood relatives of Nora and Larry Carden. If Anna were the biological child of the Cardens, she would have shared centimorgans with Joel and Robin. That takes the idea of Nora Carden having an affair off the table." Scarlett was almost giddy as she continued. "I knew it; I knew it; I knew it. But this confirmation makes it incontestable."

"It also emphasizes the question of where is the baby born to the adoptive mother, since we know it couldn't have been a baby swap in the hospital," Jake said.

"It looks like you have opened the quintessential Pandora's box," Pete said.

"All you need to tie a bow around the biological parents is a DNA confirmation Marielle Devereau is her mother," Jake said.

"I don't have it yet, but I will. I know it. That leaves us with only two questions unanswered. Who killed Vic Lanza? And what happened to the baby Nora Carden gave birth to?" Scarlett said.

"Actually three, Harvard." Jake held up three fingers. "Third one, how did the Lanza baby end up with the Cardens? Although, I'm smelling a rotten aroma of Jorgensen being part of that."

"Are you planning to call the client and give her the results?" Pete said.

Scarlett paused for a few seconds, contemplating her reply. "No. I want all the info. Now, I'm going to spend time putting together all I can on Vic Lanza and give her the whole package in person when she arrives on Saturday."

"Maybe wait until after she visits with her adopted relatives," Jake said. "I'm not so sure I want Jorgensen clued in on what we've found, and I don't trust a client's discretion. What she doesn't know, she can't let slip."

"He's got a point, Scarlett."

She looked from one to the other. "You guys are right. She could slip. This is not easy."

Jake smiled. "Want to go back to family law?"

"Very funny. But I would like to go out for dinner. Let's go back to that Italian restaurant. The food was great, and we can take Kai."

"That'll work. And we can address the next step."

CHAPTER 37

B y the time the group reached the restaurant, a breeze provided relief from the midsummer heat, creating an ideal condition for outside dining. As soon as the server left their table with dinner orders, Jake opened his portfolio and said, "Okay, let's assess what we've got. Pete, you were going to comb through the evidentiary records provided by the Charleston County Sheriff to see if there was any mention of Lanza's address book we saw at the museum. Did you find anything?"

"Nada. If they reviewed it, there's no indication in the file. How far do you want to go with this investigation, considering the inmate isn't interested in release, and the client is in the dark? The billables have got to be stacking up."

"We're here to find out if this woman is the client's mother. Until we prove she is or she isn't, we're here. Might as well use our time productively."

"Right. Just admit it. You love a challenge, Shepherd. But I'll ride the wave with you."

"Well, I don't like a miscarriage of justice. An innocent person convicted means a guilty person got away with it. What do you hear from D.C.? Everything okay without you?"

"Smooth as the coat of a greyhound. Sonny's got it under control. He's forwarding the office calls to Liz when he's on the street. The whole team is working a big party tonight for a visiting ambassador."

"You can count on Sonny."

"Jake, have you gotten permission to access the museum items you want to examine?" Scarlett asked.

"Not yet. Rowland said it might take a little time. But I think I want to get a copy of any names in that address book before we visit the prison." He jotted a note on the pad in his portfolio. "If I don't hear from Rowland by tomorrow, I'll give him a little nudge—at least get the clearance to photograph the interior of that book." As he spoke, the server brought a tray of appetizers, forcing Jake to close the portfolio and place it on the seat of the empty chair at their table.

As both men filled their small plates with bruschetta, meatballs, and stuffed zucchini blossoms, Scarlett said, "I need you guys to give me an opinion."

"Fire away, Harvard."

"I told Robin Sawyer I would let her know the results of her DNA test. She certainly has a right to know. But with the situation with her father, I'm not sure it's a good idea, especially with the Myrtle episode and with Anna planning to visit with Robin and Jorgensen. How is that going to work?"

Pete looked toward Jake, apparently expecting a reaction.

Jake hesitated for several seconds before saying. "Let me think about it, but my knee jerk response is wait."

"This lawyer, Jorgensen, is Robin's father, right?" Pete said.

Scarlett nodded.

"Then my vote is wait."

"Pete's right. Let Anna have her visit with the family. She might learn something. I know you want to keep your word but neither Anna nor Robin should know everything, yet. You're the super conscientious, compassionate one in the office, but we have too many unanswered questions that could blow up if Jorgensen learns the substitution of babies has been documented—and we know the identity of one of Anna's parents."

Jake's phone pinged notification of a text. After reading it, he said, "Rowland came through with access to everything on display at the museum, but any private areas may require a warrant. When we arrive, we're to ask for a Ms. McClain. He says she is the museum director." He paused to take a drink of water and to pick up an appetizer. "One of you needs to stay at the hotel with Kai."

At the sound of his name, Kai lifted his head from his paws where his chin had rested and looked toward Jake as if waiting for instructions.

"It's okay, boy. You can relax." Jake reached down and scratched the shepherd on the head with his left hand as he popped the tidbit in his mouth and then swung his right index in an arc going from Scarlett to Pete while swallowing, he said, "I'll leave it up to you as to who goes with me tomorrow morning."

"Take Pete," Scarlett said. "I'll need to go with you to the prison, and it isn't fair to leave Pete with all the dog sitting."

***

Jake and Pete arrived at the museum at opening time again and after presenting ID and requesting to see Ms. McClain, they waited while a clueless docent went to fetch her. It took nearly five minutes for the director to appear.

"Mr. Shepherd, I'm Rose McClain." She extended her hand to shake with his.

"It's nice to meet you, and I appreciate the courtesy you're showing us."

"I understand you want access to some of our exhibits in order to take photos. Is that correct?"

Jake nodded. "Absolutely. And this is my partner, retired FBI Special Agent Peter Cooper."

As the gray-haired woman shook Pete's hand, Jake thought he detected a shred of respect in her demeanor.

"You have my word. We'll be extremely careful not to damage what we photograph in any manner. In fact, we'll wear gloves."

"I appreciate that," she said. "But, and I may be so bold as to ask, but why are you wanting to take photos of exhibits in this museum?"

"Fair question," Jake said. "At this point, I'm only at liberty to say that we are working a case that has connections to this area and noticed an exhibit that could offer information. Please feel free to accompany and observe us. I completely respect your concern for the integrity of irreplaceable items."

"I was planning to send one of my docents, but I think I would like to accompany you."

"Please, do what you need."

She reached into a pocket on the smock she wore and removed a ring of keys. "Is the item you're interested in on our top floor in the Lanza room?"

"It is."

"Let's take the elevator. You can point it out to me. Then we'll take it to our breakroom for you to photograph without interest or interference by other visitors."

When the trio reached the Lanza room, Jake led the way to the display cabinet containing the book he wanted. As she unlocked the glass door, McClain asked, "Which item is it that you want? One of the scripts? The photo book?"

Jake pointed to the brown leather book with only Lanza's initials on the cover. "That one. We suspect it is an address book but could be a day planner or a journal."

She reached in and removed the item, gingerly opening it. "It's a planner and has a section for addresses. If you want the scripts, I'd prefer we take one at a time, so as to not deprive our current visitors of the entire contents of this case."

"Right now, I'm not interested in the scripts but appreciate the offer. As we learn more, I might come back, if that is acceptable."

Once they returned to the first floor, McClain led them to the staff breakroom and cleared a table for Jake and Pete to work on. Both slid latex gloves, used at a crime scene, onto their hands. As Pete turned the pages, Jake snapped photos with his phone. McClain watched with interest. It took them approximately twenty minutes to complete the process.

As Jake reviewed the photos, Pete closed the planner.

"I think we're good to go," Jake said, closing his phone. "Thank you for your time and trouble."

As they started to leave, McClain said, "It just occurred to me that we have a box of items you might want to look at. We didn't have enough display area to showcase everything that has been preserved. Would you like to see it?"

Hell, yes, Jake thought but smiled and said, "I would. Thank you."

"Wait here. I'll have someone bring it up from storage. And please help yourselves to a cup of coffee while I'm gone." She pointed out a Keurig coffee maker on the counter.

After the door closed behind McClain, Jake looked at Pete who was grinning. "Would I like to look at it? You damn right I would like to look at it," he said, shaking his head with a scowl on his face.

While they waited, Jake took out his phone and began scrolling through the images of Lanza's Day Planner while Pete helped himself to a cup of coffee.

"This is going to be fun," Jake said, sarcastically, after checking three of the pages. "Very few of the entries have a surname."

"Send them to Liz," Pete said. "She's a genius with computer research. She'll probably be able to come up with names of his known associates with matching first names. Might not find them all but as high profile as he was, I'll bet most will turn up."

It took McClain over twenty minutes to return, accompanied by a bearded man carrying two banker's boxes. Jake's patience was about to expire when she arrived, accompanied by the man in coveralls.

"Just put them on the table, George," McClain said and turned toward Jake and Pete. "I'm sorry it took so long. George had to move some furniture in order to reach the shelves in our storage room." As she spoke, the man left without saying a word. "George is our grounds keeper and handyman."

Pete and Jake both stood and watched as McClain took a quick look inside each box.

CHAPTER 38

"I have a telephone conference scheduled. I'm going to leave you with these items. I know you'll respect the integrity of the items," McClain said. "If you finish before I return, please let one of the staff know you're leaving so that the boxes can be returned to storage."

"We will," Jake said. "And, again, we appreciate your cooperation."

As she left, Jake addressed the first box, which held paper documents. Some were in manila folders; some were loose. He thumbed through the folders first. The files were labeled and probably were once stored in a cabinet. After reading the labels on each, he gathered them up, took them out of the box, and passed them across the table to Pete. "Those look like financial records and a few official documents like contracts. You look through them and snap a photo of any that might be relevant while I sort through the rest of this stuff."

Pete pulled the stack closer and began visually scanning them.

One by one, Jake removed items remaining in the box. There were scripts from several feature films, theater programs from plays Lanza did in the early years of his career, and photos of actors and actresses. At the very bottom of the box were several hand-written letters.

"Ah ha," Jake said, causing Pete to stop reading and look up.

"Ah ha what?"

"Personal letters. You know, the way people communicated before email and texts."

"That could be of interest."

"For sure. One is torn in half but still sealed. He must have recognized the handwriting and wasn't interested in reading it."

"I'd say a love affair past its expiration date," Pete said.

"I'd bet money on it." Jake eased the pieces of the letter out of the envelope, matched the torn sections, and read the missive before taking photos. "Whoa."

"What?"

"Definitely an ex-lover, and she's pissed. Calls him names usually found scratched on the walls of a men's room at a gas station—even threatens to kill him. Apparently, he had something she wanted."

"Case solved. Classic motive one-o-one. Got a name?"

"Nope and no return address."

"You sure it's from a female?"

"Completely sure. She describes some things in detail that will send you to a cold shower."

"Don't tell me. My old body couldn't handle it. But, it could be from your client's mother."

Jake shook his head. "No way. This is written in grammatically correct English. From all the information we have, Marielle could barely speak the language back then."

"Sometimes, a person can write better than speak a foreign language."

"Not this good, especially with some all-American expletives. Words not found in *Webster's French-English Dictionary*." He set the letter to one side.

"Any other letters that might be from the same person?"

"No. I don't think so. There's a couple from New York that look to be from family. The postmark on this hot one is L.A. and dated the month he was killed, which is likely why he still had it. If the relationship was history as everything suggests, this one might have been retrieved from a wastepaper container where he tossed it." As Jake started to return the miscellaneous papers to the box, he stopped. "Wait." Taking his phone from his shirt pocket, he pulled up the photos.

"What are you doing?"

"I am remembering that three entries in Lanza's address book were crossed out." He scrolled through the photos taken earlier. "Yep. There are three. Damn. One of these has got to be the ex who wrote that letter." He turned the phone toward Pete and thrust it forward.

Squinting to see, Pete said, "I think you nailed it, but you still don't have a name. It's almost like the guy wrote his contacts in code."

"That it does, but it's a start. We have to comb through all the publicity pieces and find who his women were." Looking back at his phone, he pulled up favorites and hit a listing. "Liz, do you have access to a directory of phone numbers from the '80s and '90s?" He listened for a few seconds. "I thought you would. We'll be sending you some to look up." Pete watched as Jake stuck the phone back in his pocket. "And Marielle might know who Lanza had been involved with close to when he was killed," Jake said as he put everything back in the box but the damaged letter. "I'm going to bag this."

"You're not planning to take it, are you?"

"No." Jake frowned. "But I want to increase protection of it and make it easy to find. I've got plastic bags in the car."

"Well, you came prepared—gloves, bags."

"It's a crime scene." Pushing the box out of the way, he pulled the second one over and began sorting through it as Pete resumed review of the folders.

"Interesting," Jake said.

"Whatcha got now?"

"An assortment of stuff." Jake lifted several items out of the box and shuffled some around. "Got a few framed photos that are probably his family. A Roman Catholic missal in Latin." He fanned the pages. "So, it's probably pretty old." He pulled two volumes from the box. "School yearbooks from a Catholic high school—and a baseball cap."

"Sounds like nothing relevant."

Jake stared at the baseball cap for a minute. "Hold that thought."

"What are you thinking?" Pete stopped what he was doing with the files and gazed across the table at Jake.

"I've not seen a photo of Lanza in a baseball cap." Jake gently turned the cap around and upside down, examining it.

"Just because you haven't seen a photo doesn't mean he didn't have one."

"He was a New Yorker. If he had a cap, I'm betting it would have been a dark blue Yankees cap, not a red Atlanta Braves."

"Wasn't his show filmed in Atlanta? He might have picked it up as a souvenir or was gifted it."

"This cap has been worn. There's a sweat stain. And how did it come to survive the fire? His clothing was destroyed."

"I see that brain of yours smoking. What's your theory?"

"Just a hunch. I would like to know where this was found."

"You're thinking evidence."

"I'm thinking evidence. I want to know where all these things were in the house that saved them from the fire. They must have been on the first floor. Otherwise, there should at least be traces of smoke damage.

I'm thinking Lanza had an office on this floor. If the door was closed, the contents were probably spared. But I don't see a reason for this cap to have been in an office. Of course, it could have been. But maybe it was found outside. Maybe someone dropped it."

"Maybe his killer?"

"Maybe. Sweat equals DNA."

"It's been thirty-five years, Jake."

"I know. It's a long shot but not impossible. Stored in this building in a box should have helped retain the integrity of the DNA. Worth a try. I think I have a bag large enough to hold it. We need to comb through the crime-scene photos. It might show up."

"Might be Marielle's cap. Women do wear them."

"True. Or the author of that letter. I'll feel Marielle out when I interview her. For now, I'll just bag it. We need to get Ms. McClain back here to give as much credibility to the chain of custody as possible. She knows we did not come in with a cap, and she opened the box, so she would have seen it. If it turns out to be of any use, we have to protect the chain."

"Why don't you contact Rowland? Have him send someone over here to take the letter and the cap into custody. That'll protect the chain. He owes you big time, and if someone got away with murder, it's his jurisdiction. You can agree to pay for the lab work, with the client's okay. Don't you have his cell number?"

"I do. Good idea. But I'm going to photograph it from all angles, in the box with this room included, and do a photo that includes the museum director, just to have a record in case Rowland isn't around, and we end up with an uncooperative SOB in the sheriff's office or the prosecutor."

"Good thinking. But, say you get a profile, unless the unsub has a record, how will you get a match? The guy or gal might even be dead."

"The same way Scarlett has been getting matches for the parent search. Genetic genealogy."

"Aren't you straying a bit far from the purpose of your investigation?"

"Probably, but my gut tells me it'll all tie together."

"Right. I think there's a little bit of Shepherd the hell-bent cowboy who can't stand an unresolved case at work."

Jake grinned. "Maybe. But I'm not done here. I definitely want to come back with Kai—after I meet with Marielle Devereau."

CHAPTER 39

"We've got our work cut out for us, Harvard." Jake dropped his portfolio on the dinette table in the suite as he and Pete arrived from the trip to the museum. Kai sprang forward to greet them and was rewarded with a pat on his shoulder by Jake. "We've got names to track, crime scene photos to scour, answers to find, and miles to go before we rest as someone once said. But first, I'm starved—and craving barbeque."

Scarlett looked up from the sofa where she sat with her computer resting on her lap. "It's 'miles to go before *I sleep*'—Robert Frost. Surprised you know it. And of course, you want barbeque, but I'll have to change."

"No need. We can do that DoorDash, Uber Eats thing and have it brought here. You've got your computer on. Pull up a menu, we'll place our order and get to work." He turned around toward Pete. "Know what you want?"

"Put me down for a pulled pork sandwich and fries. While you do that, I'll take Kai out so you can arrange the files you want to work on this afternoon."

At hearing his name, Kai switched his presence to Pete.

Without looking up from the screen where she was scrolling through a menu, Scarlett said, "What did you guys find at the museum?"

"More than I expected," Jake said. "I photographed the pages of Lanza's address book and calendar for that year, which I'm going to take downstairs to the hotel business center and make prints. Plus, we found what may be a couple of clues."

"What kind?" She said, looking up with interest.

"A handwritten letter with an articulated threat and a baseball cap that I believe does not fit the Lanza persona nor the scene."

"Wow. It *was* a productive trip. What about going back to the prison? When are we going to do that?"

"I'm holding off until we've analyzed the data from the book for potential names of Lanza's intimate circle. Most of his entries give partial names, initials, or symbols. Rarely did he include a full name. I believe our suspect is in that book. Only ten to twenty percent of murders are committed by strangers. Liz may be able to eliminate some of the entries with one of her deep dives. I want to run them all by Devereau but want to have as many identified as possible. She may know more about the relationship between Lanza and his contacts. You've done some research on his background and lifestyle, how about you take charge of gathering names of his romantic relationships through historic media. Maybe we can identify the author of that scathing letter. I'll search the records of all his film and TV roles for names of those he worked with, and Pete, you go over the crime scene photos again."

∗∗∗

By seven-thirty, Jake and Scarlett had come up with potential identities for thirty percent of the listings in the book, but the author of the torn letter remained unknown. The trio had not left the dinette table for hours, eating as they worked. As Jake pushed his chair back, stretched his arms, and was about to speak, Pete said, "Jake, take a look at this. I think I just found your baseball cap or its twin brother."

Jake immediately leaned over. "Where's that magnifying glass?"

Scarlett passed the tool to Jake and within a second, he said, "Damn! We've got it. We need to enlarge this image and have it enhanced. Why didn't forensics tag it?"

"At least they preserved it, if it's the same cap," Pete said. "When you talked to Rowland about his taking it into custody, what was the temperature of his interest?"

"Pretty hot. I think he's good police and wants to see justice done. He suggested the filing of a post-conviction relief petition. After I talk with Marielle, the client, and weigh what we've discovered, I'm going to talk to Phil about it. There's no one who knows more or is better at exoneration of an innocent party. It helps that the case is so old that no one in the agency would have been a part of the investigation—no one's feathers to rustle—good for them, less good for us because we can't question an original investigator. It seems they are all dead or have dementia."

"Can you tell from the photo where the cap was located?" Scarlett asked.

Jake pushed the photo across to her. "It was almost under that statue in the landscaped area the driveway circles in front of the house."

"That statute probably kept it from being trampled in the chaos that would have gone on during the fire," Pete said. "Someone must have picked it up because it's not in all the photos. Only that one, which was probably taken early on. Could have been grabbed up by a fireman, which might explain how it missed being considered evidence."

As Jake stared at the image, he said, "Who knows? But it was preserved. Probably not great evidence because of the integrity factor, but it could at least help identify a suspect even if it can't help convict him or her. My guess is the killer had parked his vehicle on the circle, was crossing the center in haste, and something caused him or her to lose the cap. Could have run into that statue, stumbled, or even a sharp wind. With time of the essence, the cap was abandoned. Lanza would never leave his cap on the ground outside."

"Jake, do you think there is any possibility Jorgensen could be the killer?" Scarlett said.

Jake glanced over at Pete who had stopped what he was doing to pay attention to Scarlett. "Your mind is working on overtime, Harvard. While I doubt it, stranger things have occurred. Jorgensen certainly was hiding something, and Myrtle's actions reinforce suspicion."

CHAPTER 40

Thursday morning, Jake and Pete worked out in the hotel gym before breakfast. They had agreed the night before that once they organized the case file, they would table all talk and thoughts about the case until after breakfast. Jake appeared to follow the plan, but Scarlett's mind did not have an off button.

As they waited for their breakfast orders to arrive, Scarlett said, "Okay. What's first on the calendar?"

"Your call, Harvard. It's your case. I'm just along to make sure you don't get yourself killed." He reached for the coffee carafe and topped off his cup.

"Oh. Is that what you're here for?"

"Why else would I be carrying a concealed Glock in a family style restaurant?"

She leaned forward over the table and barely louder than a whisper said, "Maybe because like your famous credit card, you never leave home without it." Straightening up, she continued in a normal tone, "But, let me rephrase. What do you suggest I do with *my* case?"

Pete followed the verbal volley with a grin on his face. "Why don't you two just break down and get married? Everyone knows you're a couple."

Scarlett turned toward him with a dubious look.

"Everyone but Harvard," Jake said.

"Now you're ganging up on me. We're not a couple. We're a team."

Jake looked toward Pete. "She's right, Coop. I'm employer; she's employee; and together, we're a team." With one eyebrow cocked, his eyes projected a mischievous expression.

"Can we be serious? Today is Thursday. Anna will be here Saturday with your favorite doctor. I think we need a formalized plan."

"How about this? Today we work through identifying the numbers in the Lanza address book until after lunch and meet with the Charleston County prosecutor this afternoon. I think they call him deputy solicitor here. Tomorrow we make the trip to Leath. You suggest to the client that she visit her family on Saturday. That way she maintains a somewhat normal relationship with Jorgensen, and we don't risk him learning too much. Then we meet with her on Sunday and give her all we know."

"I didn't know we were meeting with the prosecutor."

"I didn't tell you?"

"No, Sherlock, you didn't. What time?"

"Three o'clock."

***

The suite was still when Jake closed his portfolio at two p.m. "Awfully quiet over there, Harvard. Found anything?"

"I found a biography of Lanza and downloaded the digital edition."

"Good work." He nodded approval and pushed his chair away from the table.

"The author did a great job of interviewing sources. I'm skimming through it, but when I have time, I'd like to give it a close read."

"Found any candidates for authorship of the letter?"

"Unfortunately, it looks like there are several, which wouldn't include any deranged fans." She looked down at her watch. "I'd better get ready. What time do you think we should leave?"

"According to the Internet, it's a twenty-minute drive in normal traffic. To be safe, we should probably give it thirty to forty."

"I'd better hurry." She shut down her computer and left the room.

***

When Scarlett and Jake entered the office of Deputy Solicitor Brad Curtis, he rose from behind his desk, shook hands with both, and said, "You two have made quite a stir here. I've been looking forward to this meeting. I need to both congratulate and thank you, Mr. Shepherd, you are now a legend in your own time."

Scarlett beamed at the praise while Jake said, "I hope not. I just did what I was trained to do. But thank you."

"Please have a seat. Can I offer you anything to drink?"

"I'm good," Jake said.

"Thank you for offering but I'm fine as well," Scarlett said.

"So, you're the victim in this case, Ms. Kavanagh. How are you doing?"

"Absolutely no problem."

"Well, if any need arises, Charleston has excellent victim services." He turned his focus toward Jake. "My research tells me you spent some time as a criminal prosecutor—Federal. So, I'm sure you know that I need to take statements from each of you, but separately."

"We're both lawyers. No problem. We know the drill. Who would you like to speak with first?"

"Ms. Kavanagh. It shouldn't take long. You can wait in reception if you don't mind."

"Before I leave the room, I have a couple of questions that Scarlett has as well."

"Fire away."

"Is Paul Jorgensen representing Ms. Malone? I ask because he is likely a witness in the case we're working. And second, what are you charging Ms. Malone with? I know she was released on a bond, which gives me a bit of concern for our safety. For that reason, I have a partner of mine providing us backup security."

"Is that the retired FBI negotiator at the scene of the daycare shooting?"

"It is. I also have my trained K-9 with us now."

"Probably a good idea. You never know with some people. To answer your first question: Jorgensen is an attorney of record, but he is not showing up. He has an associate doing the work. I do know that Ms. Malone is his long-time paralegal. As for charges, I have filed for assault and battery of a high and aggravated nature plus false imprisonment. Both are serious felonies. The evidence we have is going to make building the case a slam dunk, especially the photo you were able to take, Ms. Kavanagh."

CHAPTER 41

The interviews were uneventful with Scarlett and Jake both providing a description of the hostage situation. As they prepared to leave, Curtis brought up the Lanza case, asking what had brought it to their attention.

"In my investigation into our client's birth parents, his name has come up as her likely father," Scarlett said. "But we don't have conclusive proof as to her mother's identity."

"But you suspect she may be the woman who is serving time for his murder?"

"She's one possibility," Scarlett said.

"Interesting. But where does Jorgensen and the defendant in my case fit into all of this?"

"We're still trying to figure that out," Jake said. "But I know he does. He was a P.D. when Lanza was killed, and he represented the woman convicted of the murder. Your defendant is a longtime employee and maybe paramour of Jorgensen."

"I see what you mean. I'd like to be kept up to speed with what you uncover. I've never heard negative comments about Jorgensen although I think of him more as a civil lawyer. In my eighteen years in law, I've never seen him in criminal court."

"Apparently, he left criminal law. We'll keep you in the loop," Jake said.

***

As Jake and Scarlett got ready to visit Marielle Devereau on Friday, they skipped going out for breakfast and ate an early continental breakfast in the hotel with Pete instead. Afterward, the three sorted out the data to assist Jake with his interview. As the research had progressed and each produced a potential ID for an entry in Lanza's book, it was forwarded to Liz. While they used whatever name or initials Lanza had entered to match with his publicly known friends, relatives, and associates, Liz used her technological skill and resources to find all available information on the person. Her research had eliminated some of the figures from a potential suspect list by way of articles indicating they could not have been in the vicinity at the relevant time. Some she found were deceased. She only failed to find data on two low priority names with three entries remaining with no potential ID. From her research and the Lanza biography, Scarlett identified five women in addition to Marielle as former dates or relationships with Lanza.

"Should we take the names of women Lanza was dating more than a year before his death off the list to consider?" Scarlett asked as they wrapped up the work.

"No. Anyone who ever had or thought she had an intimate relationship with him is a potential suspect. Some people, male or female, harbor feelings for a long time."

***

When Marielle Devereau entered the interview room, she appeared more relaxed than when she met with Scarlett three days before. After Scarlett introduced her to Jake, they sat with Marielle on one side of the table and Jake and Scarlett on the opposite side.

"Ms. Devereau, this case began with the purpose of identifying the client's birth parents. I don't typically handle that type of case, but Scarlett was impressed with the client, who is believed to be your daughter. I came onboard when information Scarlett obtained began to take on a far more complicated nature. After arriving here in Charleston and reviewing Vic Lanza's murder file, as a former prosecutor, based on the scanty, circumstantial evidence, I was surprised by your conviction. I would never have taken the case to trial. Scarlett tells me you aren't seeking release, and you're denying you have a daughter. But Scarlett's convinced you are the mother of Anna Carden and that you were wrongfully convicted. I'm not here to talk you into my taking your case. I'm here because I don't like guilty people getting away with a crime and don't like innocent people incarcerated for crimes they did not commit."

Marielle listened intently to Jake, never breaking eye contact. When he said, "Did you have anything to do with the death of Vic Lanza?" She did not flinch nor blink but responded softly, "I did not."

Jake studied Marielle's face for at least a minute before continuing the dialogue. "I believe you. I'd like to prove your innocence." He paused, giving her an opportunity to respond. When she didn't, he said, "Otherwise, the killer who committed this crime will *never* be held accountable."

It took Marielle several seconds to speak, first looking toward Scarlett as if seeking help.

"He's right, Marielle," Scarlett said. "Don't worry about what you will do when released. Trust us, the state will owe you a lot of money for your wrongful conviction. Certainly enough to take care of you while you rebuild your life. Most of all, you will get to know your daughter and your future grandchildren."

"What do you mean the state would owe me money?"

"When someone serves time in prison for a crime they did not commit, they can file a claim with the state for compensation. It does have a limit, but if there were any wrongful acts committed by government officials that caused the wrongful incarceration, you can also file a civil suit for damages."

Jake looked at Scarlett. "You've been doing research."

She smiled. "I am a lawyer."

"Tears suddenly ran down Marielle's face as her head moved in an affirmative manner. "*Oui*, yes! I want that." She pulled her shirt out of her prison pants, exposing a white tee shirt, and tipped her head forward to wipe her face.

"Then, let's get started," Jake said, opening his portfolio and taking out his pen. "This is preliminary. I want an overview of your relationship with Lanza and everything you remember about the day he died. I found an address book of his at the museum where he died and would like your help learning about the people listed. Are you with me?"

"Yes."

"Scarlett says you've pretty good with English, but if you have any doubt about the meaning of any question I ask, stop me, and I'll rephrase it."

She nodded.

"Okay. Let's start with how you came to be in this country."

"All my life, from little girl, I wanted to design dresses. I learned at home, but I read about schools in America, so I applied to school in Atlanta, and they accepted me."

"How did you enter the country? Student visa?"

"*Oui.*"

"How did you get the job on the TV show?"

"Some friends from school. We went to a big park—Six Flags—one Sunday. We were waiting in line for a ride. The line was slow, and the man behind me heard us talking. He asked where I was from—my accent, you know."

Jake smiled.

"We started a conversation. We had plenty of time as the line was long. He told me he worked on a TV show, not as an actor. He took care of the guns. We ended up spending rest of day together. We started seeing one another. When a person in wardrobe had an accident and left the show, he helped me get the job."

"So, you worked on the set and met Lanza? What was the name of the guy, the armorer, you were dating?"

"Carl. That was his name. Carl took me to a cast party, and I met Vic. He never noticed me on set. I worked on the women's wardrobe—not the men. Carl introduced me to Vic. They were friends since kids in the same neighborhood in New York."

"That fits. So, you were in a romantic relationship with Carl. What was his last name?"

"DeLuca. Carlos DeLuca."

"Was it a serious relationship?"

"Not so much for me, but I think he liked me more."

"When exactly did your relationship with Vic Lanza begin?"

"Not long after the party. We didn't talk about it. I think Vic felt a little guilty about Carl. He wanted to wait before telling everyone.

I wasn't in love with Carl. I didn't feel the *une alchimie* or what you Americans call chemistry for Carl. He was nice, but it wasn't like it was with Vic. But half the women in America had chemistry for Vic. He was, he was handsome—very sexy."

"Do you think Carl might have found out or suspected you were involved with Lanza?"

She looked down at the table between them. Jake gave her a minute before repeating his question.

"Marielle, did Carl find out?"

She finally looked up and locked eyes with Jake. "I don't know, but I don't think so. He didn't tell me."

"Are you sure Carl did not know?"

She paused again but finally said, "We didn't exactly break up. I told him I was too young to be serious, and I wanted to get to know other people—date others. But I don't think he knew I was seeing Vic."

Scarlett's eyes appeared glued to Marielle as Jake pressed for answers.

"Tell me a little about Carl. Did he get angry easily—have a temper? Have strong reactions if someone annoyed him?"

"I never saw him angry. He might have had a temper." She stared at Jake for a moment. "I don't know."

Jake paused to flip through the files in his briefcase. Taking out the photos of the baseball cap found at the museum, he slid them across the table toward Marielle. "Do you remember anyone who wore a cap like the one in those photos?"

It took her only a second to respond. "A lot of people had caps like that. Sometimes, Carl wore one like that."

"Did Vic ever wear a cap like that?"

She shook her head. "I never saw him wear a baseball cap."

As he pulled the photos back and returned them to the folder, he said, "Looking back at the day Vic died, I read in the police file that a witness gave a statement saying you and Lanza were fighting that day. I believe it was an employee of Lanza's by the name of Ron Brinson who said it. He said you were angry and made threats—like, 'You'll be sorry.'"

"The police and Mr. Jorgensen told me that, but that wasn't right. We were having breakfast on the terrace. Mr. Jorgensen said the witness thought Vic was breaking up with me. He wasn't. I didn't make a threat. I didn't say that. We had argued that morning, but it wasn't about breaking up. I had a ticket to fly back to Atlanta early. I had to go because of the terms of my visa and my school. Vic wanted me to stay. Sometimes, I had trouble with English and maybe I was loud. But I never told Vic he would be sorry." She took a deep breath. "I had to go to Atlanta. They could send me back to France if I didn't do what I was supposed to do. I had the ticket to go back that morning. But Vic kept insisting I stay. So, he loaned me a car to drive so I could stay longer that day."

"I am surprised that being new to the country you could drive yourself back."

"It was new car—a Mazda—and had a what you call? You know, the gadget that talks to you—tells you when to turn."

"Are you talking about a GPS?"

"Yes, yes. That's it—a GPS. Vic set it to help drive back so I could stay longer."

"What time did you leave?"

"I left a bit after five that afternoon. I wanted to get to my apartment before dark."

"How long did it take you to reach your residence in Atlanta?"

"I got there maybe ten minutes after nine."

"Did you stop anywhere on the way?"

"No. The car, it was filled with *l'essence*. I drove straight."

"*L'essence*?" Jake said.

Scarlett smiled and said, "*L'essence* is what they call gasoline in France."

He turned toward her with a you-knew-that expression. Again, focusing on Marielle, he said, "Did you live alone?"

"No. I had a roommate, but she was away with her boyfriend and didn't come back until Monday morning."

"Could anyone in your building have seen you arrive home?"

"It was all quiet. I didn't see anyone."

"Did your attorney have an investigator talk to any of your Atlanta neighbors?"

She shook her head. "I don't think so. He didn't tell me that."

"You mentioned security being at the mansion. Would at least one of them have seen you leave and known Vic was alive when you left?"

She shook her head. "It was Sunday. The two bodyguards, I hardly knew them. I don't remember the names of both, but the one who gave the statement to the police was named Ron something. There were different guards all the time. They only worked until three o'clock that day, and the next two did not come until eleven that night. Vic said thieves take Sunday off. The afternoon and evening on Sunday did not have guards."

Jake made several notes on his pad before resuming the interview. "Okay, so you sort of broke up with Carl to date Vic. And you don't know if Carl was upset."

"He was a little mad when I stopped seeing him so much."

Did either Vic or Carl know you were pregnant?"

"No."

Jake made a note but not a comment. "Do you know of anyone who had a grudge against Vic, or any reason to take his life?"

"No."

"Tell me a little more about Vic. When you began dating, was he seeing anyone else?"

"He said he wasn't."

"Do you know who his last girlfriend was?"

"I think he said her name was Diana . . . . No. Wait. It was Delta. But he said it was over—that she was a bitch."

Jake looked around toward Scarlett. "Do you have a Delta?"

Scarlett flipped through her notes. "I do. Delta Fontaine. There's not much about her in the media I found—only one or two photos of them attending an event. I'll do a deep dive on her tomorrow."

Jake pulled the photo of a page of Lanza's address book and passed it across the table to Marielle. "Look at the entry that has an X across it. Could that be Delta's number?"

Marielle gazed down at the image for only a second or two and shook her head. "I don't know. That looks like a heart crossed out and a pig. I don't know what that means."

"Before we start looking at the names and numbers found in Vic's address book, tell me about your arrest. Who arrested you?"

"Two officers from the Atlanta Police Department came to my school. They had a warrant. They took me to jail in Atlanta and kept me there until officers from South Carolina came for me."

"Did the South Carolina detectives interrogate you—ask you questions—before Paul Jorgensen came on to represent you?"

"*Oui*, yes."

"Did they read you your rights?"

"*Oui*."

"Did they read them in English or French."

"In English."

"Did you have an interpreter?"

"No."

"I saw in the file that you were given a polygraph and failed."

"I didn't know what it was then. They just told me to do it."

"Did the polygraph examiner ask you questions in English or in French?"

"English."

"Again. Was an interpreter present?"

"No."

With a flourish, Jake circled a note on his pad. "Okay. Let's take another look at the pages from Vic Lanza's address book. Would you look through all of them, and point out any names you recognize?" He pushed the entire stack of photos across to her.

Marielle nodded and began turning page by page over. After turning about six pages, she identified five entries with Jake writing each in his notes. "Those are the only ones I know." She pushed the page back across to Jake.

"Tell me who they are and what you know about them."

"Two worked on the gate. They were the security people for Vic and the house. See." She pulled the sheet back and pointed to a name. "That's . . ."

"Ronald Brinson, the guard who said you and Lanza were arguing."

"*Oui*. And that one"—she pointed to the name above. "Lloyd McIntyre, he was there that day, but they both left before I did."

"I already told you about Carl. Barnes Reddick was the director on the show. And Mary Shular was an actress that I helped with her clothes."

⁎⁎⁎

When Jake showed her the torn letter, she confirmed it was not written by her. With that, Jake wrapped up his questioning but had her copy a line from the letter on his pad to give him a sample of her handwriting. It clearly did not match that on the letter.

With Jake having completed his interview, Scarlett asked if Marielle would be willing to provide a DNA sample. Her face instantly registered reluctance.

"Marielle, we know you're Anna's mother. We know Paul Jorgensen was your attorney. When we spoke before, you said if someone had a baby girl, Jorgensen would find a good home for her. Did you release your daughter to Paul Jorgensen?"

Marielle curled her lips in for a second, took a deep breath, and said, "I did."

"Did Paul Jorgensen tell you who would be adopting your baby?"

"No. He said it was illegal for me to know who had her—not that I could ever bother them."

Scarlett looked toward Jake with an expression of satisfaction. Turning back to Marielle, she said, "Marielle, did you hold your baby before she was taken away?"

Marielle turned an empty gaze over Scarlett's shoulder as if she moved into another mental place. Her lips quivered. "Only once."

Scarlett's eyes grew glassy as she reached across the table with both hands and took one of Marielle's. "Anna Carden is your daughter. Let us prove it. . . . You can decide later if you're willing to meet her. Even if you do not meet her, I believe Anna will want us to continue the investigation. Don't cause her more delay, expense, and anxiety. She wants to know you and her heritage. She wants her children to know who they are descended from. Let us match your DNA to hers. She'll be in Charleston this weekend, and I plan to tell her about you."

The vacant glaze continued as Marielle stared across the room at the blank wall. After several seconds, she turned her focus to Scarlett and quietly said, "*D'accord.*"

Scarlett smiled.

"I have one more question," Jake said as Scarlett took a DNA kit out of her briefcase. "Where were you when your baby was born? What hospital? I assume you weren't here."

"No. I was still in the county jail. I had just been sentenced when I went into labor." Her brows pinched creating a puzzled expression. "They took me to a big hospital in Charleston. I remember when they took me back to the jail, and I knew I would never see my baby again. It was the worst day of my life. Why do you ask that?"

"Jurisdiction."

CHAPTER 42

As Jake and Scarlett drove to a FedEx location to fast-track the DNA sample to the lab after leaving the prison, he said, "Well, we know now why Jorgensen wasn't going to talk to us. Apparently, Myrtle knows his secret. I don't know South Carolina law, but I suspect giving a baby to his wife's sister without the legal process is a felony. Looks like we'll have another agency involved. The inmate would have been considered in the custody of the jail and subject to that jurisdiction, but the baby's custody is most likely with the hospital, which in this case is different. The baby wasn't an inmate."

"I figured that was why you wanted to establish where Anna was born. One mystery solved, but what happened to the baby born to the Cardens in Augusta, Jake? The real Anna-Claire Carden. And what is our Anna's legal status? Her Social Security number?"

"Legally, she doesn't have a Social. You know what? That's not our problem. That's one for a good lawyer to sort out. I suggest Anna see Phil Madison when this all gets laid out."

"Who are we going to turn all of this over to?"

"Good question. I think we need a joint Zoom meeting with both Rowland and Lester. Let them bring the right agency onboard, but not until we have the DNA results."

"What a mess. I liked Robin, and this is going to tear her world apart. Her's mother's critically ill, and her father could be arrested if he implemented an illegal placement of a baby. But I can't help thinking about the other baby. What happened to her? Where is she?"

Jake turned into a strip mall parking lot. "Harvard, you and I both know that baby died. It's the only thing that makes sense. The only question is was it accident, negligence, illness . . . or murder? I think we can rule out illness. There would have been a legal adoption. That baby died someway that had to be covered up. Marielle's baby, our client, was a substitute. That's why they moved, stayed away from the rest of the family."

"Why would Jorgensen take such a risk? I dread telling Anna. Her real mother is in prison for a murder she probably didn't commit; and her adopted mother, who she loved all her life, may have been a criminal."

"You can make that *was* a criminal. All parties to an illegal adoption break the law, right? You're the family law attorney."

"Right. People sure screw their lives up. Even worse is the collateral damage."

CHAPTER 43

Scarlett, Jake, and Phil had a late breakfast at Cracker Barrel on Sunday. After a brief debate, they decided the meeting with Anna would include everyone. Scarlett had first thought she should meet with Anna alone, but after weighing all the information she would be sharing and the effects it might have on Anna, she decided the fiancé might be needed for Anna's emotional support.

"If he's at the table, so am I," Jake said. "And we might as well include Pete in case the jerk acts out."

"Translated, that means in case Shepherd develops a bad case of insufficient anger management," Pete said, laughing.

Scarlett chuckled. "Good idea."

***

At one o'clock, a knock came on the door of the small hotel conference room, causing Kai to utter a low growl. Jake calmed the shepherd as

Scarlett opened the door to greet Anna and Dan. Larsen's attention immediately went to Pete.

"It's good to see you," Scarlett said. "You remember Jake of course, and that is Retired Special Agent Peter Cooper, Jake's partner who's been assisting us here in Charleston."

Dr. Larsen projected an antagonistic attitude causing a quick response from Jake. "Before you jump to judgment, you need to know there was an incident putting Scarlett in serious danger last week. For her safety, I had Pete and Kai come down as backup. He heads the security section of the company. But let's all get comfortable, and we will fill you in." Jake pointed toward a side table. "There's coffee and water. Help yourself."

"What kind of incident?" Larsen said.

"A woman, who works for your uncle, Anna, broke into our suite and held Scarlett hostage at gunpoint. But take a seat, and we'll fill you in on everything that happened."

Anna's face projected shock as they all sat.

Larsen turned toward Jake. "Gunpoint. My, God. Did you call the police?"

Scarlett cringed, expecting Jake to say, "No, jackass, I called the frigging Door Dash." Before he could respond, she said, "I sent Jake a message, and he made sure the police were called. A SWAT team responded, but it was Jake who disarmed her. But let us give you everything we've learned in the correct order. It'll make a lot more sense to you and save time."

Anna reached over and put her hand on top of Larsen's. "Please do."

"Anna, I have good news, but I have some that may be distressing. Bear with me. First, we know who your father was. Unfortunately, he is deceased. He was an A-list celebrity—a famous actor by the name of Victor Lanza. He was starring in a hit TV show called *Atlanta P.I.*

at the time of his death and owned an antebellum mansion outside of Charleston that is now a museum."

Anna's expression went from anticipation to astonishment as Scarlett pushed photos of Lanza, the mansion, and copies of publicity articles on Lanza across the table for her to look at. Larsen leaned over toward her to see the images.

As Anna took her time looking at each photo, she said, "That's my father? I don't know what to say. He's handsome for sure."

"We have duplicates, so, those are yours to keep." She handed Anna the folder the photos had been in. "There are also articles about his death. It happened about eight months before you were born." Scarlett paused for a few seconds. "Unfortunately, his death was a homicide. He was murdered in the mansion."

A gasp escaped from Anna. "Murdered?"

"I'm so sorry. He was shot. Apparently, a candle was knocked over at the time, setting the house on fire, but it has been restored. As I said, it's currently a museum."

Anna sucked in her breath and gazed down at the photos. Larsen pulled a couple over for a closer look. "My father. Oh, my gosh. I can't believe it."

"He was Italian, which matches your Ancestry report. His sister lives in New York. I've talked with her, and she is excited at the idea of having a niece. He had no other children. She would like to meet you. Her name and contact information are in the file, but reaching out to her is your choice."

She looked up at Scarlett. "My mother. What about my mother? You said you might have someone who could be my mother."

"This is the hard part." Scarlett took a deep breath. "The woman we believe is your mother is in prison—"

Anna gasped.

"Before you develop a wrong image in your mind, Jake and I believe she is innocent. She's a French national and was here to study
fashion design before it all happened, which explains why we had a
hard time tracking her. France does not allow citizens to send DNA
to companies like Ancestry, so none of her family members would be
in a database. Jake and I have both talked to her. When I first met her,
I could not believe she was capable of violence. Jake agreed after he
interviewed her. During our initial meeting, she did not want to admit
to having a baby, but your photo brought tears to her eyes. On Friday,
I was able to convince her to give us a DNA sample. It's at the lab, and
I may have the results as early as tomorrow."

"What, what is she—"

"There's no easy way to tell you this. She's in prison for the murder
of your father. But remember, Jake and I feel she didn't do it, and we
would like to collect enough evidence to exonerate her."

"How do you propose to do that? It sounds like all that happened
thirty-five years ago," Larsen said as tears formed in Anna's eyes. Seeing
her distress, he put an arm around her shoulders.

Jake spoke up. "We've reviewed the police file and discovered a
couple of leads. The good news is the local law enforcement officials
are being cooperative."

"Anna, your uncle, Paul Jorgensen, was her public defender," Scarlett said. "He convinced her to accept a plea. She was a young girl,
alone in a foreign country. She barely knew the language and had no
support system. I don't know why he was so quick to persuade her to
plead guilty. After the three of us reviewed the entire police file, we all
agreed, the evidence sufficient to convict just wasn't there. Jake was a
federal prosecutor before he joined the FBI. He said he would never
have taken the case to trial. They had no witness, no murder weapon,

nothing but the testimony of an employee who heard her arguing with your father the morning of his death."

Larsen addressed Jake. "Federal prosecutor? That requires a law degree, doesn't it?"

"Yeah." Jake glared at Larsen. "I've got one of those."

"Federal prosecutor, FBI agent, what else, an astronaut?" His sarcasm was palpable.

Pete sat up straighter in his chair, anticipating Jake's reaction.

"Affirmative as to AUSA and agent. Although I've fast-roped out of helicopters, never made it to space. I might look into it."

Scarlett closed her eyes and took a deep breath, hoping there would not be another verbal volley.

"So, basically, right now, you have no proof this woman is Anna's birth mother?"

Anna sat silent, staring down at the table.

Scarlett wasted no time in responding before Jake could address the question. "Not yet. The police record states she and Lanza were in a relationship." As she spoke, Scarlett removed copies of newspaper articles covering the murder and arrest from a file and pushed them over to Anna. "If you look at the photos of Marielle in the newspaper articles and even the mug shot, you can see how much you resemble her."

"Marielle?"

"Marielle Devereau. We believe that Jorgensen placed you with his wife's sister who had apparently just lost a baby. The Cardens gave you the identity of the baby they had. We don't know what happened to that baby, but Nora Carden did give birth in Augusta, Georgia, to a baby girl on the date you were told was your birthday. You were born four and a half months later. You're actually a third of a year younger than you thought."

"Wait a minute. If Paul took the baby, which was me, and gave me to my parents—he knows who I am. He looked me in the eye and told me my investigation was a waste of money. He knows and covered it up. Why? How could he pretend all these years that I was Nora and Larry's child?" Although filled with confusion, anger infused Anna's reaction. "What kind of man is he? Did they all know? My aunt? My cousins?"

"If Anna was born here in South Carolina, why have you not found her real birth certificate? Hospitals have to file one with the state," Larsen said, his tone condescending.

"How would we have been able to find her birth certificate when we did not have the name of her mother, her father, her date of birth, or her name—if she was given a name?" Scarlett said.

Larsen frowned.

"Did they all know? My aunt? My cousins? Did everyone know but me?" Anna asked.

"We're asking those questions as well," Jake said. "This brings us to Scarlett's incident with Barbara Malone. She is Paul Jorgensen's longtime legal secretary and suspected paramour—or wannabe. She gained entry to our hotel suite and held Scarlett hostage, demanding Scarlett and I leave Charleston and cease investigating. Although she kept a gun aimed at Scarlett, we don't think she wanted or intended to commit any further violence but could have done so accidentally. Baffled at first, we now believe she knew what crime Jorgensen committed in placing you with members of his family without legal documents. She was apparently afraid we would expose him to an arrest."

"I wanted you to meet with your family before we told you all this, Anna," Scarlett said. "Because we didn't want to ruin your visit or for you to bring any of this up to your uncle. We met with him when we first got here. He was not receptive. It was right after that when his employee broke into our suite."

"This is astounding. I didn't know him well, but he was always very nice to me."

"How was your visit with him?"

"I'm not sure. You're right. This is all hard to process. But as I think about the visit, he acted a little strange. He hardly spoke with me. My aunt is so sad. She has FTD, which happens with some ALS patients."

"FTD?"

"That's frontotemporal degeneration—dementia. She didn't even recognize me at first. At one point, Uncle Paul"—Anna caught herself, questioning her choice of words—"*Paul* said it was ridiculous of me to be trying to prove Nora and Larry weren't my parents. He actually seemed angry, which I didn't understand. Now it makes sense. But where is the real Anna?" She turned to face Larsen. "Dan, you see. I was right. I'm not Anna Carden. There is another one. When we get married, I want to know my real name. I want you to marry who I really am." She looked back toward Scarlett. "I'm living a stolen identity."

Seeing the raw emotion in Anna, Scarlett said in a near whisper, "I probably shouldn't tell you this."

"What?"

"The first time I visited Marielle and showed her your photo, she whispered the name Lara. I think that was what she named you. She wouldn't admit it at the time because she was still denying she ever had a child."

"Lara. That's who I really am. Lara. I like it." She looked down at the table for a minute. "Why am I feeling weird? And I can't stop thinking about the real Anna Carden. What happened to her? Is she out there?"

"Anna, we don't know what happened to her, but . . . we suspect she might have died. There's no real explanation for how you came to be raised by the Cardens. It can only make sense if something happened to their baby."

"That makes me feel even more weird. I'm the substitute for a dead baby? I took her place—her entire life." She shuddered.

"You have to stop that. You had nothing to do with whatever happened. Why should you feel weird?" Larsen asked, reaching for the hand he held earlier.

Anna shrugged her shoulders. "I don't know how to explain it. I wanted this. I want it. I want to be who I really am, but thinking about answering to Lara feels funny—unreal. But something inside of me doesn't want to be called Anna any longer. It's not my name. It belongs to someone else."

"I am sure that's a normal reaction," Scarlett said. "You'll have to give it time."

"I want to meet Marielle, and I don't. I don't know what I would say. She's my mother, but she's a stranger. What would I call her? But we've got to help her. I'm rattling on and on, aren't I?"

"You're fine. I'm not a psychologist, but I understand. Sometimes the anticipation of an event is exciting, but the culmination is daunting. I think Marielle feels the same. She wants to know you, but she's afraid. Add to that, she's in prison. She said she would not want you or your fiancé to know. She feels you would be ashamed of her."

"Not if she's innocent."

"You don't know that she's innocent," Larsen said. "But if the DNA proves the woman is Anna's mother, then your job is done, right?" he said to Scarlett.

"Absolutely," Jake said. "Unless Anna wants us to get her mother out of prison."

"That wasn't part of your assignment," Larsen said, raising his voice and rising to his feet.

"Dan, if she's innocent, I can't just leave her in prison. She may be our future children's grandmother."

"It's not your job to get her out. And we don't even know that she's innocent. They could be just telling you that to stay on your clock!"

Larsen's comment brought Jake to his feet, which brought Pete up as well.

"I take exception to that comment," Jake said. "I don't tell you how to operate on a patient, and you don't question how I do my job. A medical degree doesn't make you omniscient, and believe me, I don't need your business. I've got a backlog of cases sitting on my desk as we speak. We can pack our bags and head back to Virginia this afternoon." Jake's piercing stare would have cut through steel.

"No. Please don't do that, Mr. Shepherd. Dan, please. Don't mess this up for me."

"How about both of you sit, take a deep breath, and let Dr. Carden and Scarlett work this out," Pete said. "Jake. Cool down."

"How do we know that even if this woman is innocent that you can do anything about it?" Larsen's eyes shot sparks and his nostrils flared.

"I won't dignify that with an answer," Jake said.

"I'll answer," Pete said. "Dr. Larsen, you obviously come to this table with little knowledge as to Jake Shepherd and what he is. Let me enlighten you. He is brash, confident to the point of arrogance, has no patience with unlawful acts or dishonesty, and is completely devoid of courtesy or humility. That said, who would be my first call if I needed help? Jake Shepherd. Why? Because he is also intuitive beyond measure, near genius, extremely well-trained in his field, focused, fearless, and fervent to the point of vicious in the pursuit of justice. You think you've ever known a badass? I promise you, you've never known one like my friend and colleague Jake Shepherd. And that comes from someone who has lived his entire adult life in law enforcement."

Without responding, Larsen looked toward Jake.

Jake adjusted his stance with an air of confidence and control. "Wow, Cooper. Great speech. Couldn't have said it better myself." He aimed a piercing look at Larsen. "He's right. I am damn good at what I do. Innocent, I'm your best friend. Guilty, I'm your worst enemy. Now stay the hell out of this, Larsen. We work for Dr. Carden, not you." Jake shifted his focus toward Anna. "Dr. Carden, Anna. Your instructions?"

Her pupils dilated, Anna locked eyes with Jake. "If Marielle is my mother, I want you to do whatever you need to do to get her out of prison—please."

The corners of Jake's mouth curled in a smug smile. "You've got it. Now, we'll continue with this meeting." Pointing to Larsen, he said, "If you can't keep your mouth shut, then pack up your F-ing God complex and get out of Dodge. You're an observer here, not a player."

Larsen's anger smoldered as he inhaled and exhaled like a bull about to kick dirt and charge, but he said nothing while Anna reached into the purse in her lap, took out a tissue, and wiped away the tears streaming down her cheeks.

All the while the verbal exchanges took place, Scarlett sat quietly observing.

Suddenly, Larsen swung an arm downward with the unmistakable sign of anger and started for the exit. "I'll be in the bar."

Scarlett popped up to follow, bringing Kai to attention. As Jake reached to stop her, Pete grabbed his arm.

"Let her go, Jake. She can handle it. He might punch you, but he's not going to hurt Scarlett."

CHAPTER 44

Once in the hallway, Larsen moved at a brisk pace.

"Dr. Larsen, Dan, wait." His stride caused Scarlett to break into a run to catch up. When he failed to stop or turn, she circled him, forcing him to stop.

"I have nothing to say to you, Ms. Kavanagh. Now please move out of my way."

"I have something to say to you, and if you love Anna, you'd better listen," she said with clipped words and resolute tone.

"What do you know about how I feel?"

In rapid fire delivery, Scarlett responded. "You've asked Anna to marry you—share your life. Unless you're a con artist, I suspect you're in love with her. I get it. You're a man of science. You go into an operating room and cut into the flesh and organs of living patients. That takes not only skill and training but also confidence. Emotion can't distract you. Jake is the same. When he's in a life-or-death situation, he has to have that same confidence and same ability to block emotion. What you may not know about me is I practiced family law for over ten years—dealing with constant emotions. I also handled a few cases of adoptees wanting to find their biological parents. In many cases, where contentious relationships between parents had to be dealt with by the court, I was appointed to be a guardian ad litem for the child or children and had to do deep investigations to make a recommendation to the court of a post-divorce parenting plan. As a G.A.L., I had several cases involving adopted children in which I did extensive research and met with psychologists. There is research indicating a newborn who has any physical contact with the birth mother instantly forms a bond they carry through life—even though there is no conscious memory. Marielle held Anna before they took her away. I believe that bond is driving Anna to find and know her mother. You said it yourself. It's like a fire burning inside of her. She needs your support."

"You certainly talk fast."

"Think about what I said." Scarlett tipped her chin and raised her eyebrows to affirm her comment and then left him standing.

CHAPTER 45

When Scarlett reentered the conference room, Anna's face was buried in her hands. Jake and Pete sat awkwardly silent, obviously at a loss as how to comfort the young physician.

Hearing the door open, Anna raised her tear-stained face and said, "What did he say? He's angry with me."

Scarlett glanced from Jake to Pete. "Guys, could we have the room? Take Kai up to the suite." Her brow formed a frown. "Avoid the bar."

"Yes, ma'am," Pete said, rising. "Come on, Rambo. Let's give the ladies some space."

Once the men were out of the room, Anna said, "Does he want to cancel our engagement?"

Scarlett eased down in a chair opposite Anna and reached over for her hand. "He's not breaking up with you. I gave him something to think about, which I hope will bring clarity to his perception of your position." Scarlett gave her a few seconds to gather herself together. "Do you feel like answering a few questions for me?"

At first, she only nodded, but then said, "I can. I want to do everything possible to get the truth. What do you want to know?"

"A little more about your visit with your aunt and uncle. Please tell me everything he said, even if you don't think it's related to your adoption."

"He didn't say much. It has been a long time since I visited here. The last time I saw them was at my mother's funeral. You know how funerals are. You talk to everyone and don't remember anyone." She withdrew her hands from Scarlett's grip and reached into her purse for another tissue. Wiping away a stray tear, she said, "It suddenly feels awkward calling Nora and Larry my parents, but what else . . . never mind. What I'm trying to say is that we've never had a lot of contact, but Paul was definitely different. He never smiled or seemed happy to see me. And Irene was pitiful. The ALS is advanced—a horrible disease."

"Was there any reference to your being adopted?"

"I didn't bring it up, but he did. He said Robin told him I believed I was adopted and wanted to find my birth parents. He said I was wasting my money." Her tone rose, "How could he look at me and lie? He knows I'm adopted. Dan agreed with him, but of course their reasons were different. Dan thinks it doesn't matter who my parents are or were. Paul had the nerve to say Nora and Larry were my parents. He said if they knew what I was doing, it would break their hearts. And he said it with a condescending, judgmental attitude."

"Did you give him any details about the investigation?"

"Only that you thought you had found who my father was and he is deceased. Was I wrong to tell him that?"

"No. Not at all," Scarlett said. "Did he comment?"

Anna paused as though contemplating her response. Her gaze flickered from side to side. "Yes, but not a comment. More of a reaction—almost a hostile reaction. He made me feel like a traitor—that I was doing something inappropriate."

"Anna, he denied knowing who Victor Lanza was to us. Jake called him out. Vic Lanza was a high-profile celebrity, murdered here in Charleston. You can see from the news articles I've given you how much publicity the crime received. And Paul Jorgensen represented the woman accused of killing him."

"He really said he didn't know who my father, Victor Lanza, was and he represented the person accused of killing him? What is he hiding?"

"We'd like to know."

"I'm beginning to feel like I am so alone. The people I always believed were my family, aren't my family. I'm not even sure they will be my friends because of what I am doing. I almost wish I had never done a DNA test and discovered I'm adopted."

"Do you want us to stop pursuing it?"

"No. I can't stop. No matter what, I have to know exactly who I am. I want to know my real mother. I always thought I was drawn to medicine because of my heritage. People would say, 'You're going to be a doctor, just like your father.' But I don't have Larry's DNA. Maybe I'm in the wrong profession."

"Don't think that. If you like what you do, you're in the right career. People choose medicine for different reasons. Some are interested in the science, but some want to help others. From what I know of you, I think you are one of the latter. I don't think you'll lose any family members except maybe the Jorgensen's. I talked to your Carden relatives, and I'm sure they'll still consider you a member of their family. And you may meet new relatives and become part of their family. I know your birth father's sister wants to meet you."

For a minute or two, Anna stared down at the table without speaking. After taking a deep breath, she made eye contact with Scarlett. "I can't go back home today. I'm going to call in for emergency leave. If the results of Marielle's DNA analysis prove she is my mother, I want to meet her. Dan is not going to like me staying, but I'm going to get a room in this hotel. If he doesn't love me enough to understand, it might be wrong to marry him. This is my life."

CHAPTER 46

With a newfound strength, Anna stood. "I'm going to the front desk now to check in. Afterward, I'll talk to Dan."

Scarlett tore a sheet of paper from a pocket-size pad and wrote Pete's room number and the number of hers and Jake's suite. As she handed it to Anna, she said, "Ask for a room as close to us as possible. Jake and Pete will want to ensure your safety."

***

Monday morning arrived with a July heat wave. Anna chose to stay in her room the night before while the three investigators dined in the hotel restaurant. To Jake's satisfaction, the clerk had been able to assign her the room next to Pete's, which shared a wall. Although, he believed Barbara Malone no longer posed a threat, a heightened distrust of Paul Jorgensen brought forth a need for caution.

As the server topped off coffee cups at breakfast in the hotel restaurant, Pete said, "What's today's plan?"

"Track down all we can of Lanza's known associates," Jake said. "Look at members of that security team. In short, talk to anyone who might have known if he had any enemies and what was going on the day of his death. Most of all, we need to look at Devereau's ex and the mysterious author of that letter. I've got a feeling it's Delta Fontaine. Author of the letter, or not, she bears a look."

"I'm guessing you're comfortable moving forward with a Shepherd innocence project even though you don't have DNA confirmation that Ms. Devereau is the client's mother."

"I don't need it. Scarlett and I are both certain based on Jorgensen's role, her known association with the father, and the physical resemblance. If I'm wrong, we won't bill the client for this time."

"And we all know you're never wrong, so that's not a concern, right?"

Scarlett grinned.

Jake gave Pete a look. "I try not to be."

Scarlett's phone pinged notification of a text. Seeing it was from Liz, she immediately opened it.

> It's a match! You've got the mom. See your email.

"Guys, Liz just texted me the DNA is a match. We're good to go."

Jake turned to Pete, eyebrows raised. "And you doubted me?"

"I should know better. Now what?" Pete said.

"Liz should be working on a Zoom conference with Lester and Rowland since the DNA has given proof Marielle is Anna's mother."

"Jake," Scarlett said. "Maybe we should add the prosecutor on Myrtle's case we met with last week to the conference."

"Good idea. Shoot Liz a text. While we wait for that to happen, I'm going to work on who might have been close to Lanza." He reached into his shirt pocket and took out his cell phone.

"How are you going to do that after so many years? Do you know anything about the TV and movie industry?" Pete said.

"Not a damn thing, but I know who does."

"Yeah. Who would that be?"

"Deke Weston."

"Your former partner?"

"That's the one. Deke worked financial crime in LA before we were partners in violent crime. Some of it involved the entertainment industry. He might still have contacts. The sources are in that address book. I just need to narrow them down to one or two who were close to Lanza. I'm sending Deke a text."

***

Jake had just signed the breakfast check when his cell phone rang. Glancing down, he opened the call with the device on speaker.

"Deke, thanks for calling. We're in South Carolina working a case involving the murder of an actor thirty-five years ago, top-tier-level guy. When he died, he was starring in a popular TV series. I have his address book but not sure where to start with interviews. It's not likely to be easy tracking people down. Can you help me speed up the process by telling who a star might have the strongest connection with from your experience?"

"Good question. Like everyone else, they can have friends of all kinds both inside and outside the business. But what I saw most when I worked in LA was alliances between a star and a director whether professional or personal. Look at his IMDB page for projects with repeat names, which shows a relationship. The greater the number of productions they worked together on, the closer the relationship. Directors tend to work with actors they like and trust, which strengthens the bond."

"Thanks. Buy you a drink when we're back." As Jake terminated the call, he glanced over toward Scarlett who was absorbed with her phone.

Looking up at Jake, she said, "I've got his IMDB page. We know his director on the *Atlanta P.I. series* was Barnes Reddick.... And it looks like Reddick directed two feature films he starred in."

"Good job, Harvard. Is Reddick still with us?"

"I'm checking Wikipedia. . . . Yep. Alive and well but looks to be about eighty-two now. I'll text Liz to see if she can find current contact information on him."

"If she fails, I'll text Deke. Maybe someone he knew in the business can help. Let's hope dementia hasn't set in with the guy," Jake said.

"When you're tracking witnesses in a thirty-five-year-old murder, finding one still alive and *compos mentis* may just be a challenge," Pete said.

Jake gave a fake puzzled look toward Pete. "Damn, Cooper. You going all Latin legal on us? Next thing I know you're going to be talking *res judicata* and *habeas corpus*."

"Very funny. But do the math. Anyone who was over thirty-five back then is over seventy today."

"While you guys debate language, I'm going up to tell Anna the news," Scarlett said. "See you later." She scooped up her phone, purse, and a carry-out cup of tea and left the two men at the table.

After dropping everything but her phone and key card in the suite, Scarlett headed down the hall to Anna's room. Identifying herself as she knocked, Scarlett felt conflicted. While the news she would deliver had been the goal of the investigation, the fact that Marielle Devereau was in prison cast a chilling effect. When the doctor opened the door, it was obvious Anna had not slept. Dark circles underscored her eyes.

"Hey. Are you okay?" Scarlett said.

It was all she needed. The tears streamed down Anna's face.

"It's okay."

"No, it's not. Nothing is okay. I don't know what I've done."

"You haven't done anything except want to know who your family is."

"I've ruined my relationship with the only family I've ever known. I may have ruined my relationship with Dan. All for a strange person I don't know. Maybe I should have just left it all alone. Other adoptees don't chase their ancestors. I wanted to know who my mother was, but now I don't know if I want to see her. I don't know what to call anyone. All night long, I thought about meeting her. What do I say? Hello, Marielle? Hello, Mom? Neither one sounds right."

Scarlett moved closer and put her arms around Anna. "I can imagine how you feel. You've thought about it so much in the past weeks, probably fantasized about how thrilling it would be, and now it feels like an anticlimax. You've come this far. If you were to walk away, you might regret it. No matter what you decide to do, it should be based on how you feel. Not how Dan feels or anyone else feels." They stood without moving for a minute. "Anna, if Dan is the right man for you, he will get over it. If he doesn't, you haven't lost anything because sooner or later he would have failed the commitment. Better to know now, before you've wasted years with him—had children with him who would be torn in a divorce. Believe me, I'm a former divorce lawyer. No one wins in divorce, and the children lose the most."

"It wasn't supposed to be this way. When I found out I was adopted, I imagined an exciting reunion—meeting my birth parents. Did you ever see the show or movie *Annie?*"

"I did."

"Remember how she dreamed about her parents coming for her in the orphanage? I guess I felt like I was Annie and would have a huge happily ever after."

"Let's sit down." Scarlett glanced around the room. "I see you have the same coffee maker as in our suite. Can I make you a cup of coffee or tea?"

Anna nodded.

"You sit, and I'll make it."

When the tea was ready, Scarlett took it to Anna and then pulled the chair from the desk near the one where Anne sat. "It may sound silly to you, but I think I know how you feel. When I received my acceptance to Harvard Law, I was ecstatic for about an hour. And then I thought: What have I done? I'm going that far away from home—alone? At the time, I had a boyfriend I thought I was going to marry. We both applied. I was accepted; he wasn't. That didn't turn out well, or so I thought. But I was wrong. He showed who he really was. He cared more about himself than he cared about me."

"You broke up?"

"We broke up when I learned my twin sister was pregnant, and he was the father."

"Oh, my gosh."

"Exactly. He married her. We didn't speak for over twelve years and then I learned what a bullet I dodged. He made her life miserable. I don't know Dan or how he will handle all this, but what I do know is that if he doesn't support you, he's not the man you want to pledge your life to. In times of trouble is when the strength of character and commitment comes out."

Anna listened to Scarlett without speaking.

"As for Marielle, you don't have to meet her. You can walk away right now. Jake and I will find an innocence project to take over the quest to exonerate her. I promise we won't desert her. Don't feel guilty if you decide to walk. It's okay."

"She may be my mother. If she is, I can't walk away—no matter how I feel about it."

Scarlett took a breath. "Anna, I have something to tell you . . . . Marielle is your mother. The DNA results came back this morning."

"Oh!" She put her cup down and leaned back in the chair. "You know, I was almost hoping she wasn't. I know it sounds insane. I was thinking if she isn't my mother, I'll just stop the search. Try to go back to where I was a year ago when I didn't know I was adopted. How could I be thinking that when I have been determined to learn the truth? Am I crazy?"

"I'm not a psychologist, but I think you're just human. It's a big event—one most people never face. I think we all have doubts when we're about to take a big step. When I decided to leave the practice of law and work with Jake as an investigator, I was excited at the prospect of solving cases, doing detective work. But when I actually took the step, my stomach was so full of tension I couldn't eat. I woke in the middle of the night, thinking, what have I done? But it all worked out. I love what we do."

"I think there's something special between the two of you."

Scarlett smiled. "We won't go there."

"I am so confused, conflicted, and a little scared."

"Take your time. Maybe write down all the reasons to stop every-thing, and all the reasons to keep going. Like one of my law school professors drilled into us. It's about the balancing test. Weigh the pros and the cons."

CHAPTER 47

When Scarlett walked into their suite after leaving Anna, Pete was alone, working on a computer. "Where's Jake?"

"Walking Kai. Anything wrong? You look serious."

"No. Yes. Well, maybe. Anna is having a meltdown. She's questioning whether she wants to pursue meeting her mother."

"People are unpredictable. You just hand her your invoice, collect your fees, and move on to the next case."

"You know it's not that simple." She put her key card and cell phone on the dinette table and sat in one of the two plump chairs.

"I do. But whether she wants to move forward or not, you and Jake have the criminal situation to deal with. You were victims of a crime and are the state's key witnesses. Plus, you've collected evidence of another crime—all aside from working on the exoneration of your client's mother."

"How do you think Jake will react?"

"React to what," Jake said, coming in the room with Kai, who immediately darted across the room for attention from Scarlett.

Startled by his voice, she winced and then reached down to pet the K-9 as he reached her side.

"We're about to find out," Pete said.

"What are you two talking about? React to what?"

"Anna's having second thoughts," Scarlett said.

"So? You didn't think she would be affected? Her idiot boyfriend is giving her a hard time. Her mom's in prison, and her other mom may have murdered the child she was supposed to be. Damn heavy stuff. We've got a Zoom conference with the cops and the deputy solicitor at five-fifteen, and Liz found the director. He is living in a retirement community in Arizona. She set us up with a Zoom meeting with him at two o'clock."

"You're not disturbed by Anna's meltdown?" Scarlett said.

"No. Should I be? She'll get over it."

"And what makes you so sure?"

"Don't ask him that, Scarlett. He might tell you, but knowing him as long as I have, he's probably right."

Scarlett shook her head. "Maybe one day, I'll stop being surprised at how you think. So, Liz found Barnes Reddick. I'm amazed that he would do a Zoom meeting. His bio on IMDB, says he's in his eighties. I wouldn't think someone his age would be tech savvy."

"Turns out he has grandchildren living in Vermont that he likes to see on Zoom. His son in Arizona set him up with the equipment. It was his idea. He told Liz he likes to see who he's talking to. Sure makes our job easier and cheaper than traveling out there to interview him."

***

While Anna chose to stay in her room through lunch, Scarlett checked in on her, found she was feeling better, and coming back around to her original goal. Five minutes before two o'clock, Jake, Scarlett, and Pete sat in front of the large screen TV in the suite's living room. Jake had made a quick run to a nearby Walmart and purchased an HDMI cord to connect his laptop to the TV making it easy for all three to observe the subject. He also bought three folding TV tables for their computers. Shortly after opening the meeting, Barnes Reddick entered the waiting room, and Jake admitted him.

"Hello, Mr. Reddick. I'm Jake Shepherd, and I want to thank you for allowing us to speak with you. I have my associates, Scarlett Kavanagh and Pete Cooper, here with me. Do I have your permission to record this session?"

The man on the screen appeared younger than his years. He was immaculately groomed and wore a classic, Ralph Lauren oxford shirt in light blue with the sleeves rolled back to mid-arm. The color intensified the blue of his eyes and white of his hair.

"Record all you like. I don't get many calls for interviews these days. Your lady I spoke with said you want to talk about Vic Lanza. Is that right?"

Jake smiled. "That's right. We saw that you worked with him on a number of film and TV projects. I assume you knew him pretty well."

"Sorry thing that happened to him. I didn't even know it until after his funeral. When on a hiatus between seasons, I always headed to Europe in those days to backpack in the Alps. No phones, no harassment. Just me and nature. But what can I tell you about Vic? I did consider him a friend on and off the set."

"I'll try to give you a concise version. My associate, Scarlett Kavanagh, accepted a case with the purpose of locating the biological parents of a young woman who had recently learned she was adopted. As it turns out, Vic Lanza was her father."

"No. Vic had a child? You have proof of that?"

"We do. Through forensic genetic genealogy, we were able to trace her DNA to his immediate family. She has one-thousand, six-hundred, forty centimorgans in common with Lanza's sister, which denotes a sibling. Lanza had no brother. Subsequently, we also have DNA proof that the woman convicted of his homicide is her mother."

"Good, God! Who was the woman? I can't recall her name."

"Marielle Devereau."

"Oh, yes. I remember now. She was in the wardrobe department. Vic was fooling around with her, but I did not know that at the time. By the time I gained communications, Vic was buried, and the show was canceled. I read about her conviction but know only what I heard on the news. Replacing Vic in that role would have never worked."

"Mr. Reddick, we believe Marielle Devereau is innocent, so my questions to you are first, were you aware of any enemies Vic Lanza had? Did he owe anyone money?"

"Vic was a likeable guy. Considering his popularity, he was less egotistical than most. Now don't get me wrong, Vic was aware of his fame. The last show put him over the top. But he never flaunted his position. As for owing money, I don't think so. He made good money, didn't do drugs, no gambling issue."

"What about relationships? You say you didn't know about Ms. Devereau, were you aware of any other relationships? I understand he was never married."

"I only know of two. The first one got tired of waiting for a ring. She called it off. I can't remember her name, but they were a couple for several years. You should be able to find information about them in newspaper and magazine archives. Vic wasn't the type to settle down.

The last woman he dated had been his manager. She was older, a cougar before we knew there were cougars. It was a messy breakup. He ended up firing her and signing with a new manager."

"Was her name Delta Fontaine?"

"That's it. I remember now because her name always reminded me of that Tanya Tucker song, 'Delta Dawn.' I never understood the attraction, but who can account for chemistry? However, I would qualify that by saying, I suspected the relationship was always one-sided. She wanted him a lot more than he wanted her."

"You say the split was messy?"

"With a capital M."

"Can you describe what you mean by messy?"

"Vicious. Nasty letters, nasty phone messages, vandalism to his car—which couldn't be proved. She was an aggressive hothead with no boundaries—foul mouth as I recall."

"Did she ever spend time or even visit the mansion here in South Carolina?"

"I don't know how much time she spent there, but when the renovations were finished, Vic threw a big party to show it off. The entire cast and crew were invited. He loved showing that place off. Delta was there. What stands out most in my memory was his showing us the secret room."

"Secret room? Tell me about that. Where was it in the house, and how was it accessed?"

"People with houses of that era liked to have those rooms. It was in the library. One of the bookcases opens to a secret room. Probably used to hide in during the Civil War. Vic loved it. Probably bought the house because of it."

Jake made a note on the legal pad next to his laptop.

"Do you happen to know how the moveable bookcase worked?"

"Vic chose a certain book, wiggled it or tilted it, which released the mechanism. It was quite clever."

"You don't happen to remember the location of that book or the title, do you?"

"I don't."

"Was the book high, low, eye-level?"

"A little above my eye-level. I'm just shy of six feet tall."

"That is interesting. Going back to Delta Fontaine. She was angry about the breakup and an aggressive woman. Do you believe she could do serious harm—even kill?"

"Was she the type to kill someone? If you're asking me if she appeared to have the ability, that's going pretty far, but I would almost say yes. I felt a little bad for Vic when he was trying to shake her, but he chose to hook up with her. You reap what you sow as the cliche goes."

"Were there any other scorned women in his past, maybe wannabes or obsessed fans?"

"I only know of the two. He had a casual date here and there, but nothing extended. A lot of celebrities have stalkers. If Vic had a stalker, he never told me."

"What can you tell me about Carlos DeLuca?"

"Carl DeLuca? Oh, yeah. The weapons handler on the show. He was a friend of Vic's from the old neighborhood. They grew up in Little Italy, went to school there, and took acting classes together. When Vic's career took off, he tried to help Carl, but the acting thing never worked out for the guy. He liked guns and was good with them. So, Vic brought him on as the armorer on the show. He didn't come close to having Vic's charisma."

"Was there ever any trouble between them?"

"Funny you ask. I never got to talk to Vic about it, but Sharon, our showrunner, told me Vic insisted she not renew Carl's contract at the end of the last season. I have no idea what brought that about."

"Did she inform Carl he was being dropped?"

"She did."

"Did Carl know Vic was responsible for his losing the job?"

"I don't know. But I suspect he did. There are no secrets in the industry. Why are you interested in Carl?"

"His name came up in some of our research. Do you happen to know where he is now?"

"I don't. Here in Arizona, I'm out of the loop."

"Thank you for speaking with me today. I'm going to let you go now, but before I do, I have a favor to ask."

"What's that?"

"Would you send me a list of anyone you believe I should talk to about Fontaine and DeLuca?"

"I can do that, but I'll need to give it some thought. Nothing comes to mind right now."

"Thank you. Just use the email address that sent you the link to this meeting. And thank you again for your time."

CHAPTER 48

After Jake ended the meeting, Pete said, "Well, it looks like you've got yourself at least two persons of interest."

"You're damned right. Isn't love great? Two exes with plenty of motive to seek revenge against our victim," Jake said. "All we have to do is eliminate one and prove the other did it," Jake said. "I'd bet a year of my life that torn letter was written by Delta Fontaine."

"I'm not taking that bet. How many women could he piss off to that degree? But I'm leaning more to the guy as the trigger man." Pete held up a finger. "One, best friend steals his girlfriend—major betrayal there." He held up a second finger. "Two, the friend gets him fired. And three, if he wasn't the killer, why didn't he step forward to help Devereau? And don't forget, he had access to guns." He held up four fingers to emphasize his position.

"Strong case. But he might have thought she was guilty. Pete, that letter spews venom, suggests anger control issues, and expressly threatened to kill him. A female employee turned lover gets both dropped and loses a lucrative client. I'm sure you've heard the saying 'Hell hath no fury like a woman scorned.'"

"I feel like I'm at a gender reveal party," Scarlett said. "Pete says boy; Jake says girl."

"Guess you're the tie-breaking vote," Jake said, grinning. "But we both may be wrong. There may be someone else out there."

"If only solving a crime were as easy as taking a vote. But what if it was a collaboration? They both had grudges. Or even a murder for hire?" she said, tapping her fingers in a steady rhythm on her laptop.

"Well, that's a novel thought," Pete said. "But unlikely they would choose the same target. DeLuca was betrayed by both his friend and the woman he thought he had a relationship with. But would his motive have been revenge or eliminating the competition to get back in the game? On the other hand, Fontaine's motive would definitely be revenge on a theory of the bastard done me wrong."

Scarlett closed her laptop and stood. "I'll let you guys work on that. I'm going to do another check on Anna before the meeting with law enforcement."

Jake nodded, but Pete said, "I'm going to my room to check on the office and any correspondence I need to address. I'll be back before the Zoom call."

***

By the scheduled time, all parties were present for the meeting.

"We appreciate all of you working us into your busy schedules," Jake said as the last participant came on the screen. "I set this up to save time as I think you'll all want to know what we've learned as it pertains to each jurisdiction. The city of Charleston is also likely to be involved, but I don't have a contact in that agency. And Augusta, Georgia, may have a connected case. To wrap it all up, I'm going to need your help."

"Not a problem, Shepherd. You're a force to be reckoned with, and one we can't ignore," Rowland said. "Fire away. Whatcha got?"

"As it turns out, we have a couple of things working. At first glance, they may appear unrelated, but actually they do tie together. Lester, you may not know that we have found a connection between Paul Jorgensen and the event you've been investigating involving his employee holding Scarlett hostage. We found that the woman convicted of killing the celebrity, Victor Lanza, thirty-five years ago in Charleston County is our client's mother. Her name is Marielle Devereau, and Jorgensen was her attorney. Genetic genealogy points to Lanza as her father. We interviewed Devereau and believe she was wrongfully convicted."

"Now that's news," Rowland said. "Any evidence other than the woman's word?"

"At this point, it's more a matter of the lack of evidence showing she was the killer. Not to throw stones, but it's looking more and more like a rush to judgment. The people working the case had a terrified suspect who wasn't capable of helping her own defense because of a language barrier. Jorgensen did not speak French. She was polygraphed without an interpreter. Of course, she failed. And her attorney obviously took the easy way out of what might have been a difficult case by scaring her into accepting a plea."

"So, are you looking to file an appeal based on ineffective representation by counsel?" Curtis said.

"No. I'm looking to give you the person who actually committed the crime. That's what I do."

Pete grinned.

"Your lack of modesty is outweighed only by your skill, Shepherd," Rowland said. "So, who did it?"

"Not quite there—yet. But closing in."

"Are you implying that Jorgensen wants you out of the picture because he threw the case? Maybe covering up for the killer. You don't think he was the killer, do you?" Lester said.

"No. No, I'm not thinking that to either proposition. *But*—Jorgensen has something to hide all right. I don't think he killed Lanza or threw the case with malicious intent. What I think he did was opportunistic. He took the baby Marielle Devereau gave birth to in March of 1991 and gave her to the Cardens to replace the child they actually had the previous December. He ignored legal requirements. We believe that baby is most likely deceased. Hospital records will prove the date our client was born. We could not find her birth certificate as we had neither her true date of birth, nor her mother's name. I doubt the original birth certificate has a name for the baby, or if it does, it's fake."

"You have proof your client is Devereau's daughter?" the deputy solicitor Brad Curtis asked.

"Confirmed DNA evidence. I don't know how much you know about DNA units, but the lab found that our client and Marielle Devereau have three thousand four hundred and ten centimorgans in common. For the record, an individual has six thousand eight hundred centimorgans—half come from the mother and half from the father. Do the math, guys."

"You think he was using his employee to go after you because he what? Fraudulently placed a child in the custody of his relatives?" Curtis said.

"He may or may not have sent her. I suspect she operated on her own. But, yes, he fraudulently placed Anna with his relatives—no legal process. With Devereau facing life in prison, the baby would have to go to a relative or be put up for adoption. Devereau was a French national. No relatives in this country. He took the baby, promising to place her in a good home but filed no paperwork, no legal placement or adoption proceeding. I'm betting he knew something illegal had happened to the other baby that was never reported. How easy for them to simply move to another state, which they did, and give the Devereau baby the deceased baby's identity—name, Social Security number, birth date. Who would check? The few months difference in age would smooth its way out after a while. Throughout our client's lifetime, they passed her off as the biological baby they actually had."

"My, god, what a case," Lester said.

"You think he set his client up to take the fall to get the baby?" Rowland asked.

"No. I think whatever happened to the real Anna-Claire Carden, abuse, accident, whatever, occurred at the right time for the substitution. All this is easily proved with a look into the records. You don't even have to take Devereau's word for it. No one else could have visited a prisoner in the hospital but her lawyer. That's where Lester and possibly Charleston PD come into play. Devereau gave birth in a hospital in the heart of Charleston. While the county had jurisdiction over the mother, the site of birth would be the proper jurisdiction for the child. I'm going to leave it to you guys to follow up on that. This is also your prosecutorial jurisdiction, Curtis. Am I right?"

"Absolutely right. I'm going to have a team of Charleston PD detectives assigned and call Mr. Jorgensen in for a chat. I have a question as to why an upstanding attorney would risk his reputation and criminal charges to participate in the switch for members of his wife's family."

"Maybe you can get that out of him in an interrogation," said Jake.

"So, we fit into your investigation by talking to Jorgensen?" Lester said. "I see Charleston County with the question of exoneration and the city of Charleston needing to probe into Jorgensen's misconduct, but North Charleston only has the case against Barbara Malone."

"But you can explore Malone's motive to strengthen your case." Jake took a sip from a can of Pepsi. "I'm betting she knows what Jorgensen did. Only explanation for her bold assault on Scarlett. In some moment of weakness, he confessed to her. Curtis, you have leverage, which might come in handy. I know you are bound by the speedy trial rule, but don't push it or offer her a plea deal until we have Jorgensen nailed. If he refuses to cooperate, she may be the weak link."

"That leaves me," Rowland said. "I'm sure you've got something in mind."

"Funny you should ask. Yes. You helped me with the intro to the director at the Marley Museum, which worked out well, but I want to be able to do a search of the entire building—with Cooper and my K-9. Can you and Curtis get a warrant to cover all but the private property of employees such as their desks, file cabinets, and lockers? A friendly judge should be able to see that no one's rights would be violated. The owner of the property was the victim, and he is deceased. We will not violate the privacy of the museum employees as the locations of their personal property will be precluded from the search. That leaves only the unsub. Anything he or she left should be characterized as both abandoned and evidence of a crime."

"What are you looking for?"

"It's a crime scene. I'll know it when I see it. However, I need a little more than just permission from the director. I need to have someone from your department along to protect the integrity of anything I find. I want no challenges to authenticity and chain of custody."

"You really think you're going to find evidence of a murder that occurred that long ago?" Curtis said.

"I won't know until I look. But if something is there, I assume you'd also want it found."

"Of course, I would. We all would."

"If I find something that needs testing, Curtis, can I rely on you to make that request?"

"It is not my job, desire, or character to keep an innocent person in prison. I can't reopen the case at this point, but if you show up with credible evidence, I'll see that it is properly processed and preserved."

CHAPTER 49

With the Zoom meeting wrapped up, Scarlett closed her computer and stood. "I'm going to check on Anna."

"How long is she planning to stay?" Jake said.

"I'll find out. She's not really doing anything here but maybe decompressing. I don't think Marielle is ready to meet her, so there's really no reason for her to stay."

"She may be testing her relationship with the doctor," Pete said.

Scarlett thought for a minute. "You could be right."

"Invite her to join us for dinner. I'm thinking about the Italian restaurant with outdoor seating so we can take Kai with us," Jake said.

"Good idea. She can't keep staying in her room alone. But I need to be available at seven-thirty for a potential call from Marielle, which would be awkward at the restaurant."

"She doesn't know about the DNA results, does she?" Pete said.

"Not yet. She can't receive calls. I plan to tell her tonight. I would prefer to tell her in person, but with the drive there and back taking over six hours, it's a full day event just to tell her one thing."

***

Anna met Scarlett at the door, her makeup fresh, hair neatly tucked into a ponytail, and wearing a red gingham shirt with jeans. She looked more like a pretty college student than a physician.

"You look better than when I left you," Scarlett said.

"I am much better. Come on in."

Anna sat on the edge of her bed, while Scarlett settled on the upholstered chair. "Have you talked to Dan?"

"He's left messages, but I haven't returned any. He needs to think a little more, but he is coming around. He says he doesn't want to lose me."

"That's a good thing."

"I think it is, Scarlett. But he needs to develop a little more compassion. I thought about what you said, and you're right. I need to pay attention to how he reacts before I marry him, regardless of how much I'm in love with him. I don't need more drama in my life."

"I hope it works out for you. I came to not only check on you but to invite you to go with us for dinner. We're going to an Italian restaurant we've enjoyed since we've been here."

"Thank you. I would like that. But I need to tell you that I want to confront Paul tonight or tomorrow with what you've learned. I want answers from him."

Scarlett slowly shook her head. "I don't think that's a good idea, Anna. He won't like being backed into a corner. He knows what he did."

"I have to. He arranged the transfer. He allowed me to believe I was someone I wasn't for my entire life. And what did my parents do to the real Anna? Did he cover up a crime for them? He knows what happened to that baby. I doubt they rehomed her like a pet no longer wanted."

Scarlett stood. "Let's go to dinner, and we'll talk about it with the guys. I don't think Jake is going to want you to confront Jorgensen alone."

As she slid off the bed, Anna smiled, and said, "Sounds good. I'll grab my purse."

***

Once the server left the table with their dinner orders, Scarlett brought up Anna's desire to confront Paul Jorgensen, evoking a frown from Jake.

"Paul Jorgensen committed a crime he knows is about to be exposed. A position like that can push someone to commit an act out of character. Let law enforcement handle him."

"He might tell me something he won't tell the police. I want to know what happened to the real Anna-Claire Carden."

"It's not worth him going off the rails and possibly harming you. I can't stop you, but I can't—"

"Jake," Scarlett interrupted him. "What if Pete went with her? Neither of us could go because he knows we're investigating her birth, but he doesn't know Pete."

They all turned toward Pete.

"Create an excuse for me to be with her, and I'm onboard."

Anna spoke up. "I could say you're an uncle of Dan's who is driving me to the airport because Dan got a call from the hospital and had to fly home."

"Good call," Jake said as the server arrived with drink orders. "But this confrontation is better done tomorrow at his office. The environment should keep him civil."

***

The group arrived back at the hotel shortly after seven o'clock and dispersed to their rooms. At seven-thirty, Scarlett's phone rang. Glancing down at the caller ID, she said, "It's from Leath—Marielle."

Marielle came on the line after Scarlett accepted the call and immediately asked if the DNA results were provided.

"I got them earlier today. You are a match, Marielle."

The phone was silent for several seconds. When she finally spoke, her voice quivered. "She's my daughter?"

"She is definitely your daughter."

"I've dreamed of a moment like this, never believing it would happen, and now I don't know what to say except does she know?"

"She does, and you don't have to say anything."

"How did Anna react?"

"It was both thrilling and startling to finally know who she is. But I also have some other news. Jake talked to Barnes Reddick about Vic. Do you remember him?"

"Oh, yes. He was the director on the show. Mr. Shepherd talked to him?"

"He did. Reddick provided some interesting facts about Vic and his relationships. We've also had an online meeting with police and a local prosecutor about your case. We're looking at a couple of suspects in the death of Vic as well as the misconduct of Paul Jorgensen in giving

Anna to his relatives. A lot is happening. Have you given any thought to meeting Anna?"

Again, there was a delay in Marielle's response. "I've given it a lot of thought, Ms. Kavanagh. As much as I want to meet her, I can't meet her here in prison, wearing prison clothes—not the first time. Please help her understand that I do want to see her, but I want it to be beautiful. You've been here. You know what this place is like—how I look."

"I think I do know how you feel. There's time. Maybe you can talk to her."

"I don't know what to say. Not yet."

After Scarlett ended the call, she looked across at Jake. "I don't think I realized the emotional impact this would have on both Anna and Marielle. It's probably better that neither wants to rush into a meeting."

"You're the investigator with a finger on the emotional aspects of a case, Harvard. While you were on the phone with Devereau, I received a text from Lester. Curtis has invited Jorgensen in for a chat with him, Lester, and Cannady on Wednesday morning, which means Jorgensen will likely be rattled when Anna and Pete see him tomorrow."

CHAPTER 50

As planned, Pete and Anna made the trip to Paul Jorgensen's office on Tuesday morning. When she reached the desk of his receptionist, Anna said she was on her way back to D.C. and wanted to say a quick goodbye. The woman said Jorgensen had not come in. After waiting for the woman to make calls to Jorgensen and receiving no answer, Anna gave up on seeing him and they returned to the hotel. Scarlett and Jake were in the restaurant having an early lunch.

"He wasn't in his office," Anna said as she reached the Shepherd table.

"He wasn't there?" Scarlett motioned for them to sit.

"No. And they couldn't reach him," Anna said, taking a chair between Scarlett and Jake. "Penny, the receptionist, tried his cell, the house phone, and even called Robin."

"The call from Curtis must have spooked him," Jake said.

"Enough to put him in the wind?" Pete said.

"Guilt is a tough burden to bear. He's smart enough to know that the records are going to expose him, but run? That would surprise me. By the way, Brad Curtis got a warrant to search the mansion and set it up for this afternoon. Rowland is providing a detective to lead it but told the guy it's our search. It's one of the detectives we met at the daycare shooting. We're to meet him there at two o'clock. I know it pushes us, but they assured the judge we wouldn't shut the museum down for a decades-old fishing expedition. So it's today or wait a week since Tuesday is the day the place is regularly closed."

Wide-eyed, Anna listened intently until a lull came in the conversation. "Dan is having a hard time understanding why this is all so important to me and why I'm willing to spend so much money on it, but I think I am more determined than ever." She hesitated, looking around the room but not appearing to focus. "Last night, my mind played out all the things that changed my life and wondered what it would have been like if any one of those things never happened. If someone hadn't killed my father, would my parents have married? If my uncle, my phony uncle, had worked harder to clear my mother, would I have grown up with her? And if my uncle hadn't given me to the Cardens like a puppy, where would I be? I thought about the person who killed my father and got away with it, and an anger I've never felt in my life took control of me. I was denied the chance to know and maybe really love my true father." She picked up the knife in front of her and began twirling it on the table like a top. "Dan says he doesn't want to lose me, and he will try to understand. But I am not setting a date for a wedding until I know he really understands, until I have a name, and until my true mother can be at the wedding. Am I wrong?"

Neither man responded, leaving the floor to Scarlett. "I can only guess how deep your feelings are, Anna. But I don't think anything you just said is unreasonable. You have to live with the decisions you make now for the rest of your life. I might not should say this, but I don't think you should compromise your inner feelings."

Jake looked at Scarlett with an obvious sense of admiration. "I'm an insensitive kind of guy, Anna, as anyone will tell you. But what Scarlett said makes sense to me."

"Thank you. I want you to do everything you possibly can to find out who killed my father and free my mother. I trust"—she looked around at each one—"all of you. I believe you are smart and good at what you do. I've also decided to go back home and let you do your thing. I've made a reservation to return to D.C. tonight. Scarlett told me that Marielle is not ready for a meeting, so, there's no point in my staying. I would like to see the mansion that was my father's home, but it's not going anywhere. I think it's best I leave. I'm sure I'll be coming back, and I'll confront Paul then if there's still no information on what happened to the other Anna."

"What time is your flight?" Scarlett asked.

"Seven forty-five."

***

Traffic almost caused the team to be late. When they arrived at the museum, Detective John Blackwell was sitting in his car on the circular drive in front of the massive structure. Jake parked the Yukon directly behind him. A landscaping crew was scattered around the property, cutting grass, working the flower beds, and doing routine grounds maintenance. As the detective exited his car, Jake, Scarlett, and Pete opened their doors, got out, along with Kai, who wore a vest bearing the phrase: K-9 Certified.

"Extending his hand, Jake said, "Jake Shepherd, and you're Detective Blackwell. Right?"

Blackwell shook Jake's hand. "Guilty. I saw you guys at the daycare shooting, and I've heard a lot about you the last few days. Happy to meet"—He looked toward Pete—"and you must be Peter Cooper, retired FBI negotiator, right?"

Pete nodded and shook hands with the detective.

"And this is my associate, Scarlett Kavanagh," Jake said.

After acknowledging Scarlett, Blackwell looked down at Kai, who emitted a low growl as Pete passed the lead to Jake. Jake issued an order in German to calm the dog.

Blackwell said, "A working dog, I take it."

"He is," Jake said. "Certified multi purpose—detection, tracking, and security. He alerted for your weapon."

"Handsome animal." He reached in the chest pocket of his jacket and took out a folded piece of paper. "I've got the warrant right here. Our contact is the property manager. His office is over the carriage house turned garage in the back. He knows we are coming. If you're ready to get started, I'll give him a call to come let us in."

"Let's rock and roll," Jake said.

After Blackwell made the call, the group started up the stairs toward the building's entry. As they reached the grand portico, Blackwell said, "I hear you're working to exonerate a woman convicted thirty-five years ago of killing a guy in this house. What are you looking for? It's hard to believe there would be any evidence here after all that time."

"It's a long shot. I'll give you that. But I tend to be a bit anal. It never hurts to check it out. Have you looked at the old file?"

"I haven't. I just got the assignment this morning."

"It's pretty thin. After going through it, I was surprised a prosecutor filed the charge and even more surprised that the defense attorney agreed to a plea. I clerked for one of the best defense attorneys in the country and served a couple of years as an Assistant U.S. Attorney before going into the FBI."

"Impressive. You think there was a coverup or conspiracy?"

"Not necessarily. I suspect there was a lot of media pressure on the case and a convenient suspect. It happens, unfortunately. Law enforcement anxious to solve the case meets a defense attorney who doesn't put up resistance."

Jake hardly finished his sentence when a golf cart came around the corner of the building. "Has this guy got a name?"

Blackwell grinned. "Most people do. It's Carson. George Carson."

"I think we sort of met him the last time we were here," Jake said. Before we go in, you need to check that we are not taking anything in with us but what we're wearing, gloves, our phones, flashlights, my keys, and papers with research on the place." Jake began turning his pockets inside out as did Pete. "We want no questions raised concerning the integrity and authenticity of any evidence we find."

"Knock yourself out."

As Carson reached the stone entry, Blackwell took out his credentials and held them up. "Mr. Carson, I'm Detective Blackwell, Charleston County Sheriff's Office." From the inside breast pocket of his jacket, he removed a folded paper. "Here is a copy of the search warrant for your files. And these folks are Jake Shepherd, Pete Cooper, and—"

"Scarlett Kavanagh," Scarlett said.

"They are private investigators from D.C. We'll try not to take too much of your time. As you can see from the warrant, we'll be looking around the building but avoiding any areas of personal space belonging to the staff."

CHAPTER 51

O nce inside the museum, Blackwell said, "Where do you want to start? Bottom up or top down?"

"Second floor," Jake said. "The top floor burned and was totally repaired and renovated. I doubt anything remains of what was there back then. The victim was shot on the second floor according to the file. We'll start there. The murder weapon was never found and no shell casings, indicating it was probably a revolver. Not likely that the assailant would pick up casings if the place had caught fire. He or she would want to get out."

"How was the fire started?" Blackwell asked.

"According to the arson investigator's report, the fire started from a candle being knocked over and igniting a flammable fabric on a piece of furniture, which traveled to the drapes, probably pretty quickly. Fire travels upward, so the first floor was spared."

***

A search of the second floor produced nothing of interest, which Jake expected. Once on the first floor, his attention was directed to the library where he expected to find the secret room described by Barnes Reddick.

As they entered the wood paneled room, Pete said, "That is a hell of a lot of books. Some of them look like they might go back to the original owners of this place, but most look fairly modern. You think Lanza was that big of a reader?"

"Not necessarily," Scarlett said. "I've read there are companies that stock libraries with any type of books you like. They do it for movie sets but also for private homes who want an instant library."

"Reddick said pulling a certain book releases the mechanism controlling the movement of the bookcase. All we have to do is find that book," Jake said.

With a quick survey of the room, Blackwell said, "There's a lot of books in here."

"I think we can narrow it down by eliminating the front wall," Pete said. "That window indicates there's no hidden space between the bookcase and the outside wall."

"And the same would be true for the wall dividing the library and the entry hall," Scarlett said.

Blackwell surveyed the entire area. "You're looking for a secret room in here and need to find a specific book to gain access. Good luck with that. And what makes you think there would be any evidence to help your case if you find it?"

Jake ran his fingers across the row of books. "No forced entry equals victim likely knew attacker. Classic homicide one-o-one. According to a witness, Lanza showed off the room to his guests, which suggests a known unsub would have knowledge of the secret room."

"Are you thinking you're going to find the murder weapon in this so-called secret room?"

"Probably not, but gotta look."

"That's why you brought the dog."

"Never underestimate Jake," Pete said. "He's got instincts the rest of us read about."

"It's not rocket science. Look at it this way. I just shot a guy. The house is on fire. No doubt this place could have a fire alarm that's going to send a signal to the fire department and the cops. Even if I get out, I could be stopped, and I don't want to be caught with the weapon. So, what do I do? Ditch it where it's not likely to be found—at least not for a long time."

"Thirty-five years and counting?"

"Guns don't decompose, dissolve, or self-destruct." Jake worked the wall of books to the right of the entry, searching for the magic book.

"And what about the renovations? Wouldn't a weapon have been discovered?"

"The first floor escaped the fire," Jake said. "No need for reconstruction, but no sense debating. We'll see soon enough. Might be absolutely nothing. This has got to be the wall. It's the only one where a space would be disguised. Who could tell if five or so feet existed between this room and the music room on the other side?"

"Jake, I think I've found it," Scarlett said from her position near the far end of the wall. "This book isn't a book. It's wooden with a book cover, and it's next to the side of the bookcase."

Jake moved over to where she was, with the other two following.

"Well done, Harvard." He pulled the book, but it seemed attached. So, he removed a couple of books from the side of his target, jiggled the wooden book, and tilted it outward. The latch sprung loose, allowing the case to pop slightly forward. "You found it, Harvard."

"Damn. I didn't know they had such mechanical skills in that century," Pete said. "How many people have been in and through this place and never knew that was here?"

Jake pulled the case to fully open the entry. It was dark inside. "Obviously, they were crafty but no electricity in here." Jake took the flashlight from a holster on his belt and proceeded in, Kai at his heels.

"By the time electricity was invented, this room was probably forgotten and didn't get wired," Pete said.

The room ran the length of the library wall and was approximately seven feet wide. It contained no furniture. "Lanza must have cleaned out anything in here from its history," Jake said.

All of a sudden, Kai began barking.

CHAPTER 52

The shepherd's bark was ear piercing as it reverberated in the empty room with concrete walls.

"What's got him riled?" Pete said as Kai positioned himself over the floor at the end of the room that bordered the exterior.

"He's alerting. He knows there's something here," Jake said.

"The room is empty, Shepherd. He's barking at nothing," Blackwell said.

"He doesn't do that."

He doesn't," Scarlett said.

"Look around. There's nothing in here," Blackwell said.

Jake shone his light on the floor where Kai was positioned. "There's something under this room."

"Well, even if there is, you're not going to get to it from here," Blackwell said, shining his flashlight around the floor. "There's no trap door in this wood floor."

"Take a closer look. The planks of this floor are cut in what? Three-foot pieces. Not the way a hardwood floor is usually done. Why get fancy in a room no one sees with crude walls. I'm betting Kai is standing on a removable section." He gave Kai the command to stop barking, lightly pulled him away from where he had been, and turned to Pete who was closest. "Hold Kai's lead for me and give me some light."

Jake made a fist and began tapping the floor until a section wiggled. "Here it is. Blackwell, do you have a knife on you I can use to pry it up and get a grip on this section?"

The detective reached into his pocket and took out a knife and passed it to Jake through Pete.

Once Jake had the section repositioned, a set of open steps, leading down about seven feet, became visible. "Here I go. Hold on to Kai, and keep the light handy."

"Ten-four," Pete said.

When Jake reached the floor of the cellar, he flashed his light around. Spider webs were abundant.

"What's down there, Shepherd?" Pete called out.

"Empty shelves. A few wooden crates." He pulled a crate slightly off the lower shelf and shone his light inside. "Some empty wood boxes. Maybe used to store food back before supermarkets—probably potatoes." The bottom shelves were about six inches above the stone floor. Jake got down on his knees and flashed the light underneath.

"Bloody F-ing damn!" He said aloud to himself reacting to something white, pushed back under the shelf. "Got something," he shouted.

Blackwell instantly responded. "What? What have you found?"

"I'm about to find out." With his flashlight on the floor, he reached a gloved hand under the shelf and eased the item out. Once his find was in front of him, Jake paused, staring at it.

"Shepherd, what have you got?" Blackwell called out.

Jake didn't immediately respond.

"Shepherd, what the hell? Tell us what you have."

"The Comstock Lode. Blackwell, bring me an evidence bag." He took his cell out of his pocket and snapped several photos of the discovery.

Blackwell immediately went down the crude stairs, shining his light in front of him. "What have you found?"

Jake moved aside so the detective could see the revolver laying on a man's white handkerchief. "Smith & Wesson 38. Bag it and be careful with both the gun and the handkerchief. I'm thinking a good chance DNA could have survived in these conditions."

"F-ing shit. You were right," Blackwell said.

"I usually am. With a bit of luck, there may be enough DNA for a profile."

"Touch DNA couldn't have survived this long."

"I'm not thinking touch. That handkerchief could have sweat, mucus, spit whatever. The assailant probably used it in an attempt to wipe the gun clean of fingerprints. Not many perps were thinking DNA back then. Any cartridges remaining in the cylinder just might have a usable print."

"Does the caliber match up for your homicide?"

"Yep. But I think it's technically *your* homicide—my exoneration project."

"It could be your client's DNA on that handkerchief."

"It could be, but I seriously doubt it. Be sure the lab analyzes the DNA for gender," Jake said.

"Why? Do you have a suspect?"

"Let's just say I have a couple of persons of interest. Gender could help with elimination. And one more thing. How about taking this beauty to your car *before* you call George to lock up? No need for anyone else to know about it right now."

"Got it."

Blackwell led the way back up the stairs and as the detective neared the secret room, Kai went into attack mode.

Pete called out, "Jake, what's the word to calm Kai?"

"*Ruhig.*"

***

As the trio, plus Kai, was entering the SUV for the trip back to the hotel, Jake's phone rang.

"Detective Lester. What can I do for you?"

Jake stood by the vehicle, an intense expression forming on his face as he listened. "That is a shock. Who found him?" He turned his head toward the inside of the SUV. "Thank you for letting me know. I'll be in touch soon." Tucking the phone back in his pocket, he got into the driver's seat of the vehicle and closed the door.

Scarlett stared at him, waiting for him to speak. "Is something wrong? Who was that on the phone?" she asked.

"Lester. Jorgensen is dead. Took his own life. The Malone woman found him at his beach house this afternoon."

She gasped. "Oh, my gosh. How?"

"Carbon monoxide."

CHAPTER 53

Except for the panting of Kai, the car was silent for the first fifteen minutes of the drive back to the hotel. As they neared a turn, Scarlett said, "With Jorgensen gone and his wife with dementia, we'll never find out what happened to the real Anna."

Jake glanced her way. "Maybe not. But there's a good chance Myrtle knows."

The conversation aroused Kai's interest. He moved forward, stuck his head over the center console, and nuzzled Scarlett for attention. She reached across and rubbed his chest with her right hand. "You think she would tell?"

"Who knows. But she's got a pretty serious charge hanging over her. Curtis could help with getting her to give it up. What do you think, Pete?"

"Good leverage for a plea negotiation. It can't hurt Jorgensen now."

"I hope Anna doesn't blame herself for his suicide. I can see her doing that."

"From what I saw of her yesterday, I think her anger will mitigate any guilt," Jake said.

"Did Lester say whether they found a suicide note?" Pete asked.

"Didn't mention one, but I'm going to talk to him tomorrow."

Pete removed his sunglasses and rubbed his eyes. "I'm gonna admit, although I know you have instincts like an African bush elephant, I did not expect you to literally find the smoking gun. Of course, the credit goes to Kai for finding it."

At the sound of his name, the shepherd turned his head toward Pete.

"Blackwell was F-ing gobsmacked. The color literally left his face."

"African bush elephant? Didn't know they were known for instincts," Jake said. "But yeah. I'm expecting Charleston Sheriff's Office to have a ballistics report within a few days. Blackwell said he would push to expedite all the lab work despite the age of the case. Speedy exoneration should be a priority but I'm not sure it is."

"How long do you think it will take to get results from the DNA analysis if they are able to recover DNA from the handkerchief or the gun?" Scarlett asked.

"Hopefully, within a few days, but no way to know. Blackwell said he would petition for it to be sent to one of the best private labs, and I said we would help with the cost if necessary."

"If they do the gender thing you asked for, that could eliminate one of the suspects and maybe solve the case," she said.

"I am not sure about that. I think we'd be making a mistake to only look at those two. As I'm thinking about means, motive, and opportunity, I'm not sure those two fit. Motive looks like a given. Means definitely works with DeLuca without too much digging, but *opportunity?* That is the wildcard. I want to take a look for any others who might check all the boxes. You can help me with that, Pete."

✳✳✳

It was after six o'clock when Jake pulled the SUV into the hotel parking lot. "You guys want to do room service or find a restaurant?"

"It's been a full day for an old man," Pete said. "I'll opt to eat in tonight. Kai can stay with me if the two of you want to go out."

Scarlett glanced down at her watch. "I'm sure Anna has gone. I'm fine either way."

"I think a quiet night sounds good. Let's put the case aside and relax tonight," Jake said.

***

On Wednesday morning, Jake and Scarlett waited for Pete in the hotel restaurant before placing their breakfast order.

"Here he comes," Scarlett said, raising her hand to signal Pete Cooper.

"Good morning," Pete said as he pulled a chair out to sit. "Everyone cool today after the events of yesterday?"

"All good," Jake said.

"What's on your calendar?"

Jake slid a menu over to Pete and said, "I hope to find out a little more about Jorgensen's suicide from Lester and to talk to Curtis about using Barbara Malone's criminal charges to extract information about Jorgensen's role in the client's custody. I think Scarlett is working with Liz to find out as much as possible about Fontaine and DeLuca."

"How much longer do you expect to remain in Charleston?" Pete said as he poured himself a cup of coffee from the carafe.

"Scarlett and I were talking about returning home tomorrow, but I haven't decided. While there's not much more we can do here until the lab results are in, I do have a couple of thoughts I want to check out."

"What are you thinking? If they do the gender thing you asked for, it should eliminate one of the suspects and solve the case."

"Maybe. But like I said, I think we'd be making a mistake only to look at those two. Tracking the registration on that gun could tell something about who had possession of it. I think Rowland will pursue ownership, but I was able to see the serial number and snap a photo of it. I'm going to have Liz run it through any of the sources she has the ability to access. But opportunity is the wildcard. Just because those two may have wanted him dead, doesn't rule out the possibility of someone else doing the job."

"Where do you plan to start today?" Pete said.

"Do a deeper look at any other known enemies? Did he have any stalkers—a deranged fan? Who had opportunity? You can help me with that."

"I'm sure it has crossed your mind that the model of that weapon was the most popular gun for law enforcement, military, and private security at the time."

"That it has. But it was also sold in the private sector. How about you pull up videos of Lanza's cop show? See if you can tell what model gun he carried on the show that DeLuca would have had access to as the armorer."

CHAPTER 54

By four-thirty, Scarlett had closed her computer and announced aloud, even though she was alone in the suite, she was done for the day. Her research found Carlos DeLuca disappeared from the film industry after Lanza's death. He seemed to totally disappear.

After preparing a cup of tea, she sat back in a plump chair with her feet on an ottoman. She was about to switch the TV on when Jake came in the door.

"How did your visit with Curtis go?"

"I think we're on the same page. He did say the baseball cap we found at the museum had enough DNA for a profile but no match in CODIS or the state database. Lester stopped by while I was there and filled us in on a little more about Jorgensen."

She put her cup down on the table beside her chair. "Really. What did he say?"

Jake walked over to the refrigerator and took out a can of Pepsi. After popping the top and taking a swig, he sat down on the sofa perpendicular to her chair.

"He left a note, but it didn't say much—only that he was sorry for any pain he caused his family, but he was in a place of no return. Certainly nothing about Anna or Devereau."

"What did that mean?"

"Good question. Lester said his daughter, the one we met, told them he had recently been diagnosed with pancreatic cancer, which she believes caused his suicide. Although Jorgensen assured her it was caught early, and he expected to beat it, she thinks it may have been more advanced than he admitted."

"Could he have been making that up in case we uncovered the truth of what he did with Anna?"

"Of course it's a possibility, but he might have been telling the truth."

"Knowing he was seriously ill should help Anna avoid guilt, but unless he told Barbara Malone the whole story, the chances of knowing what happened to the other baby died with him." She took a sip of her tea and gazed out the window.

"He dodged the humiliation and disgrace of a potential arrest and the possibility of spending what life he had left behind bars. As for the mystery baby, I suggested to Curtis that he try for a warrant to take cadaver dogs to the house where the Cardens lived when their baby was born."

She turned back toward him. "You think they killed the baby and buried her in their yard? That gives me chills."

"Strange as it may seem, the backyard turns up as the burial site for a lot of victims. It avoids the risk of being stopped in a vehicle with a body."

"Did you talk to Brad Curtis about Barbara Malone—what she knows about Jorgensen and Anna?"

"I did. He's onboard with our investigation but he's not the top man in his department. He said he'll support us any way he can but doesn't expect his superiors to give him the go ahead to reopen Devereau's case. He will try to get information about the custody arrangement. He said he will offer her a deal in exchange for information if you, as her victim, agree. What did you and Liz turn up today on Fontaine and DeLuca?"

After filling him on what little she learned about DeLuca, she said, "Liz found out Delta Fontaine also left the entertainment industry not long after Lanza's death. She moved back to Indiana where she was from and worked in real estate. She married, but it didn't last. No children. Apparently, she took her aggressive attitude with her because she had two Orders for Protection entered against her. One for a neighbor she threatened, and one for her ex during the divorce. Liz emailed me copies of the court papers. No criminal record other than traffic violations. She's in her seventies now but still working part-time. She looks like a stronger candidate for our killer than DeLuca."

"Interesting." He took out his phone and tapped a contact. "Pete, I'm back. Want to come to the suite, and we check out what we all have?"

Pete was at the suite within a minute, carrying a portfolio.

"Come on in. Want something to drink?" Jake said after opening the door."

"I'm good." He walked across the room to where Scarlett sat and was greeted by Kai. Addressing Scarlett, Pete said, "Hello, pretty lady. How was your day?"

"Pretty good. And yours?"

"I've seen enough of Vic Lanza to last me the rest of my life, but overall, it went well."

"Let's spread out at the table," Jake said.

Once seated, Scarlett and Jake shared their data for the day and waited as Pete opened his notes.

"Lanza did carry what looks to be a Smith & Wesson revolver. The few times he drew the weapon on the show, either the scene was too dark, or the camera did not move in close enough for me to identify the gun until an episode in the fourth season. After reviewing all those TV shows, I tracked security companies in the area until I found the one who provided services to Lanza. As expected, the guy I spoke with could not give me names of their employees without a court order, but I did get him to say that the company provides weapons to their armed guards. The guards are also free to carry personal weapons upon approval. The ballistics report is vital for multiple reasons. You have the serial number. If it is determined to be the murder weapon, it should be traceable to who purchased it, but it will take a subpoena, warrant, or court order. The good thing is the manufacturer should have the information."

"While Fontaine and DeLuca are looking good for the homicide, we can't close the door on the perp being someone else," Jake said. "Thanks for looking into the security company, Pete. They come up first on my list of those to consider. Access and opportunity are givens. Motive? Not so obvious. We need to at least look at any household staff such as housecleaners, but especially the security details. They would have had the most knowledge of the property, security system, routine, and access to entry keys."

"Motive will be the big question, but sometimes people in those categories have sticky fingers," Pete said.

"I understand you don't want to think security guard since we are in the business, but a dirty bodyguard is just as possible as a dirty cop. Until we have a definite suspect, we should look at eliminating anyone with access to the house." Jake's cell vibrated in his pocket. Taking it

out, he read the caller ID and said, frowning, "This should be fun."
Opening the call, he said, "Jackie. What can I do for you?" Pointing to
the phone, he mouthed his ex-wife's name for Scarlett and Pete as if
they had not heard him address her.

"Good that you called. I was about to tell the team since we're in
a holding pattern down here waiting for test results, we need to trek
back to Virginia for the weekend. I have some stuff to do up there.
Sabrina can spend the weekend at my place. You and the ASAC can
have your weekend getaway."

Scarlett and Pete exchanged puzzled looks.

He ended the conversation with, "Now see how easy that was."
After terminating the call, he shrugged and said to Scarlett and Pete,
"We don't really have anything to do here until we get the ballistics and
DNA reports. Curtis is meeting with Malone's defense counsel next
week to talk plea deal." Shifting his focus to Scarlett, he said, "When is
that concert you're chaperoning for Sabrina?"

"It's a little over four weeks away. What do you need to do in
Virginia?"

"I want to meet with Phil Madison about the legal steps in securing
an overturn of Marielle's conviction once we have sufficient evidence.
And remind me to keep the time clear for you to be in the D.C. area
for that concert. Pete, do you have any problem with driving back
tomorrow?"

"None. Works for me. I need to check in at the office."

Scarlett stood up and took her empty teacup to the trash bin under
the sink in the kitchenette. "I'm really glad we're going home. Casper
and Ebony need to know I'm still alive and well."

"Casper and Ebony?" Pete said.

"Scarlett's cats."

"Okay. By the way, don't you have a rabbit?" he said to Jake.

"A rabbit lives with me. It's not my rabbit. It's Sabrina's, which fricking duckhead Kirby won't let her have at their house."

CHAPTER 55

After spending the weekend in Virginia, the trio, plus Kai, drove back to South Carolina on Monday. To streamline the trip, Jake had retained their hotel accommodations and chose to drive the rental GMC Yukon with its eight-passenger capacity. Pete left his Rav4 in the hotel parking lot. While stopped for a lunch break, Jake's phone rang. He answered, laying the cell on the outdoor table with the speaker activated.

"Blackwell. Have you got something for me?"

"You're gonna like this, Shepherd. We got the ballistics, and you were right. It's a match."

Jake nodded toward Pete and Scarlett with an I-told-you-so expression on his face. "Good to hear. Any evidence found on it or the cartridges?"

"You're gonna love this even more. They were able to lift a couple of prints on the cartridges but no match in the FBI's IAFIS database, which means your lady probably didn't load it."

A big smile zipped across Scarlett's face.

"And increases the probability she didn't fire it," Jake said.

"Not gonna argue about that. You're too damn prophetic. Are you still in Charleston?"

"We're on our way back. We're at the border having a quick bite. Any word on the DNA?"

"Not yet. I'll keep you posted."

"Scarlett and I will be in Curtis' office tomorrow before his plea negotiation conference with Malone's lawyer. Have you given Curtis this info? He's having trouble getting his boss to take our exoneration case serious."

"I've had the reports emailed to him. I'm not surprised he's having that trouble. The guy's tough, and you know how reluctant most all agencies are to have a case overturned and a false imprisonment case arise."

"I hear you. If you're free, maybe you and/or Rowland can meet us there. We've collected some new information."

***

Blackwell was waiting in the lobby of the Charleston County So-licitor's office when Scarlett and Jake finished providing their official position to a plea deal on the felony charges against Barbara Malone. They agreed to a five-year probation and no jail time, if she would reveal what she knew about Jorgensen's transfer of physical custody of Anna to the Cardens.

"What if she doesn't know?" Curtis had asked. "You know if I take it to trial, the two of you will need to show up to court to testify."

"No info on Jorgensen, no deal for us. We'll show up to court. She may not know everything, but she knows enough to have caused her to commit a felony trying to block our exposing him. Don't let her or her attorney fool you. She wants to walk on this? She's got to give something. His death makes it even more reasonable to expect her to pony up the truth," Jake said. "Whatever has to be done, we'll do."

"Then your final word is give us the info or risk a conviction."

Scarlett hesitated, but Jake was firm.

"Noted," Curtis said. He addressed Scarlett. "You are sure this is your position?"

"I am."

"I'll go with it." He addressed Jake, "I bet you're hell in interrogations, Shepherd."

Jake smiled. "I hold my own."

***

As Blackwell stood to greet them in the lobby of the solicitor's office, Jake extended his hand. "Good to see you."

"I've locked in an interview room here where we can talk. If Curtis is available, he might want to join us."

"He's with Malone and her lawyer. Why don't we leave a message for him to join us when he's done? I'm hoping he'll have something to share." Jake checked his watch. "Better idea. Let's grab a cup of coffee in the cafe here in the building and leave a message for Curtis to meet us in about forty-five minutes. That way, we'll only be telling our story once."

***

By the time Jake, Scarlett, and Blackwell made it to the interview room Blackwell reserved, Curtis was there with a leather portfolio in front of him on the table.

"Who wants to start?" Blackwell said.

"I'll go." Curtis opened the portfolio. "Ms. Malone decided talking was better than serving time. Between choking and crying she got out that the baby, Anna-Claire Carden, born in Augusta, Georgia, to Nora Carden, sister of Paul Jorgensen's wife, died at the age of approximately four months old of heat exhaustion as the result of being left in a closed automobile. Allegedly by accident."

Scarlett gasped, while Jake gave a slight nod.

"And Jorgensen provided a substitute—the baby born to Marielle Devereau," Jake said.

"He did."

"Why? Did money change hands? Did she say why he would jeopardize his career, possibly his freedom?"

She said he hated defense work but had not been able to find a job with a firm doing something else. Dr. Carden was desperate. Even though the baby's death was a negligent accident, Nora Carden was suicidal. He had already made the mistake of not reporting the death and had buried the remains of the baby. At that point, he would be in serious trouble if he reported it. He offered Jorgensen fifty thousand dollars to facilitate the transfer of custody of the Devereau baby to him and his wife. Jorgensen saw his chance to fund a start-up law practice, and took it, never thinking anyone would ever come looking for the Devereau baby. Figured it was a no harm, no foul."

"Did he purposely kick Marielle to the curb in order to basically sell her baby to his family?" Scarlett asked.

"She says not. It was a coincidence that her baby was born close to the death of the Carden baby. Did he do a good job representing her? I think Shepherd is about to prove he did not. But the plea and conviction were done before the baby deal."

"Even though we all suspected something like this happened, it's still hard to process," Scarlett said.

"The remains of that baby are out there—no proper burial," Blackwell said. "We need to find them. The warrant to search the Augusta home of the Cardens should be easy to get now."

"I've got my paralegal preparing it," Curtis said. "But it does raise a question as to who will take charge of the burial if remains are found. Wouldn't be appropriate to rebury them on private property. There's apparently no immediate family member available."

"I'll take care of it," Scarlett said. All eyes turned to her.

"You'll assume responsibility for the burial if we find the baby?" Curtis said.

"If no one in the family volunteers, I will. I can't let that innocent baby who never got a chance at life be denied a decent burial and resting place," Scarlett said.

Jake stared at her with unmistakable admiration. "We're responsible for finding her. We'll take responsibility for taking care of her."

The room fell silent for several minutes.

CHAPTER 56

After approximately three minutes of deafening silence, Blackwell spoke. "I almost hate to take this meeting any further, but I suspect you all want to know the results we have so far in the testing of the DNA taken from the material wrapped around the gun that killed Vic Lanza."

They all nodded.

"The good news is they were able to build a profile. The bad news is there's no match in the system—neither SLED nor CODIS."

"You can't win them all," Jake said. "But I'll take having a profile any day. Were they able to determine gender?"

"They were. It is definitely male DNA. Since you have been so interested in a determination of gender, I'm thinking you had suspects of both genders on your radar," Blackwell said.

"Spoken like a detective," Jake said. "Yeah, you just eliminated someone we've been looking at. Might have been easier if it had been the reverse because I'm looking at several men and only one woman. But I'll take what I can get. You'll have to admit it certainly clears our client since she's in the system."

"You know I can't say that," Curtis said. "And you know I don't have the official go-ahead from upstairs to reopen the case, but we're listening. Right, Blackwell?"

"Ten-four."

"I don't need you to find the killer. I'll do that."

"Did he just say what I think he said?" Blackwell gestured toward Scarlett.

"Trust me, he did."

"Damn." Blackwell said, "Is he always that arrogant?"

She laughed. "Yep. He is. But he's usually right."

With a snap of his head in a gesture of disbelief, Blackwell said to Jake, "You told us your team has new information. Let's hear it."

"We're looking at a person of interest with a giant-size package of motive plus the means—but uncertain opportunity," Jake said. "And we have a list of possibles with opportunity but unknown motive or means. Having the gender established allows us to pare it down. I don't expect your boss to reopen the case yet, but try to keep him out of my way."

Curtis tapped his pen on the legal pad in his portfolio. "Should I be on the lookout for a Petition for Post-Conviction Relief?"

"It's coming. I've talked with Phil Madison about it. He's got a connection here in South Carolina who will file the paper and seek to add Phil *pro hac vice.*"

"You certainly speak the language," Blackwell said.

"He's got a law degree from Yale, John, and was an assistant U.S. Attorney in D.C. before joining the FBI." Curtis turned toward Jake. "And by the way, I've read about Madison. He ranks up there with F. Lee Bailey and Gerry Spence. How did you get him involved?"

"Clerked for him back in the day. Now, I'm his lead investigator."

"Of course you are. Keep me updated on your progress. From what I see, you're going to have enough to reopen. I won't oppose."

"We're close now. But while you never know where the evidence is going to lead, this looks like it's heading for a new day for Ms. Devereau and maybe a big apology from the State of South Carolina."

"Maybe more than an apology."

"Right," Jake said. "The lady lost her child and a big piece of her life. They might not have found the gun back in the day, but they put her in prison with nothing I can see to prove her guilt. Is the solicitor originally assigned to prosecute her case still around?"

"No. I looked that up when this first hit my desk. He was near retirement age at the time. He left the office in 1997 and subsequently passed away. Do you mind telling me what your next step is?"

"Bring you DNA to compare with what you found. I assume you'll do the testing."

"If you give us probable cause, I'll get it done. But how the hell do you plan on getting DNA from a suspect?"

"Haven't figured that out, but I will."

CHAPTER 57

When Jake and Scarlett returned to the hotel after the meetings with Curtis and Blackwell, Pete was out walking Kai.

"Quite a morning, Harvard. We've got our work cut out."

"You mean how are we going to get a DNA sample from DeLuca when we can't even find him?"

"DeLuca and maybe a half dozen others." Jake dropped his portfolio and key card on the table, crossed the room, and opened the drapes.

"Are you talking about the security guys?

"Looking at the security team would be first, but there may be others—pool guy, a maintenance man—anyone with knowledge of the house and access. Maybe a close professional relationship, like an agent."

"It's got to be DeLuca. What motive could any of those others have?"

"Never rule anything or anyone out until you have all the facts, Harvard." He took out his phone and texted Pete to let him know they were in the suite.

"Before we start making a plan, I'm going to change into something comfortable," she said. "Be back in a few minutes."

***

By the time Pete reached the suite with Kai, Scarlett had changed into jeans, track shoes, and a knit shirt. Jake had changed from his khakis, which were his concession to business attire, to denim. The table was covered with the case materials.

"Help yourself to something to drink from the fridge," Jake said to Pete as he came in with Kai.

After grabbing a can of Sprite, Pete sat down at the table and listened as Jake and Scarlett filled him in on what they learned in the earlier meetings. "So, where do we start?"

"Obviously, our strongest person of interest at this point is Carlos DeLuca," Jake said. "We need to concentrate on finding him and go from there."

"Jake, I had a thought while I was changing. DeLuca grew up with Lanza. Maybe Lanza's sister has stayed in contact with members of Deluca's family and either knows where he is or knows how to find out," Scarlett said.

"I like it," Jake said.

"I could call her now. I need to let her know that her DNA was a match with Anna."

"I wouldn't let on that he is suspect in a homicide. She might let it leak and put him on notice," Pete said.

Jake agreed.

"I don't think she would even connect it because she doesn't know I met with Marielle, but I'll be careful. I'll make the call right now."

Scarlett went to her room, came back with a folder labeled contacts, and sat down at the table. Pulling out a sheet, she took her cell out of her jeans pocket, tapped in a number, hit the speaker icon, and placed the cell on the table between them.

When a woman answered, Scarlett said, "Mrs. Salvadore, Veronica, this is Scarlett Kavanagh. I'm sure you remember me from a week or so ago. I'm the private investigator you provided with a DNA sample."

Jake and Pete both stared at the phone, listening with interest.

"Yes, of course. Have you found anything out from my DNA?"

"We have. The sample you gave confirmed what the prior report suggested. Your brother was my client's father. The number of centimorgans, which is the unit of measure in genetics, you have in common with Anna is more than adequate to determine you are a sibling of her father."

"Oh, my. That is . . . that is incredible news. Vic's daughter."

"Her name right now is Anna-Claire Carden. I'm pretty sure she will be calling you. It's all very new to her, but exactly what she wanted to know."

"I would like that."

"Anna is a physician in D.C. She's engaged to another doctor. I'll let her tell you more when you get to know one another."

"A doctor. She must be smart. Unbelievable. My children and my sister are going to be so excited. What about her mother? Do you know who she is?"

"We do. But I'm afraid I can't tell you who she is right now, but I'm sure I'll be able to soon. I do have a question for you. Your brother had a friend from his youth who worked on the TV series with him."

"Oh, that would be Carl DeLuca. They were best friends growing up and both set out for the same career. Carl never quite made it in the movies."

"Do you happen to know where he lives or what he does now? Maybe you've kept in touch with some of his family or friends."

"I do. Carl and his wife live in Montreal. He owns a gun range up there."

"That's interesting. So, he left show business?"

"He never worked in TV or film after Vic died. In fact, when Vic died, Carl was in a Maryland hospital."

Scarlett's expression changed, taking on a look of great surprise. Jake and Pete shared puzzled looks.

"I am so sorry to hear that. What was wrong?"

"He was in a bad auto accident on his way up here to visit his mother the day after the show finished filming for the season. He had a serious head injury and had to be put into a medically induced coma. He didn't even know about Vic's death until weeks after it happened."

"Oh. What a tragedy. Do I understand right that his accident was before Vic died?"

"It was. He had been in the hospital about a week when all that happened with Vic."

"What a tragedy. Do you by any chance know where it happened?"

"I heard it was on I-95, just outside of Baltimore, Maryland. He was lucky to be near a city like Baltimore that had great hospitals."

As soon as Scarlett ended the call, Pete said, "Pretty good alibi, I'd say. Reasonably easy to verify. Your suspects are dropping like snowflakes in a blizzard."

"I'm shocked. I was sure it was DeLuca," Scarlett said as she tucked her phone into the pocket of her shirt.

"I told you not to be too married to anyone until all the facts were accounted for," Jake said. "I think it's time to hit the backup list."

"His living in Canada makes sense as to why Liz and I didn't find him and the accident is why he didn't step up to defend Marielle," Scarlett said. "So, now where do we start, Jake?"

Jake picked up one of the folders on the table. "The obvious place is the security guards. Pete's found the company providing them, but it will take a subpoena, warrant, or court order to obtain the full list. We'll start with the two we have from the police file, and if we eliminate them, talk to Curtis about getting the others. The two we have names for worked the day of the murder. I'm especially interested in the one whose statement was relied on to charge Devereau."

"And Marielle said it wasn't accurate. What a convenient way to divert suspicion," Scarlett said.

Jake flipped through the folder. Taking out a sheet, he scanned the document. "Here it is. Ronald X. Brinson and Lloyd Isiah McIntyre. Brinson provided the damning statement."

"I wonder what the X stands for. But it might help in the search." She took her phone out of pocket. "I'm texting the names and what we know to Liz and hope she can work her magic. Really hope they didn't leave the country—and they're still alive."

"The latter would complicate obtaining DNA," Pete said.

CHAPTER 58

Wednesday morning, Jake received a text from Brad Curtis as he and Scarlett waited for their breakfast orders at Cracker Barrel.

> We've reached out to Smith & Wesson for a trace on the registered purchaser of the murder weapon. They say it will take time to research historic files. Will let you know what develops.

"Well, it looks like we're making progress," Jake said as he closed the text app. "It sounds like his office is beginning to give the case legs."

Scarlett reached for sugar packets and said, "I sent Liz what we know about Ronald Brinson and Lloyd McIntyre. She's going to do background checks and search all the state databases for security guard licenses. While it's not likely either one has a criminal record since there was no match in the databases for prints or DNA, there could be civil cases that show a propensity for violence, like orders for protection.

I'm going to cover social media and people searches. What exactly is Pete doing this morning?"

"The company's got a couple of big events to cover in D.C. and he felt like he should coordinate the teams. I think he just doesn't like being left out of what's going on at home. Cooper & Shepherd Security is his baby."

"Are we taking him food back?"

"He's ordering room service."

She stirred her tea and took a swallow before saying, "Jake. I've been thinking about how we can get DNA from these guys when we find them."

"Without badges and warrants, it'll have to be old school. We'll have to either put a surveillance team on them and follow until they discard a usable item—or raid their garbage."

Her arm hit her water glass as she reached for her cup of tea, causing her to grab it before it spilled. "Yeah. I know all those techniques, but they are going to take time. I have a better idea."

He paused his coffee cup in midair and stared at her for a second before putting it on the table. "You have an idea? What kind of idea?"

"I could pose as a writer and say I'm writing a book about security guards or a bio of Lanza. Invite one of the guys to lunch and then save the utensils, glass, can, whatever he drinks from or eats with. You could even pick it up from the table if I act like I'm leaving when he does."

"Kavanagh undercover. That's your plan?"

"Yeah. Undercover."

"No."

She put her teacup down with a force that caused some to spill over. "What do you mean no?"

"Webster's simple definition of the word. Not in this lifetime."

"Why not?"

"Do I have to spell it out? One of these guys may be a killer. He smells a rat and . . . . Although it's not a bad idea. Just a bad idea for you to be the one in harm's way."

"Well, you couldn't pull it off. He'd see through you in a second. A woman would be far less suspicious."

He shook his head. "No way."

"Don't say that. You and Pete would be close by. It's been thirty-five years. Why would he even begin to think the case was open? As far as the guy knows, Marielle is in prison, and no one suspects a thing."

"A person who commits murder never stops looking over his shoulder, Harvard. This is non-negotiable. We might figure a way to do it, but it's not going to be you. In fact, we could bring Brenda in to handle it."

"You never give me credit for being able to do anything. I can do this. It's my case."

"Yeah? And it's my firm. That's why you aren't a partner. It's my call."

She stood, dropped her napkin on the table, and stormed off as the server approached with their food.

When the server reached Jake, he said, "Would you box those up? Something's come up we have to take care of."

***

By the time Jake reached the suite with the takeout boxes, Scarlett was in her room with the door closed.

"I brought your breakfast," he called out, loud enough for her to hear. "If you don't want it, I'll put it in the refrigerator."

Her door opened, and she came out but did not speak.

"I get it. I've pissed you off. But you need to eat."

"Really."

"Do I need to call a negotiator?"

"Very funny. You treat me like I'm helpless."

"No. I treat you like someone I give a damn about. It has nothing to do with you being helpless. Undercover agents go through extensive training before going out on an assignment, Harvard. You're still learning the fundamentals of investigation and self-defense. It's high-risk. Why would I want to put you in a high-risk situation?"

"You never think I can do something until I do it. Back in Florida on Faith's case, you threw a fit about my going in with Jessica's sister, but I handled it fine. Even Hal Kirby said so. I handled the situation when Myrtle held a gun on me. I'm more competent than you give me credit for being. If I don't actively participate, I'm nothing more than a secretary."

"My ex-wife's husband's approval does not impress me. He got off on taking the opposite position from mine."

She glared at him, sparks shooting from her eyes.

"So, it means that much to you?"

"It does. I know I'm not your equal in the field, and I would never volunteer to do this if I didn't know I had you for backup." Her delivery grew faster as she spoke. "We need the DNA from these guys. One of them is sure to be who we are looking for. Marielle has been in prison for years. I want to get her out as quickly as possible. If we don't do it, there's no guarantee law enforcement will. They might, but they won't be in as big a hurry. Look what the poor woman has already lost."

"Slow down. I'm listening."

"I'll be in a public place, Jake. We can choose a restaurant and have you and Pete there. I'll tell him I've interviewed Vic's sister and that TV director—almost true. I'll ask a few questions about what Lanza was like, who all visited the mansion—nothing to make him suspicious. I can act like I think Marielle was guilty if the murder comes up."

"What's today? Wednesday?"

"What's that got to do with what we're talking about?"

"Pete's got two big events to cover this weekend. We don't have a location for either one of those guys, yet. I'll go along with your little plan, but only on the condition that Sonny and Brenda are also on the team. But you will follow my instructions without deviation. Now, can we eat? Our food is getting cold."

She gave him a sharp look.

"Let's eat. Your closing argument was compelling, counselor. You win."

CHAPTER 59

When Jake returned from taking Kai for a walk on Thursday afternoon, Scarlett handed him a sheet of paper. "Liz found an address for McIntyre in Nevada. I've located Brinson in North Carolina. He moved a number of times according to the expired security guard licenses Liz found in his name. But he is working security at an industrial park in North Carolina. According to Liz, McIntyre moved from South Carolina to Las Vegas a year after the murder and worked security in casinos until he retired as the security director for one of the smaller casinos."

"Good job—both of you." He scanned the information on the sheet. "We'll look at Brinson first. His location and questionable statement to law enforcement puts him at the top of my list."

"I've been thinking."

"Why do I have a feeling I'm not going to like this?"

"Stop it. I can send Brinson an email today but set the meeting up for next week."

"Wait. Table that thought. Before you make any contact with him, there are things that have to be put in place. The only way you're meeting with him is if Sonny and Brenda are there along with me and Pete."

"Really? What if they're tied up?"

"Then we wait."

"We need to get Marielle out of prison."

"So, you want me to put you face to face with a possible killer while you try to set him up with only Pete and me for backup? You couldn't think I would agree to that. And another thing. We've got to set up your fake identity. You can't just fire off an email."

Although she didn't verbally object, there was no mistaking her displeasure with his position.

Jake placed the paper on the table. "Dig up a little patience, Harvard. You don't want this guy to learn who you are or discover you're a private investigator. We have to create a fake identity for you."

Her lips curled inward as she gave his statement thought. "Yeah. I guess you're right."

"I usually am."

She made a fist and punched his shoulder. "You're incorrigible. . . . What if I use my old email account from my law practice? If he looks me up, he'll see a family law attorney and not think criminal activity."

"Maybe. But a little risky. There may be another way. Do you have any social media accounts still live from your law days?"

"One. I just never took it down."

"So, it has followers, posts. Let Liz scrub it for anything that identifies you completely. Change either the first or last name. Do you have a middle name?"

"I try not to tell it."

"Well, drag it out and dust it off because this may be the time it comes in handy. What is it?"

"Armstrong."

"Perfect. Scarlett Armstrong. It's still your name but unconnected to your public identity. You can set up a new email account using Armstrong. Once we have the social media account edited for the new name, you can send the email."

***

On Friday, Scarlett, Jake, and Pete attended the plea hearing for Barbara Malone. When it was over, Brad Curtis waved Jake down.

"I thought you would like to know that Augusta has taken the case of the missing baby, and a search warrant has been issued to allow cadaver dogs to comb the property. I'll let you know how it goes."

Scarlett listened intently. "If the dogs find something, what happens?"

"It'll probably take a second order to proceed with the excavation, but they are using multiple dogs. So, if they get an alert by more than one, a judge is very likely to give them any order they need."

She looked up at Jake. "That makes me shiver."

"I'll keep you posted," Curtis said. "If they do alert, I plan to drive over for the excavation."

***

Friday evening, Scarlett received a call from Anna.

"Your text said you have new information," Anna said.

"I do. Things are happening. After you left, Jake found the gun that fired the fatal shot in a hidden room at the mansion." After filling Anna in on all the events of the week, she said, "I am hoping to meet with a prime suspect next week."

"I had to sit down. They know where the real Anna is buried."

"They have a lead, and Georgia law enforcement is following up on it."

"Scarlett, did the couple who I called mom and dad my entire life kill their baby?"

"According to Barbara Malone, it was an accident. But it was never reported to the police. Let's hope it was an accident. You probably know much better than I do what causes of death can be found by the medical examiner after all this time."

"Only traumas to the body such as gunshots, blunt force, and maybe knife wounds—but only if the wound struck a bone—are likely to be found. All the tissue would have decomposed."

"Jake and I were talking about the problems with identification if the remains are found. Obviously, the real Anna had no siblings, and the parents are dead. It would be a big deal to exhume one of their bodies for DNA. But we do have DNA from your cousin and from your uncle Joel."

"And that would be important?"

"Yes, you and Joel Carden have absolutely no matching centimorgans, which again proves you were not related by blood. However, if they do find an infant's remains, it could prove the baby was Anna Carden."

"What are you planning to do next?"

"We're going to attempt to obtain DNA from one of the suspects. It's going to mean a trip to North Carolina, but I'll let you know."

CHAPTER 60

Despite having little to do, the team stayed in Charleston over the weekend and prepared Scarlett's cover for the meeting with Ronald Brinson. Once social media, her email, and a burner phone were in place to conceal her identity, she sent a short email informing Brinson she was doing research on Vic Lanza for a book and asking if he would be willing to give her an interview. At Jake's recommendation, she offered him two-hundred-dollars compensation for his time. His response was surprisingly positive. They agreed to meet at a large coffee shop on Tuesday afternoon at five o'clock as Brinson worked the nightshift and had to be on duty at seven p.m."

As Jake drove the three of them toward Wilmington, the tension mounted in Scarlett's gut. They had left Charleston at eight a.m. for the three-hour drive. The Lassiters, Sonny and his wife Brenda, were driving down from Virginia and scheduled to meet Jake, Pete, and Scarlett at the hotel where they all would spend the night. Sonny, a retired FBI agent, and Brenda, a former Baltimore Police Department officer, were employees of Pete and Jake's security company.

There had been sparse conversation on the ride. Pete was absorbed in a book, Kai lay stretched out across the third row of seats in the Yukon, and Scarlett sat in the passenger seat, mentally going over her list of questions for the interview."

As they neared the hotel, a red light stopped them. Jake glanced down at Scarlett's hands, tightly clasped in her lap atop her script as she stared at the street ahead.

"Nervous, Harvard?"

She snapped her head around toward him. "Of course not."

"Then why are your knuckles white?"

Her eyes flashed downward, and she relaxed her grip. "They are not."

"Are you really going to lie to me? When did that ever work?"

Scarlett could feel her heart pounding. "If I'm nervous, it's not what you think."

The corners of his mouth turned up. "Do tell me what I'm thinking, Harvard."

"You're thinking I'm afraid of Brinson. I'm not, and I'm not lying. . . . At least, I'm not afraid of what you think I am."

The conversation aroused Kai, and he moved forward through the gap between seats on the second row to stick his head over the console.

"You don't have to do this. Brenda can go in for you."

"Is that why you insisted on bringing Sonny and Brenda to Wilmington—so you could have Brenda take my place? I'm fine. This is my case. I want a part in catching the killer."

"No. I did not insist on bringing them onboard to replace you. I brought them onboard because they are two of the best protective operatives we have. Right, Pete?"

Pete closed his book. "None better."

The SUV went silent again as they moved past the traffic light.

***

After checking in at the hotel, Pete took Kai and the overnight bags to their suite while Jake and Scarlett waited in the lobby for Sonny and Brenda. Brenda had texted Jake that they were less than half an hour away.

Scarlett sat on a loveseat in the lobby while Jake went for a cup of coffee. When he returned, he sat in a companion chair. After taking a swallow, he said, "Hmmm. Not bad. Could be a little stronger, but not bad."

Scarlett looked at him but didn't speak.

"Want to tell me what's bothering you now?"

"I'm not afraid of meeting with him. I'm fine."

"Okay, we'll skip over the afraid of meeting with the guy. But don't try to tell me you're not nervous. I know you are." He rested his cup on the low table servicing the sofa and his chair. "Give it up, Harvard."

"I'm just having anxiety over something going wrong, and we don't get something with his DNA. What if he takes his cup to the garbage? What if he suspects what I'm there for and leaves without anything for us to collect? This is our chance, and it could go wrong."

He leaned toward her, reached out for her hand, and said, "Calm down. Something goes wrong, we go to plan B. There's always a plan B. This doesn't work, then we track him. Raid his garbage. We'll get it."

"This is our guy. I know it, Jake. This is him."

Jake's phone pinged. He dropped her hand and took it out of his pocket. "It's Curtis." He scanned the text and with an affirmative nod handed her his phone.

Scarlett's mouth fell open, and she put her free hand to her face. "Oh, my gosh. They did it! They found the baby."

She handed the cell back to him. "They really did it. They found the real Anna Carden."

Jake smiled. "They found a baby. Remember, there's a matter of confirming its identity."

"You know it's Anna."

"I suspect it's Anna. You should be proud. I'm proud of you. You took the case and fought your way through it. Without you, none of this would have happened." As he tucked the phone back into the pocket of his jacket, he spotted a couple coming through the hotel entry. "There's Sonny and Brenda." He stood and waved them over.

As the couple reached Jake and Scarlett, Sonny Lassiter thrust his hand forward to shake Jake's and then gave Scarlett a hug.

"How was the ride down?" Jake said, as Brenda and Scarlett exchanged greetings.

"Once we got past morning traffic, it was smooth all the way. Where's Pete?"

"He took our luggage up. I've checked you in." Jake reached in his pocket and took out two key cards. As he handed one to Brenda, she looked past him and raised her hand in the air.

"There's Pete."

When he reached the group, Pete shook hands with Sonny and tipped his head to Brenda. "Glad to see you made it okay. How were the weekend gigs?"

"Piece of cake," Sonny said. "Only problem we had was one drunk politician. So, what's the plan today?"

"Let's head up to the rooms, so you can park your stuff, and I'll fill you in," Jake said.

"I'm going to give Kai a go outside," Pete said. "Won't be long."

***

Once the four were in the small suite, Jake spread printouts of the interior of the shop where the meeting would take place. "We're lucky the website of this coffee shop provided good images of the interior, but a couple of us need to run by after lunch to be sure we aren't thrown a curve. Sonny and Brenda will sit at the table closest to Scarlett. Pete and I will be across the area with a direct line of view. It's a slow time for the place and a number of tables will provide the view we need."

"Any reason you picked a coffee shop?" Sonny asked.

"We thought restaurant at first, but since they don't usually use disposable tableware, we'd be basically stealing property unless we let someone on the staff know what we were doing. Since we don't know who this guy knows, I'm not up for sharing any info. Plus, a conscientious restaurant server could clear the table."

"Do you expect him to be armed?" Brenda said.

"I do. He's security at an industrial park on the night shift. I would expect him to be carrying regardless of any suspicion on his part as to who or what the meeting is actually about. He's being paid a couple of hundred bucks to talk about Vic Lanza, the actor, who he worked security for at the time Lanza was murdered. Scarlett is using the name Scarlett Armstrong. Her cover story is she's writing a book about Lanza."

"Is she looking to get a confession?" Sonny said, picking up one of the photos.

"No. I'd rather the murder didn't come up. The goal is to get his DNA and fingerprints. One or both. If he's a match, South Carolina law enforcement will have enough probable cause for an arrest warrant. They can work on a confession."

"Who's going to go for the DNA bearing items?" Brenda asked.

"If the plan follows the right course, he'll leave whatever he uses on the table, Scarlett will head for the restroom when he goes toward the exit. Either you or Sonny will collect whatever you can. Don't worry about which cup is his. Get them all. Pete's got evidence bags and gloves for you. We brought a large purse for Brenda to carry. Use it to stash whatever evidence you collect. Scarlett will put a mark on the bottom of her cup if she can. Pete and I will keep eyes on the guy until he's clear of the area."

"What about distress signals? Is there a code word or physical signal if the meeting starts going sideways?" Sonny asked.

"Scarlett will have an open call to me on her Apple watch. I'll be monitoring the conversation. If she senses trouble, the code word is *sweet*, but I'll be the one to hear it. If I stand up, be ready. But, honestly guys, I don't expect trouble. This is all erring on the side of caution."

"How are we all traveling to the scene?" Sonny asked.

"Scarlett will take an Uber to the shop so she arrives alone on the off chance he might show up early. Sonny, you and Brenda will be there when he arrives. Pete and I will wait in our vehicle in the parking lot, signal all of you when we see him arrive, and come in after Brinson. There's likely to be very few people in the place at that time." He pointed to the center of a photo of the interior of the coffee shop. "One of these tables is where Scarlett will sit. Pete and I will be across the room by the windows or over by the counter area, depending on what's available. Sonny, you and Brenda take the table closest to Scarlett's."

"Why not have one of us show our credentials to the manager to make sure we have the seating you describe," Sonny said.

"Because the business, not wanting to risk trouble, could ask us to leave."

"What do we know about him? Any record of violence?" Brenda asked. "Do we know what he looks like?"

"No sheet found on the guy. A record would have cost him his license. As for what he looks like, he and Scarlett are exchanging photos by text for purposes of recognition. She'll forward his to all of us. Remember, our only objective is to get the forensics and to be there as back up for Scarlett should anything go wrong."

"Jake, I just thought of something. If I'm paying at the restaurant, I can't use a card because he might see my name. I've got the two hundred dollars but not sure I have enough to pay for anything extra. We need to stop at an ATM, so I have enough cash. In fact, take my cards and keep them in your wallet."

Jake took all her cards and then pulled eighty dollars out of his wallet and handed the cash to her. "This should cover the bill. Better keep one card to cover your Uber." He fanned the cards and held them up for her to choose one. "You can hide it in your purse."

CHAPTER 61

Scarlett, Sonny, and Brenda were in their places by four-fifty. A decadent chocolate drink and a croissant sat on the table in front of Scarlett but not yet touched. Next to the refreshments was a new portfolio with the initials S.A. in gold with a folder tucked inside containing a sheet of neatly typed questions. Although new, the leather object was scuffed up to look worn. Her disposable cell was open to text messages where she stared at the photo received from Ronald Brinson. For a man near retirement age, he appeared to be in good shape. His hair was not quite completely gray, and he had a neat beard. The photo was probably unnecessary since he wore black chinos, a black polo shirt with a company emblem and a patch on the shoulder in the shape of a badge. A photo ID hung on a lanyard around his neck, and his waist was outfitted with equipment, including what looked to be a semiautomatic handgun. *Doesn't look like a killer. Definitely armed. Good looking man.*

Although she would not admit it to Jake, her stomach was in turmoil. *I can do this. How many depositions of hostile witnesses and cross exams of belligerent parties have I done? I can.*

The closer the clock got to five, the more sweat accumulated on her palms. She took a sip of the drink and a nibble of the croissant, but it almost made her nauseous. *Don't look nervous. Look cool and calm. Be professional.* Her watch was set on the phone app, ready for her to hit Jake's number. He and Pete were outside, monitoring the door. He would text her if he spotted Brinson arriving.

Five o'clock came with no sign of the suspect. Five after five and no Brinson. At ten after five, she looked around at Sonny and Brenda and then tapped Jake's number, held the watch close to her face, and said, "He's a no-show. What do we do?"

"Patience, Harvard. He could be caught in traffic."

In the background she heard, "Two o'clock, Jake. He's here."

Scarlett flinched. "I heard Pete." Leaving the line open, she took a deep breath, opened the portfolio, and pretended to be reading her questions. *Stop trembling. I can do this.*

Despite expecting him, when he said, "Ms Armstrong?" Scarlett flinched.

"I'm sorry. I didn't mean to startle you."

"You're fine. Please call me Scarlett."

He smiled. "And I'm Ron. Sorry I'm late, but there was a wreck on the way. I hope it won't mess us up." He pulled a chair out and took a seat.

"No. It's fine. If we run out of time, I can always set up a Zoom meeting. Please get yourself a drink, something to eat. This chocolate drink is sinful."

"I'm good."

What if he doesn't eat or drink?

"Then let's get started. If you change your mind about getting something, don't hesitate to tell me." She picked up her cup and took a drink. After swallowing, she picked up her pen and opened the folder with her questions. "Let's start with when you began working for Vic Lanza. How long were you on his security detail?"

"From the time he moved into the big house. I was just a kid, only twenty-one. I dropped out of college and planned to enter the police academy, but I needed work. A friend of mine told me the company was hiring. I was the youngest guard they had."

"And that would have been how long that you actually worked for him?"

"A little over a year."

"Did you work when he was not there?"

"Absolutely. And he was gone more than he was there. He did come home on weekends sometimes during the shooting of the TV show, but he was gone a lot."

"What was he like to work for?"

"Okay. He didn't interact with us hardly ever. We were like invisible to him. If he had a question or request, my partner always handled it. Lloyd was older and more experienced than me. He knew Lanza better than I did. His name was McIntyre. He left the company not too long after Lanza was killed. They kept the security on until the house was taken over by whoever Lanza left it to."

"Have you remained in contact with McIntyre?" *I've got to get him to touch something.*

"No. We went our separate ways."

Scarlett took a photo out of a pocket in her portfolio. She handed it to Brinson. "Is this what the mansion looked like when you worked there?"

He took the photo and studied it for a minute.

He touched it. Thank, God. We've got something.

"I don't see any changes, but it doesn't show the grounds. There were acres of land around the building." He slid the photo back to Scarlett.

She left it on the table, afraid if she picked it up, she could destroy the evidence. After asking several more questions about Lanza, she placed the manila folder over it, hoping he wouldn't notice she had avoided touching it.

Fifteen minutes went by as Scarlett asked detailed questions about Lanza and his lifestyle. She forced herself to drink her beverage, taking sips after each question. Throughout the exchange, calm alternated with nerves.

Twenty minutes into the interview, Brinson stood and reached toward his waist.

Is he reaching for his gun? Fight or flight followed the question in her mind. *Has he figured out I'm a fake?* In a panic but determined to stay calm, Scarlett considered saying the code word but held back. *Make a wrong move friend, and there are four guns surrounding you—ready to take you down.*

Her latter thought sent a wave of exhilaration through her body and bolstered her confidence.

"Your drink has got the best of me. Going to order one."

Waves of relief coursed through Scarlett as she said, "You won't regret it," while mentally she thought, *but actually you will.*

While waiting for Brinson to return, Scarlett realized that she would have to keep the interview going until he finished drinking, otherwise, he was likely to take the cup with him.

When he returned to the table with his drink, Scarlett switched topics and began asking Brinson questions about his job, his family, his travels. If he realized she was stalling, it did not show. Ego kept him on her line.

Scarlett kept the interview going until six o'clock when Brinson glanced at his watch and said, "I'm sorry, Scarlett, but I go on duty in an hour. I'll have to stop here. If you want to ask any more questions, give me a shoutout, and we can schedule an online meeting like you said." He stood.

"Definitely. Thank you for giving me your time today."

"You're welcome. I enjoyed meeting you. Never met an author before. I'll look forward to reading the book." He looked down at the table. "I'll take the trash." He started to reach for the two empty cups, the scrunched-up paper napkins, and the remainder of Scarlett's croissant.

No, no.

"Oh, leave them, Ron. I'm going to the restroom before I leave, and there's a trash bin right beside the hallway."

CHAPTER 62

When Scarlett returned to the seating area after exiting the restroom, the entire team was sitting at the table where Jake and Pete had been during the interview. Jake stood and opened his arms. "You did it, Harvard. Good job. Brenda's got the evidence safely tucked in the bag."

She moved right in for the hug. "I'm so glad it's over. So many things happened I didn't plan on."

"It always does," Pete said. "But you rolled with it like a pro. Congratulations."

As she pulled away from Jake she said, "This is going to sound absurd, but I found myself liking the guy and feeling bad that I was setting him up for prison."

"That's undercover work," Brenda said. "Build relationships to betray relationships. You did a great job."

"I actually had to remind myself that if he's a match, he killed someone and then helped put an innocent person in prison to cover up his crime."

"Whatever thoughts you had, you stuck to the job, but I think we're all ready to get away from here," Jake said. "If Pete and Scarlett are onboard, I think we'll head back to Charleston tonight." He turned to Sonny. "You guys have a longer drive, so, stay over and use the room and expense account for a date night."

"Will do. Thanks."

"Ditto," Brenda said. "Glad it worked out without any drama."

"Okay, team. Let's get this bag back to Curtis. The sooner we get it there, the sooner we know if we can mark this one closed."

***

Jake and Scarlett pulled into the parking garage for the government building housing the Solicitor's office minutes before nine o'clock, Wednesday morning. Jake corresponded by text with Curtis the night before, notifying him of the potential evidence obtained, and set up the appointment. An entirely different Scarlett from the day before sat in the passenger seat. She held the handbag Brenda Lassiter used to store the items in her lap. Scarlett's cup, bearing a black Sharpie line, had been tossed. Brinson's cup, the photo he handled, and his napkin remained.

"I'm going to let you present your treasure to Curtis. You're the one who managed to get it. You deserve full credit."

"I didn't do it for credit. I did it because I want Marielle released."

"I know that, Harvard. But enjoy your accomplishment." He reached across the console and patted her knee.

When they checked in at reception, the woman at the desk said, "Assistant Solicitor Curtis is expecting you. I'll let him know you're here."

They were barely seated when Curtis entered the lobby. "Welcome back." Shaking Jake's hand, he said, "Good job. We could use you on our investigation squad."

With a gesture toward Scarlett, Jake said, "There's where the credit goes. Setting the guy up at the coffee shop was all her idea. She's the one who went in under a pseudonym and pulled off getting the goods."

Scarlett held up the bag.

"Come on back. I'll get the evidence logged in and expedited to the lab."

As they walked down a corridor toward Curtis's office, he said, "We received the DNA profiles your office sent of potential relatives of the unidentified baby in Georgia. They were immediately emailed to the authorities over there. Georgia told us they expect to have preliminary results within a day—two at the most."

When they reached his office, Curtis removed the evidence bags from the handbag, gave them to his paralegal, and said, "Log these into the Lanza murder file, and get them to the best lab we use ASAP with a request that they expedite the results. But before you ship them out, have our crime scene unit dust the cup and the photo for fingerprints if they can do it without screwing up any DNA."

After all three were seated in his office, Curtis said, "I have to admit, this has been an experience."

"How long have you been a prosecutor?" Jake asked.

"Coming up on five years. And you were a Fed?"

"Less than three years. I failed the dress code."

Curtis chuckled. "I've noticed you opt for casual. The other thing I wanted to mention to you is we have a sentencing hearing set for Barbara Malone. As you know, Ms. Kavanagh, Scarlett, and you as well, Jake, have the right to give an impact statement. So, my question is, do either of you, or both, want to do so?"

Both were quiet for several minutes. Scarlett was first to speak. "Brad, I don't think she is a criminal. She was a desperate woman who used poor judgment. I wasn't hurt. She's lost her job, the man she probably loved, and she did what we wanted in giving up what she knew about the baby. I don't need to say anything."

"Jake?"

"I'm fine. I'd probably be a little more harsh with her than Scarlett, but she isn't getting away with it. A conviction and probation are going to impact her life. So, I'll pass."

CHAPTER 63

The call from Curtis came on Friday. Jake was at his desk in Arlington.

"It's a match, Shepherd, and so was the DNA extracted from the cap you found at the museum. You nailed your suspect. The warrant has gone out to North Carolina. It's just a matter of time. The hearing on your client's Petition for Post Conviction Relief is set. She should be a free woman by midweek. Congratulations. And I have a little bonus for you. I got a call from Augusta. Your DNA profiles show enough common centimorgans to confirm the remains found are those of the Carden baby."

Ending the call, he buzzed Liz and said, "Meet me in Scarlett's office."

When he walked into her office, Scarlett was deep into computer research on a new case. "You're gonna want to drop what you're doing, Harvard."

She looked up at him as Liz appeared in the doorway. "You got the call," Scarlett said.

"I got the call."

"Did it?"

"It did."

She sprang up and threw her arms around him. "We did it. We did it, Jake."

"Yes ma'am. We did it. Curtis not only said it was a match with Brinson, but he also had a call from Georgia that the baby is a match to the Carden family. I think you have some news to share with the client."

"Congratulations, Scarlett," Liz said.

"I couldn't have done it without all of you. And I didn't do it. Jake did the hardest work in South Carolina." She paused for a second and looked down at Kai. "And you helped, too, boy. I can't wait to tell Anna. Have you called Pete? How soon will Marielle be released?"

"Slow up. Do you think I would have told Pete before I told you? As for Devereau's release, it should be within days, according to Curtis."

"Are we going?"

"Could I stop you if I wanted to?"

"No. Has anyone told Marielle?"

"I'm pretty sure the Charleston attorney Phil associated with has received official notice and would have notified her."

***

The hearing on Marielle Devereau's release took nearly a week to schedule, which gave Anna and Scarlett time to plan for the release and for where she would go. Marielle agreed that she and Anna would meet for the first time when she exited the prison. Scarlett and Jake would also be present to support both mother and daughter.

"Please wear your compassionate hat," Scarlett said to Jake as they were about to leave the hotel. "This is a very emotional moment for them."

"Yes, ma'am. I'll work on it."

Anna stood in the hall as they exited their suite. "I'm as nervous as a rabbit who has just spotted a hungry fox."

Scarlett smiled. "You're going to be fine. You look gorgeous. Your mother is going to be so proud of you."

"Thank you for being here. Dan wanted to be here, but his surgery schedule couldn't be changed. I'm kinda glad he isn't."

"Just remember, you may still be developing your feelings for Marielle, but she has loved you all your life. She always knew you were her daughter. You have only known she is your mother for a few weeks."

"I never thought about it that way."

***

When Marielle walked out of Leath, she wore a classic shirtwaist dress, chosen from a catalog, and sent by Scarlett. Her hair was neatly tied back at the nape of her neck, and she carried a small bag of possessions. Despite the intimidating surroundings of the prison of wire-topped fencing and bleak architecture, Marielle's appearance was stately, displaying no suggestion of the status she was leaving. Anna had purchased a few items of clothing for her that were at the hotel.

The face-to-face confrontation paused for a second before Anna threw her arms around Marielle. Tears streamed down Scarlett's cheeks.

***

That evening as the four had dinner at the Italian restaurant Jake and Scarlett liked so much, Marielle said, "I never thought a day like this would happen. How do I thank all of you for what you did for me?"

"I'm just so glad I found you," Anna said. She turned toward Scarlett. "And glad I found Scarlett and Jake. I don't think anyone else could have done what they did."

"What I don't understand is why that guard, Ron Brinson, did what he did," Anna said.

"I can help you a little with that," Jake said. "I talked to the prosecutor this morning before we left. When he and the detectives questioned Brinson, they broke him. He confessed. He claims he didn't mean to kill Lanza. He returned to the house that night, expecting it to be empty. Lanza's ex had offered him a sizeable amount of money to retrieve some, shall I say, compromising DVDs they recorded when they were together. Lanza surprised him. Panicked, Brinson drew his gun, and the rest is history."

"What are they charging him with?" Scarlett said.

"Second degree. He might even plead it down to involuntary manslaughter."

"Was it the Fontaine woman who hired him?" Scarlett said.

"It was. It's possible she wanted to use the films against Lanza. Or maybe, she was afraid he would use them to embarrass her. Who knows? They may be able to charge her with felony murder. She masterminded an act, and someone died. I think she's got a problem."

CHAPTER 64

Three weeks after Marielle Devereau's release from prison, Jake and Scarlett drove to a cemetery in Fairfax County, Virginia. "I can't believe all that has happened in the past four months," Scarlett said.

"It turned out to be quite a case."

As they reached the site, a group of people had already arrived. Most were hospital colleagues of Anna and Dan. A short distance away, Anna stood with Dan, but when she spotted Jake and Scarlett, she rushed over to greet them.

"Thank you for coming," she said, giving Scarlett a hug.

"Of course, we would come."

"Today, we say goodbye to Anna-Claire Carden, the real Anna-Claire. She can rest for eternity with her parents."

Scarlett nodded. "It's a beautiful day. I believe her parents loved her, and her loss was a tragic accident."

"I do too. That's why I wanted her to be here with them. And I wanted you to be the first to know Dan and I have reset the date for our wedding. In the end, he came through for me, Scarlett. I do think he's a little jealous of Jake. But we both hope you and Jake will come to the wedding."

"Of course we'll come." Scarlett glanced around the area. "Is Marielle here?"

"No. She wasn't comfortable about being part of this. But she's doing great, and I'm growing closer to her."

"I'm happy for you."

Anna smiled. "She will be at the wedding. It won't be Anna-Claire Carden getting married. The invitation will read Lara Devereau-Lanza. Mr. Madison is taking care of all the legal stuff, including the change of my name. It's going to take getting used to, but I like it, and Marielle is happy. To her, I've always been Lara."

"Amazing Grace" began playing softly as a priest and two acolytes walked to the head of the small grave. "We'd better take our places. Thank you again for everything." Anna reached out and squeezed Scarlett's hand and then returned to where she left Larsen.

When Jake and Scarlett reached the group gathered at the grave site, which was surrounded by an assortment of beautiful floral arrangements, Jake stood behind her. As he rested his hands on her shoulders, he leaned over and whispered, "One of these days, we might plan a life event of our own."

THE SHEPHERD &
ASSOCIATES SERIES

ACKNOWLEDGMENTS

While I may sit alone at my computer, typing out the sentences that become a book, I don't write alone. I could fill a book with those who have contributed in so many ways to the work I create—those who inspired me, those who supported me, those who taught me, those who answered my questions, and those who patiently listened. I wish I could thank each and every one. While that would be impossible, here I will acknowledge those who dominated the production of *A Raging Fire*.

As always, first on the list is my editor and good friend, the brilliant John Boles. From book one to book ten, he has been there, catching mistakes, making suggestions, and giving advice. I'm not sure any of my books would exist if I had not had the opportunity to work with John. I'll always be deeply in-debted to him for helping shape this author.

Next, my family. They are my strength and my joy. Bill, Allison, Lynda, Judson, Sarah, Trevor, Brooks, Amelia, John, Keri, Samantha, and Caroline to whom this book is dedicated. Caroline reads every book I write and asks me everytime we are together, "Did you get any writing done today?" And finally, the fourth generation, who are too young to read what I write, however, they are treasures of inspiration and motivation—Elle, Audrey, Will, Hunter, and Annabel.

And finally, the friends who support me in so many ways: Nancy Duty, Dee Boutwell, Elizabeth Ruiz, Karen Baltovski, and Eleanor Erwin.

LETTER TO READERS

Dear Reader,

Allow me to start with expressing my deepest gratitude for your interest in my books. Your enjoyment of the characters and stories I create is what provides my greatest joy.

Whether this was your first book of mine you've read, or whether you've read them all, thank you.

A Raging Fire, as you know, is the fourth book in the Shepherd & Associates Series. But Jake and Scarlett existed before the first in the series. Scarlett made a brief appearance in *Shadows from the Past*, a romantic suspense book inspired by a historical event in my family. Jake appeared in both *The Ballet* and *The Studio*, also romantic suspense. As he developed in those two novels, the desire arose in me to give him more. *Voila*. Shepherd & Associates was born.

However, the inspiration for Jake's experience, training, attitude, and skill came from my admiration for law enforcement and two former FBI agents—Perry Smith and Christopher Whitcomb. If you doubt any of the actions Jake takes, read *The Unlikely Priest*, by Perry Smith and *Cold Zero* by Christopher Whitcomb. Perry, I've met. Christopher, I would like to meet. I also had the experience and pleasure of working with a former FBI agent, Steven Stansbury and a former NYPD officer, Sean Mullholland in their roles as private investigators during my twenty-two years of practicing law, plus many other members of law enforcement.

The above being said, I hope to write many more episodes in the cases of Jake and Scarlett and hope you will read them all. In addition, my fervent desire is to see Jake and Scarlett on the screen, and welcome any suggestions as to how to make that happen, including reader suggestions for casting.

To keep up with all events, promotions, and releases, please subscribe to my newsletter at www.juditherwin.com. I will not share any of your information nor saturate your inbox.

Of course, I would be grateful for a review or rating if you enjoyed the book and would love for you to follow me on social media and join the Facebook group: Jake Shepherd, PI Fans. https://www.facebook.com/groups/1544010183683123

Again, thank you for your support.

Judith

ABOUT THE AUTHOR

On the way to author, Judith Erwin worked as a costume designer, photographer, journalist, teacher, and attorney. She served on the executive boards of four ballet companies and as a judge on the Florida Department of State Grants Panel for Dance. Although she holds a law degree from the University of Florida and practiced law for twenty-two years, to further her knowledge of law enforcement, she completed the Jacksonville Sheriff's Office Citizens Academy and the FBI Citizens Academy. She is currently a member of the FBI Jacksonville Citizen's Academy Alumni Association.

GUILTY UNTIL PROVEN INNOCENT

Preview of *Guilty Until Proven Innocent* – Shepherd & Associates Book 5

Jake did not make it through the door of his office before receiving an exuberant greeting from Kai. With ultra-keen hearing, the one-hundred-pound shepherd recognized the arrival of the Lexus LX the moment it rolled onto the driveway.

"Any fires since I left this morning?" Jake said to Liz Glover, his research analyst and office manager, as he scratched the top of the dog's head.

"Fairly quiet, but you'd better check your messages, particularly the one on top."

Jake glanced down at the spindle holding a stack of pink message slips. The one Liz referenced read, "Call Jackie. Urgent!" With the message written in letters twice the normal size, Jake's expression immediately changed to alarm. "Sabrina? What's happened?"

"It's not Sabrina. However, she wouldn't say what she wanted—just that it was urgent."

"Well, if it isn't Sabrina, then it can't be that urgent."

"You didn't hear her voice."

"She has my cell number. If it was that bad, why didn't she just call it?" he said as he tapped his ex-wife's name on the smart phone and pushed the speaker icon. "Maybe Hal shot himself loading his service weapon."

"Come on, Jake. Be nice."

"Not likely. I left nice at home this morning."

On the second ring, Jackie Kirby answered. "Jake, we've got a serious problem."

"Not Sabrina. Right?"

"No. She's fine. It's Hal."

A frown creased Jake's forehead. "Since when am I interested in ASAC Hal Kirby's problems?"

"Can you try to be civil? This is bad. Hal really needs you."

With a mock look of shock, Jake stepped back, glanced toward Scarlett, who had come out of her office and was standing in the doorway.

As his gaze transferred to Liz, she scowled, shaking her head and holding up an index finger as if to say, "Don't be a smartass, Jake."

"ASAC Harold Kirby needs me? You've got to be kidding. Did he lose his phone privileges? Why isn't *he* calling me?"

"I'm sure you can figure that one out. How hard would it be for you to ask him for help? Can you please shelve your sarcasm for a minute. This is serious."

"Actually, I don't have any trouble asking him for help. The way I see it, he owes me. But okay, okay. What's going on?"

"Ryan has been arrested."

When Jake failed to respond immediately, Jackie said, "Did you hear me, Jake. Hal's son has been arrested."

"Yeah. I heard you. What's the charge?"

"Sexual assault—rape—and domestic assault."

Jake whistled through his teeth. "Did he do it?"

"Of course not."

"You know that how?"

"I know Ryan. He's not the type to do anything like that."

"People do things we don't expect, Jackie."

"Listen to me. Ryan's a good kid. He would not."

"I certainly hope you're right, since I assume he is around my daughter periodically. But you're correct about one thing. It's serious. Where is he? I thought Hal's ex and his kids didn't live here."

"Ryan's in college here in D.C. He's a good student and hopes to get into vet school. This will ruin his chances."

"Getting into grad school is the least of his worries right now. Did the D.C. cops pick him up?"

"No. The girl has an apartment in Arlington and claims it all took place there."

"So ACPD has him. I'm guessing he's been to first appearances. Was a bond set?"

"There was, but Hal wants to get more information on the case before we decide how to handle the bond. We'll be paying for everything. Neither Lori nor Ryan have money."

Jake curled in his bottom lip for a second, again glancing between the two women staring at him. "He needs to get him out ASAP. Kirby knows that. Jail is not a happy place for the son of law enforcement.

Tell you what, Jackie. If Hal needs me, Hal needs to ask me. He knows where I am and can either come to the office or give me a call."

"Jake, are you going to make him grovel? It's his son. I thought we had buried the past."

"Have we? Oh, yeah. That's right. Buried. But I still want the request to come directly from the SOB. As I think about it, he needs to come over here. If I am to consider this, I want to have the full picture—and that's better done in person. And tell him to leave his service weapon in the car. Kai doesn't like firearms in the office." Jake looked down at his watch. "It's almost two-thirty. I think my calendar is open this afternoon. Right Liz?"

She nodded.

"He should be able to get here in an hour. If he doesn't know where I'm located, tell him to put it in his GPS or ask our daughter."

"Try to be nice, Jake. You're a father."

"Glad you remembered. But no promises. Kirby can't afford my play-nice rate."

"Right!" With that, she disconnected.

Jake turned toward Liz. "This should be an interesting afternoon."

She gave him a hard look. "You *will* behave, won't you, Jake. This sounds serious."

As he responded, Jake glanced toward Scarlett. "I'll be nice as long as he is. I know it's serious, and I bear no ill will toward Ryan. I hope the kid didn't do it."

"Do you know Ryan?" Scarlett asked.

"I don't. He might have come to Sabrina's recital. One of Hal's boys did, but I'm not sure which one. The kids are from his first marriage. He was on wife number two when he showed up as my supervisor at the Bureau. Never knew him before." With that said, Jake took the remaining messages from the spindle and started toward his office, passing Scarlett with a tap on her shoulder.

As Scarlett watched him walk down the hall, Kai following, her brows drew inward as if a negative thought had arisen.